GROWING DOWN

A Novel of Reminiscence and Remembrance

By

Sarah Kavasharov

Excerpt from *The Soul's Code* by James Hillman used with permission by Grand Central Publishing.

ISBN 978-1475063820

Photos by Martha Toon:

Cover: Pioneer Peak, Matanuska Valley
Author: Kodiak Island

This book is for my daughters – and for other daughters.
And, of course, for sons.

Acknowledgements

None of the words of this book would have appeared on a page without the patient labor of Margaret Smallwood, who typed and retyped the original manuscript. I also owe a great debt to Monty Pitcher and to Edison Thuma, who were my earliest readers; though both have since left this earthly life, their interest in the story and belief that it was worth telling, was my first inspiration. Next, I must thank my three daughters, especially Kat for her patient work of editing the manuscript. Still, the manuscript would not have become a book without Dan Duncan's critical readership and encouragement, the persistence of Nancy Streufert and Martha Toon in moving the project along, and the technical expertise of Jim Helm.

"To plant a foot firmly on earth – that is the ultimate achievement, and a far later stage of growth than anything begun in your head. No wonder the faithful revere the Buddha's footprint in Sri Lanka. It shows he was truly in the world. He had really grown down. In fact, the Buddha had begun the process of growing down early in his life, when he left his protected palace gardens to enter the street. There the sick, the dead, the poor, and the old drew his soul down into the question of how to live life in the world. . . . Until the culture recognizes the legitimacy of growing down, each person in the culture struggles blindly to make sense of the darkenings and despairings that the soul requires to deepen into life."

James Hillman, *The Soul's Code*

Chapter One

Cold was an indelible part of childhood for Annie and her sisters growing up on a homestead near to Alaska wilderness. And wind, the moan of the Matanuska wind that came down the Valley so often day or night from what they vaguely heard of as a glacier far up Sheep Mountain. Even when Annie finally saw the glacier, on a fearful ride along steep and narrow, winding road with her brother Walter driving (was he sixteen?), it was hard for her to connect the monstrous dirty hulk straddling the mountain to the invisible wind that blew through her childhood.

The third invisible thing, this one bringing terror, was War. Their father had a shortwave radio in their crowded cabin and every evening the children had to be dead quiet while he fiddled the dials and then intently listened to the scratchy men's voices that came from far away telling about War. Annie liked numbers, learned them early, but these were terrible numbers, how many killed in Austria, in Poland.

"We're going to War," their father said; "we're going to have to kill the sonofabitch." Meaning a madman named Hitler. But when the war came close it came from the other side, from some strange, slant-eyed-looking people called the Japanese. "They're coming up the Chain," people said. It was years before Annie understood that the Japanese didn't get far up the Aleutian chain, didn't get within eight hundred miles of their own Valley in Southcentral Alaska. To Annie, at age seven, it sounded like they could come right out of the sky and through the door any minute. There were air raid sirens, search lights going in the sky beyond their south field. Then they couldn't have lights without taking the blankets from their beds, until Mother made the big heavy curtains to cover the windows, and there was nothing to make them out of until someone brought into the Valley a load of something like dark canvas.

Because there were no extras in the homes of most people in the Valley; every usable thing, every blanket, was needed, every scrap of fabric used and reused.

So there were enemies on both sides. "Far, far away," Mother said, about those voices coming out of the air on one side, and she showed the map from the Book of Knowledge. It didn't look far at all to England, to Germany. And from the other side they were close, just a finger width between Alaska and the Japanese on the map. Annie didn't keep asking, she just didn't believe. Sometimes she didn't let herself think about it, but sometimes she felt fierce and thought about how to fight. They have bayonets, she thought, but we have pitchforks and pitchforks are longer. Her big brothers were good with pitchforks, tossed hay around with them like they were toys.

But suddenly her two biggest brothers were gone, signed up for the Air Force and were gone. And Walter talking about joining the Navy. The boys hadn't been really living in the cabin for a long time anyway, but they had been right up the hill, in their own cabin they had built as teenagers (Annie didn't realize for years that it wasn't usual for big brothers to live in their own place called the Boys' House), and she had felt safer having them close. This was the end of safety and the beginning of a new life.

2

Chapter Two

Annie treasured early memories of life before the war. She knew well enough that her mother and her father had their angers and their troubles over each other; it was something she grew up with, imbibed with her mother's milk. Like having a bunch of brothers and sisters that she had angers and troubles with, like the sky and the earth having angers and withholding from each other. Which was called Weather. A very important word that explained why the rain didn't come when the earth needed it and how the earth fought back by blowing dust at the sky. Or sometimes filled the sky with a blizzard of snow, trying to rid itself of piles of snow too deep to abide with. Annie loved the earth, the smell of it fresh-turned in spring, the warm dust of summer. She hated the feel of the wind even though she was sure it was the earth's main way of fighting back when the sky was ornery. And she loved the sky when it was warm and calm.

It was confusing but she liked figuring things out for herself, finding explanations, and she thought she saw that all creatures, and all things, put up with other things they didn't want. So it made her feel sort of like an equal when she had to struggle through chores or awful cold or Martin's pestering. And good things kept coming back. Or new good things would pop up: finding a patch full of plump raspberries where they had been puny the year before, discovering that she flew far ahead of all the other kids in her first race without hardly trying. And the miraculous discovery that you could have a book that was your own, or a record, if only you had the money to order from the Sears catalog.

But some things she never figured out. Like the rooster that you had to run from before he could peck your legs. That was an early memory; she was probably about five years old before being allowed to go with

3

her sisters to feed the animals or collect the eggs. And the rooster was like a trap she would fall into, over and over, in her headlong rush to learn to do what the big kids did. She was sure the rooster had it in for her personally, that he lay in wait to fly at her out of nowhere even when she remembered to be watching for him.

"Stand up to him, Annie," her twelve-year-old sister Mary would call out, again; "kick him!"

"No," argued Ellen, eight years old and friends with the rooster, with all the animals. Ellen had named the rooster Cocky and she talked to him when she collected the eggs. But she carried a heavy piece of stick. "Hold the stick down across in front of him, like I do," Ellen said. "That way he'll either peck at the stick or go away." But Annie was either too clumsy with the stick or forgot to bring her own when she dashed after Ellen at the last minute. It took her a year before she stopped running from the rooster, learned to copy Ellen and had some steadiness with the stick if she'd had the foresight to bring one.

Her older sisters, Ellen and Mary, argued a lot. (Margaret was an older sister too, oldest of all, but hardly around even in Annie's earliest memories.) Ellen said Mary was bossy, which was true, but Mary, aged twelve, was set to watch over them and their brother Martin while Mother was busy in the house with all her work and tending the two littlest sisters. And Martin, ten years old — two years exactly, almost to the day, between Ellen and Mary — Martin was a trial to anybody. That's what a neighbor said and that's what Annie agreed to with all her heart. It seemed to her that putting up with Martin's relentless pestering was worse than having to keep a rooster because at least the rooster was in a pen. At least you knew that's where the rooster was, except on those few spring or summer days when Mother opened the pen to let the hens and rooster ramble free until they went to roost. Why Mother did that was one of those mysteries and Mother's answer to Annie's wondering was an even deeper mystery: "It's part of Nature," she said, "Nature wants certain things. We don't ask why." Mother was afraid of the rooster herself, relied on Ellen to keep him occupied if he was free while Mother hung the clothes or did whatever else she needed to do outdoors. So Annie deeply wondered why they had a rooster at all, or why they had Martin. But those were questions too deep to be asked; she sensed there was something darkly secret at the heart of them. But she thought that having Martin around was at least as bad as the grain getting blight, which her father and the neighbors talked about with terrible grimness.

At least that blight came only in one year, one short time in Annie's memory of the grain growing straight and tall all through her childhood, tall enough to hide her along the edge of the south field when they played hide and go seek. Rapidly growing far too tall for her to see anything over it when she and Ellen, and then Elizabeth by the time she was allowed to come, took the path across the south field to their favorite bit of woods. In the woods they hunted out star flowers and bluebells and morel mushrooms, and found little rooms or whole houses carpeted with moss under the trees. There they would carry out entire lives for hours at a time. Correct the homemade stuffed doll and the smooth wood pieces they used for other doll children and argue like grown-ups, especially spanking the boy doll Martin until Annie got tired of it and made a pen for him to keep him out of the very serious pursuits of life as motherhood.

Life did have its other troubles — Annie's favorite kitten getting watery looks in its blue eyes and then just dying — but it sometimes was perfect, gave just the right amount of rain for the crops, gave blue skies for summer days on end to ramble around picking and eating the wild raspberries that grew everywhere. Annie's very earliest memory, one that she knew was her own and not one of the pieces of family memory that came to be tangled with hers, was of sitting alone in warm dust by the door of the old cabin. She may have been only two years old but all her life the memory would come back to her to feel at moments the warmth of that day, the sun on bare arms and legs and on her face, the tangy smell of warm dust and animal lives, the utter *happiness* of just being there. She thought she knew other people were around — Mother, brothers, sisters, thought she heard their voices — but she was completely contented in herself, by herself.

Annie loved being alone to ramble the homestead as long as she wasn't far from the cabin.

The long dusty driveway onto the homestead — which Father somehow found gravel for and kept graded to prevent the worst ruts and chuckholes — came across level land that began to slope on each side and ended at the old cabin, the first cabin built by her father when their parents came to the homestead fifteen years before Annie was born. Slightly down the slope, south and east from the old cabin, stood the cabin they lived in now, much bigger than the first, with a big basement dug into the hillside and a broad front porch standing out from the hillside above the basement. Further up the hill on the other, the northwest side to the left from the driveway, was the Boys' House.

Annie knew directions early; she knew where the sun was, where to find shade in summer and how to stay in the southeast and south for the warmth of the low-lying sun in winter. She knew the adults' names for those places without having thought about it: the north field that filled first with snow when the blizzards came, the northeast field, further away and surrounded by heavy woods even more filled with deep snow. The south field, her favorite, with the path across it to the railroad tracks and over the tracks to a road. And the west, which, beyond where the south field stretched away, was the way out of the Valley, out of the surrounding mountains. It was to the west that the railroad track, after running down from the mines and through the Valley, took people to Anchorage on rare trips. And south from Anchorage on even rarer trips into a bigger, far-off world.

The wind that Annie hated, the wind relentless in spring and bitter in winter, came from the east and northeast, down from the mountains and the glacier, and that was confusing because the sun also came from the east. But Annie was living her life from southeast to south to west and northwest before she knew it, ignoring true east and true north. She always knew, too, where the moon was: it was always where she looked for it, or very nearly so; the moon seemed to ignore the truest east just as Annie did, and if it then went true north she didn't know it. For her it was always found on a known path from southeast across the sky to the northwest. A path with its heart in the south.

Annie loved the story of their parents' arrival in the Valley in late March of 1919, asked her mother over and over to tell it. It wasn't easy to get Mother to tell a story. She wasn't talkative and she was always busy, tending to cooking or cleaning or other work and to Annie's little sisters Elizabeth and Jeannie. Mother's few words were usually reminders, mostly gentle reminders, to get something done or to stop doing something. More than words, Mother gave you a look. The look said that Mother knew you, knew exactly who you were. And knew if you were up to something. You couldn't lie to Mother; Martin tried it, but only for devilment: Martin was open as a book, not secretive like Annie often was about her inner doubts and fears and questionings.

There was a period in her early years when Annie followed Mother around, begging, sometimes, for a story. But when Mother paused in her busyness she would usually just stand and look far off. In burgeoning spring and summer Mother seemed to look to the mountains; in winter, indoors, she looked at nothing Annie could see. Long before Annie knew her mother was Aleut or knew what an Aleut was; long before Annie knew what pride was, there was growing in her a quietly fierce, proud feeling of being like her mother.

"The weather turned bad as soon as we got here," her mother said, on each of the very rare times she told the story of the beginning of the homestead. That was late in March, Annie knew, her own birth month. "It was supposed to be mild, your father said, supposed to be an early spring. But there was new snow right after we pitched the tent he brought. We had James (Annie's oldest brother) and we had to keep warm right away. So we banked the tent with the new snow and I kept a fire going all the time from the branches and saplings your father was cutting and sawing from clearing the birches and cottonwood to build the cabin.

"He worked like a demon, your father. And we were warm in that first little cabin in no time. But we had to be clearing land right away, so there was no rest. His friends from Anchorage, the Barkleys that you know, came up to help, and Mr. Losey — he wasn't "old man Losey" then like these new people like to call him; he was a lot of help, from dawn to dusk in those long days from April into May."

"How did they dig the land?" Ellen asked, though she knew the answers as well as Annie did. "Old Moke was a work horse then, wasn't he? Not sick like he is now?"

"Moke was as good a horse as I guess they come," Mother said. (Mother didn't much relate to animals as big as Old Smoke, who had been called Moke or Mokey, Annie understood, ever since Martin had been a baby who didn't say his esses. But out of her own orneryness toward Martin, Annie always called the horse Old *S*moke, emphasizing the beginning *s*.)

'He wasn't old then," Mother said, "and you know we didn't have Moke the first years," and Mother looked at Ellen with a look that said *I know what you're up to, foolishly trying to trip up the truth.* "You know we used Mr. Losey's mule that first year. And your father knew how to fashion a plow.

"And then," the story went on as Annie expected, "your father and Mr. Losey got Mr. Losey the old tractor that the Extension service was selling off."

7

"It was Mr. Losey that had some money socked away," Ellen prompted.

"And your father who fixed it up and kept it running. But he always said it was Arlen Losey's tractor, of course. And then after a couple years your father came home with the horse, Old Smoke, when they were in the middle of clearing the northeast field and the tractor kept breaking down and even your father couldn't fix it for quite a while."

"Waiting for some engine parts to come from Outside," Annie said, though she didn't know what that meant, had only heard the mysterious words about engines and the Outside.

They were out on the big porch, Mother and the four younger girls (Annie had never heard the word 'deck' but realized later that most people would call it that, that wide porch almost as big as the whole cabin). Mother was doing more of the endless washing of clothes, scrubbing Father's and brothers' big old dirty shirts and overalls on the washboard and putting them in the tubs of rinse water. Everybody carrying more water from the well as the original tubs (filled by big brothers before they went off to work) got dirty. Elizabeth helping too, or trying to, while little Jeannie was asleep nearby in a sort of cradle made by Father.

Then Mother was wringing out the clothes, putting them through two tight rollers that Father had rigged up to be pumped by your feet. Which the girls, and sometimes Martin, would push and pump when Mother's feet got tired. Mother didn't talk again while she pumped. So Annie got down and tried to push the pedals hard enough to get Mother to talk again and Ellen pushed too — they always both pushed if one started it — but Mother didn't say much more for some time, didn't go on with the story about how Father found a horse.

Having a work horse made the family special; the Bogles had the only other horse in the Valley when Annie was little and Annie would go to the fence beyond the pig pen to talk to Old Smoke. He would lie near the fence because he wouldn't have to hobble far on his old legs to get the hay or a piece of rutabaga or, very rare, a piece of apple that came from Outside. Even Annie never gave up for Smoke a whole apple of the two she remembered getting when she was little, though she prided herself that she gave up to him almost half her apple on a fall day soon before Smoke died. When Martin never gave more than a couple of pieces. And it was Annie who had discovered that, among all the other things that the children had kept poking through the fence for him, old Smoke liked a bit of rutabaga best.

But as much as she loved Ellen, and had loved Old Smoke, Annie was half-cranky that Ellen kept derailing the story before it came to the most exciting parts.

"You worked too," Annie said, wanting to get back to the beginning year on the homestead.

"We all worked hard," Mother said, "but of course I had to stop awhile." And for years, until Annie was much older, Mother didn't fill in the gaps of the second story that fascinated Annie. Annie first overheard that story from her father telling other people and then repeated by her older brothers and sisters. And of course it was years before little Annie could understand what it meant that her mother had been pregnant at the time her parents came to start a homestead. In those years Mother didn't talk, people didn't talk, about being pregnant. At least not to children.

"William was on the way," was what Mother did say, "and he came soon past the middle of May. The men had cleared a big part of the south field and I was cutting the seed potatoes for planting; people said you needed to have things in the ground in May. As soon as we had the potatoes in, I was going to ride the train to Anchorage, to have William born there. But that didn't happen; he was born right here. And after that you were all born here."

Annie heard more of the story when Father was talking to Mr. Easter or somebody: "When we knew that baby was coming, I went over to the station house and cranked up the phone, called up to Jonesville mine for the first-aid man. He said he'd get right down here on a handcar. I explained to him how to come through the woods to where we were clearing the south field. 'You can't miss it,' I told him, 'just keep heading north from the track.' But," and here Father laughed, "that fellow just didn't know north from south. He wound up on the other side of the tracks, due south, in the woods over there, which was all woods then, before Bogles made their farm, and by the time he came back over to our side he got lost and wandered around in *our* woods. Until he finally saw a faint light, he said, and thought it might be coming from our cabin.

"Which it was. It was full dusk by then, near midnight. It might have been near eight when I called him and knew it would take him an hour or more to come down on that handcar. Thought he'd surely be here by ten. In the meantime Nature had taken her course and William had arrived, long since. A lusty kid at the start, bellerin' like a calf. Though he did turn out to be the quietest one of the boys. Well, anyway, then we sat out and talked half the night, Kinney and I, with Losey, drinking too much of Losey's mule-kicking moonshine. The first-aid man's name was Bernard Kinney and he had to take the handcar back in the morning. Good man. I never stopped ribbing him, though, about not knowing north from south. 'Course it was a cloudy evening; he didn't have the sun to help him. Still, I asked him, 'how are you going to survive in Alaska wilderness without knowing that much?'"

"'I didn't come up here to live in the wilderness,' is what he said. 'Not like darn fools out clearing land with handsaws and hand plow. Happens I know something about mining,' he said, 'and got some medical training before I went over to France.'

"Which I'm glad I didn't do," Annie heard her Father say and heard him say at other times: "Better to be getting something done, something useful, than to be out squabbling and killing people. That was the most pointless damned war." He meant the First War.

Annie loved hearing her father talk to his 'cronies,' as Mother called them, though it didn't happen often. Father was usually gone, or hard at work. He sounded so different, talking to other men, from the way he talked at home. When she was a grown woman Annie learned more from her mother about early years on the homestead and about Father as a young man (though Father was late in his twenties and Mother only sixteen when they met). Drinking tea together in Annie's kitchen all those years later, Mother filled in the gaps in William's birth story. "We were afraid to cut the cord," she said; "it was after that that your father ordered those two big medical books of his — paid for them with most of the bit of money we had — and then we just delivered the rest of you at home. Until Jeannie, of course, because we had the hospital by then and your father wasn't home when I went into labor. William was the oldest one at home then, and he was scared. So I let him drive me down to the hospital toward the end. Which then of course we couldn't pay the bill, even though we were only there a few hours — I wasn't about to stay, didn't need to after Jeannie was born. It was still the Depression and people in the Valley hadn't had any money even before then; I think those doctors and nurses who came to Alaska were working for almost nothing, so anyway it seems they just wrote off the bill."

"But you started to talk about the night — or the evening — that William was born," Annie said. "What did you do when you couldn't cut the cord?"

"Waited for that man Kinney. Who was a nice young man. We had a big roll of brown paper we used for everything — I don't know where your father got it — and he wrapped up the afterbirth in the paper and put it beside me, the cord still attached, of course, and I was pretty much asleep with the baby when that young man turned up. It had been a long day and I'd already had an aching back, bending over those potato cuttings and then starting to plant them, tending to James all the while and cooking for the men. I hardly even woke up while he tended to the cord.

"I woke up a bit later, though, to realize it was done. And heard your father with young Kinney and Mr. Losey outside the cabin. They got drunk as skunks on Mr. Losey's moonshine, out there thumping things and laughing their heads off. That was one sorry-looking young man who had to pump that handcar back up to Jonesville next day. We didn't have anything like coffee those years. Your father made him some awful-smelling hot brew out of birch bark or something that got him looking less green around the gills and then I made him eat oatmeal; I remember that."

"Didn't our dad make whiskey too, a still down by the calf barn? I remember William saying. . . ."

"That was later. But long before your time. Yes, your father did that for a few years, grain whiskey, and I guess it was just as bad, and just as powerful, as Mr. Losey's. He made a bit of money at it too, asking fifty cents for a pint from the miners and such. But he stopped doing it as your brothers got older; didn't want them around it. And by that time he was gone too much anyway to keep an eye on things."

In childhood, Annie especially loved the long-lingering twilight from spring into summer, the light lingering till midnight or after while she just dreamed or played with her little sisters or watched her big brothers at their harder games, hearing the carrying sounds of other children over the hill, aware of a world full of creatures and knowing everything was growing again under skies alive with swallows and other birds coming back. She loved the way the light was so gentle, but so full of life like no other time of year. She loved the way the birch trees shimmered white long into the dusk, long after you could no longer see their leaves twinkling and moving in the sun. She liked to stay out — like they all did, like the world did — reluctant to go in even when repeatedly called, wanted to stay out until she could sometimes see the little bats that would fly when everything and everyone else was still.

Winter had its own special, long-lasting memories too. Annie and her sisters, sometimes even with their brother Martin, had marvelous times: sledding into the dark and early moonlight, shouting and laughing. For lack of sleds they scrounged cardboard, an old dishpan. Even hard knocks on the ice learning to skate — on secondhand, usually ill-fitting skates or clamp-ons because they couldn't have real ice skates that fit for such a large family — even the most wobbly attempts and hard falls on the ice would wind up in gales of laughter by the half-pond when the low part of the south field froze over every winter. Even some awful falls on the school rink at recess.

Home was the one real place in winter. Warm. Bringing you out of the cold with the smell and taste of stew or salmon patties and fresh-baked bread. Warm blankets through the night. And in daytime coming in red-nosed and radiating cold to drink the rare treat of hot chocolate or chew on buttery bread, sometimes doughnuts, around the big table their father had fashioned out of thick boards, boards that Mother scrubbed so often they were turning white. With their small and gentle mother humming around the big black cookstove in the smell of something more always cooking mixed with the summer scent of the tea she kept constantly warm or simmering on the back of the stove.

Her tea was the only thing Mother wanted for herself from the orders they sent in to the Sears catalog or to the Alaska Commercial Company in Anchorage. She said the Aleuts had learned from the Russians to drink tea like this. "Our mother told me," she said, "that when she was little they had bitter tea that tasted like weeds. 'But then we learned to make Russian tea,' she said. 'So the Russians were good for something.'"

Annie learned, at some time, that when Mother referred to "our mother," she wasn't talking about her own real mother, whom she hardly, only vaguely, remembered. Mother had been taken from her Aleut village when she was very young. "Taken by some 'Baptists," and she never even knew who her real family had been. Without knowing what a Baptist was, Annie thought it must be some kind of child stealer that couldn't get in trouble for it for some reason. Mother had known an old Aleut woman she and some of her Aleut classmates at the Baptist school in Kodiak called "our mother," a woman who made them tea and told them stories when they stopped at her house after school.

Life was full. Whether crowded or lonely it was rich, it was scary: thick with the possibilities that came out of the still cold of winter under dim, faraway sun, or from the soft velvet of summer dark, or moonlight.

Annie didn't so much like salmon cleaning time in June — days on end of smell and flies while the family cut up the piles of fish into chunks for the canning jars or strips for the smoke house, on a big makeshift plywood table in the yard. Buckets of entrails to be buried but coated with flies before they went to the ground. She felt a swelling pride when she got to really help, when she worked like everybody else, when she did correctly the fetching and carrying they let her do. But she hated the flies, shiny fat things buzzing around in clouds. She came to be just as glad for the spiders as Mother was: Mother wouldn't let you disturb the spiders or the webs they spun indoors over the three cabin windows and at the top of the door. "They keep the flies down," she said. Mother got angry at Martin, so Annie got angry too, for Martin's poking and pestering and trying to trap the spiders. Killing them on the sly. Martin didn't do it because he hated spiders, Annie decided. Not like she hated flies. He did it because he liked doing it, liked having the power in his hands to do it.

But there was more in it, Annie began to decide, more to the reasons for Martin's killing. Martin had had a little dog, Danny, the runt from the litter of the family border collie, Maggie. And just as Maggie followed Father everywhere when he was home, Danny followed Martin everywhere for most of a year. They were constant companions, that little dog always sneaking into the house and trying to hide behind Martin's legs to keep from being put back out where he was supposed to stay in the barn. But both parents began to ignore that little dog after winter was setting in, let him stay in the crowded cabin by pretending to overlook him while the little dog kept very quiet under the bench at the big table where Martin was struggling with the reading or arithmetic homework which he hated. It kept Martin quiet too, kept him from the restless silent pestering he usually indulged in when confined indoors: because Martin didn't want Danny to be noticed, it was the only time Martin didn't want family notice for himself.

Then Danny got sick and died; "must have gotten into something bad he should have left alone," Father said.

It was after that, after Danny died, that Martin really began killing things, mostly still bugs and spiders but also birds and then a kitten. Sometimes it seemed mean, but sometimes it didn't: more like Martin wanted to get some control over this mysterious thing that had taken Danny away from him. As though, if he himself caused the mysterious thing called death to happen, then it wasn't the awful, final thing that left him stunned and baffled and miserably angry when Danny turned cold and unmoving and left him. Or maybe Martin was like a scientist with his rats and mice in a laboratory that James helped Annie read about in the Books of Knowledge. Martin seemed to be repeating the same experiment over and over, thinking that he could understand how things came out. Except that, young as Annie was, she sensed that Martin kept wanting to make them come out different. She watched Martin more than others did; he was her nemesis and she had been wary of what he was up to ever since she could remember; she thought he seemed desperate a few times, to make an experiment that didn't end like all the rest.

It was the one time in her childhood that Annie felt something like kinship with Martin, when she saw how he moped after Danny died. She made him a picture of Danny on one of the few precious pieces of paper she had stolen from the Sunday school. She mixed flour paste and carefully pasted on bits of cloth and weeds, and cottonwood fluff she had been saving for herself since spring, and dark pieces from the old Sears catalog, to match the brown and white and near-black of Danny's colors. Then she was hurt and angry when Martin only looked at her offering like it was nothing and she left it lying on the big table just as carelessly as he had, vowing that she would never again care about Martin or about what he felt or thought.

Later she wanted to rescue the picture, at least for herself. She had thought she hadn't even liked that little dog; you weren't supposed to get attached to the farm animals, because they were working animals (when she had given names to her favorite three cows and the heifer Bluebell she had done it secretly, not openly like Ellen, and sneaked to be able to talk to them). It was okay, when she was little, to talk to Old Smoke because he wasn't a working animal anymore. She did begin to understand that you weren't supposed to "spoil" the working animals but she had grown up liking to watch from a distance their border collie, named Maggie, so attached to Father.

When she went back for it, her picture of Danny had disappeared. She fretted about it without telling anyone, making little hints to see if she could find out if anyone had seen it, and inspecting the burn barrel. Then, finally, she saw it, where she shouldn't have. Where she sneaked, again, to look behind the curtain that Martin always kept pinned shut over his back wall bunk in the bedroom that all the children shared. She glimpsed, because the cloth was slipping from one uppermost nail, a corner of what Martin had turned into his secret hideaway. And when she got bold to peek further into his space (which she had done before in spite of admonitions from her parents to leave Martin and his "room" alone) there was her picture of Danny, carefully pinned, by a small nail in each of its four corners, halfway down the wall above his bunk where he would see it when he lay there in his cubby hole.

Martin kept up his killing. He especially killed the fat flies in the outhouse, would trap them and torture them first, and Annie never knew how she felt about that. Then Martin and a friend from over the tracks got the bright idea to harness a fly. When the friend called Beanie came over, they would spend hours with little nooses made of Mother's thread until they each had a fly — two flies, Martin had one day — captured in their ingenious harnesses that left the fly's wings free. And then they would parade their flies around like kites on a string, trying to get the flies to land on Annie or any of her sisters. There were days Annie was sure that she still hated Martin. But he was like the one-man avenger from the weekly movie serial when it came to flies in the outhouse, where Annie hated them the most, dreading for them to land on her bare skin. On her "private parts."

In some ways she loved the outhouse in summer. She came to like even the smell of the Bu-hac kept burning there to discourage the flies and to overcome the other smell. (She remembered it later, often, that pungent Bu-hac smell that disappeared after her childhood.) In winter she dreaded being there, so she always had mixed feelings about the place. In summer you could dream there — so long as no flies pestered — dream over the old Sears catalog kept there for paper to wipe on. Dream over all the things in the book that people somewhere might have. Annie couldn't quite believe it, that actual people had some of these things, but she later began to glimpse some of them in the houses of the colonists: beautiful-looking chairs that weren't hand built, rugs on the floors. And lamps. She began to think it would be glorious to have a lamp, or even one of those pretty glass things to put over a bulb; she began to think that the bulbs hanging from the ceiling in the cabin looked ugly being so bare.

The other thing about the outhouse was that you were safe from Martin, once you were inside. The wooden slat that held the door shut from inside was heavy and strong and though Martin might pester from outside, rapping on the walls and making sounds to try to scare you, it didn't scare Annie unless it was dark, in winter. In winter the outhouse got terribly cold and the pages of the Sears catalog were so cold that they crackled and hurt your bottom. She was so proud when she was first allowed to go there in the dark, instead of using the honey jug in the cabin that Mother carried out every day. But one dark afternoon she was struck with such an awful fear that she had to fight to prove to herself that she was a big enough girl to go there. She dribbled on the seat and it froze, froze her bottom to the seat.

She was paralyzed. She felt herself frozen to the ice-cold wooden seat. She *saw* herself, frozen over the hole, forever. In such a place! With her pants down! So that even awful Martin could see her bare bottom if they had to break down the outhouse to get her out! She couldn't cry, or even cry out to her sister Ellen waiting outside.

After an agony of long moments in cold panic, the thought of Martin suddenly energized her. She broke free — it wasn't that she was stuck on the seat after all! — though it was a long time before the fear of becoming truly frozen there really left her.

In summer Annie and her sisters could hide in the outhouse, to tell secrets, like she and Ellen did. Or, with her little sister Elizabeth, Annie would go through the pages of clothes in the catalog — Ellen wasn't interested in clothes, turned up her nose, not caring what clothes she wore — but Annie longed to have a dress. Just one dress. The hand-me-down denim coveralls that she had to wear, even the occasional skirt passed on from somewhere — she felt more and more that they were ugly. She wanted something pretty once, just for once. One thing for herself that was pretty.

She wailed when she saw her parents bent over the newest Sears catalog, ordering more of the dark coveralls, more of the gray underwear, more of the heavy socks. And not even new ones for Annie, always for Mary or Ellen and Martin, so that Annie everlastingly wore their hand-me-downs. "Why don't they at least make them *red?*", she wailed about the coveralls. "Why don't they make them in a *color*?!" She loved the brilliant colors of the pansies that Mother always grew by the door, that some girls had in their dresses at school.

In high summer she was often in trouble, along with her sisters. They couldn't resist eating the peas from the garden before they grew truly fat, ate too many of the raspberries and currants they were sent to pick for jelly and jam, wandered too far when they were supposed to come back in time for supper. Got yelled at by old Mr. Hogworth for cutting across his field, breaking the grain, and punished at home for it; punished for rambling before finishing the weeding. Their punishment was never physical; Mother gave you the look that put you at a distance, put you off by yourself into a cold place, and no matter how many of you had collaborated, wanting to hide behind having done the thing together, Mother's look made you each feel alone. It made you skulk off questioning why you had separated yourself from the web of work and caring that everybody shared, or was supposed to share. Made you feel cold. Even Ellen stopped her giggling under that look.

Mother's look was more serious to Annie, in one way, than their father's punishments. When he was home, often before a weekend, Almighty Father depended on looks too, looking like a frightful thunder cloud, but he had a thunder voice too when he wasn't being stern and silent. He would make them work longer, harder. Make all of them, from the big brothers down through Walter and Mary and Ellen and Annie — and even sometimes Elizabeth — feel responsible for things not done or not done according to his specifications. Made them go without something expected or promised. And since they had so little it could be a terrible punishment to be deprived of any extra. But since they had so little there was often nothing extra to be deprived of.

But there was the Friday night movie. It was the last, the ultimate, punishment to be deprived of going to the Friday night movie. They would work like demons, even into the dark, to save themselves from missing the Friday night movie, where people put up chairs in the school gymnasium and showed a movie every Friday night, with cartoons and news reels and a piece each week of the serial about the one-man avenger. The Hoolihan family had their fifteen kids haul in huge gunny sacks full of popcorn they had made at home and they sold it in little paper bags for a nickel. It was a town-life celebration.

The only other town life that Annie remembered was at Fourth of July. On Fourth of July there was a big town picnic barbecue down by the school, with games and races in the school yard. Annie carried off blue ribbons running the fifty-yard dash, even a silver dollar whenever she won the hundred-yard dash. She and Ellen always won the three-legged race, even against the boys when they put boy and girl winners together. It was like the girls' family tradition: Mary won races for her age group, especially as the anchor in the relay, and all the sisters came along following in her footsteps. When Ellen was moved into an older age group and could no longer pair up with Annie, then Annie and Elizabeth set records for the three-legged race and the wheelbarrow race. Those were some glory days, even after the War.

For all that it had troubles and angers, it *was* a glorious life in those years. Annie could always escape outside or into a book when frightened by the anger of her father. They had few books but those they did have were treasures; you could have one when you had done your chores and washed your hands. Then Mother or Father or her oldest, gentlest brother James would take a book down from the high shelf for Annie. Annie loved especially the Books of Knowledge, a whole row of them full of pictures and stories and facts about the world. She pored over them, astonished at the variety of life. More and more she began longing to see the wonders of the world outside the Valley.

Through a path across the north field, and over the hill beyond, lived the Gearharts in a tidy log house where they had whitewashed the ends of the logs at the corners. The Gearharts were colonists, who had come to the Valley only a few years before Annie was big enough to be aware of colonists. The whole farm at Gearharts was tidy and so were their two children, a little older than Annie, a boy and girl always well-behaved on the school bus. Everything at their farm was in apple-pie order, with the only lawn that Annie ever saw growing up. There was a white picket fence around the lawn and children weren't allowed to play on it, except once when the whole family was having a barbecue picnic there and Mrs. Gearhart let Ellen and Annie stay. You had to play carefully. The Gearharts were nice people; Mrs. Gearhart in her neat apron sometimes offered milk and cookies though you had to stand in the porch to eat them and be careful, again, not to make a mess. Annie and her sisters simply accepted that they weren't invited into colonists' homes; they thought kids always had to stay outside of such homes. It made sense: they had such pretty things inside, like lamps and lovely, soft-looking furniture to sit on; why would you let kids ramble around among such things any more than Mother let you play in her sewing corner where she kept her own few precious pretty things — the silky, scarlet cloth with its intricate design and fluttery tasseled ends covering her treadle machine, the green glass swan full of buttons sitting on top of it beside the dainty little figure of a woman with gold edges on her blue cloak that Annie loved to look at. That William had so carefully glued back together for Mother after one of the boys broke it. Why would you let kids play in houses where you might knock into some special or precious thing every time you turned around? It only gradually registered with Annie over a few years that the 'white' kids were in and out of those homes, playing in them, all the time.

Further up the road from Gearharts the land kept rising until it leveled off again into the Riley's farm. Even though the Rileys were colonists too, their place was the opposite of Gearhart's, their dirt-packed front yard crammed with farm machinery and vehicles and parts of vehicles, some of them rusting. Bird Riley had a big laugh or a chuckle around a plug of tobacco always in his mouth. Annie's brother Walter, probably fourteen or fifteen at the time, laughed about how the men in town said Bird Riley was the champion cusser of the Valley and how Walter had heard him "cut loose." Annie and Ellen once hung around the Riley's yard when they were supposed to be berry picking, hoping to hear him cuss, but he didn't do it while they were there. Mrs. Riley never came out; people said she was crippled in her legs but still played the piano. All the Riley kids were older, in high school by the time Annie started first grade, one of them friends with Annie's big brother Walter. Walter was Annie's third brother, born right after Margaret, Annie's oldest sister.

When Martin was safely away, Annie would sit with the precious bit of pencil she had kept hidden from him and some of the paper she stole from Sunday school and make a list of the names of all her brothers and sisters, with the age of each one. She herself was number eight, five years old when Ellen was eight, with two little sisters younger, Jeannie the youngest of all. That's why they called her "little Jeannie." Annie spent a long time over the list, after a too-quick, careless start, asking questions about birthdays and laboriously working out the arithmetic by herself, not asking anybody for help. Becoming extremely careful about using up the nub end of eraser on her only pencil by having to make any more corrections. She was proud of her final result: ten children, ten; and she had counted them up by herself:

James	almost 20
William	almost 18
Margaret	16
Walter`	15
Mary	12
Martin	10
Ellen	8
Annie	almost 5
Elizabeth	3
Jeannie	almost 1 ½

Directly across the south field by another path that went on through the girls' favorite woods was the railroad track, for the spur line that ran up to the Jonesville mines. Then over the track was the big, beautiful farm of the Bogles, the most successful farm in the Valley; people said it had the richest soil, bottom land steeped in silt the Matanuska River had been bringing down out of the mountains forever.

At the very bottom of the south field, toward the west, was the road that ran around the homestead. The girls rarely rambled there, had their shortcuts everywhere to avoid having to follow the rigid lines of roads that outlined the farms with sharp corners. But Annie was fascinated by tales about old Mr. Losey, the bachelor who lived across the road down there. He was one of the oldest settlers in the Valley, had been there before her parents came in 1919 and long before the colonists who arrived in 1935. He was the one who had been so much help to their parents when they first came to the Valley but Annie couldn't picture that because he seemed so silent and so old. People said he didn't bother to wash his clothes, just counted on being out doors in all weather, loved a good rainstorm as a wash day, hung his clothes out and stayed out himself to let the rain wash him and whatever he was wearing. People also said they could hear old man Losey hollering and cussing at his mule, hear him "halfway across the Valley," but Annie didn't remember hearing it. Maybe it was the wind, that always blew in a direction that carried his voice away from the homestead and across the Valley. In winter, it was said, old man Losey just added layers to whatever he kept warm underneath by wearing it all the time. He did seem very old, but Annie didn't know why she thought that. He wasn't bent, or crippled; he kept up his little farm by himself with the usual help from neighbors like Father, but Annie somehow felt like she knew why people called him "old man Losey." He seemed utterly silent, gave a nod the few times the girls passed by.

But Annie had once heard old man Losey really speak, in a voice with soft edges, his voice and a deep laugh mingling with her father's, and forever after that day she connected those sounds with the surprising wonder of a good day following on something bad.

Some days before she heard Mr. Losey talking, Annie's second grade teacher, Miss Stratmeyer, had found Annie bent over, sick — so very sick, sick and hurting as she'd never hurt — in the girls' bathroom at school. And then the school nurse put her in a car, in a sleeting wind, just to go to the hospital, a distance anybody would walk; the school and the hospital were hardly far apart. Annie woke up to new smells and to find out the doctor had taken out her appendix.

"Here you are then, my girl," the funny-looking, grizzled doctor with the big chin said to her. "This squiggly-looking thing is what was making you sick." And he gave to Annie her appendix floating in a jar, a part of herself to marvel at and show off, compare to the colored pictures in the magical see-through overlays of the human body in her father's big medical book at home. The nurses gave her a teddy bear, her brother William brought her a book and someone gave her a jigsaw puzzle. The puzzle was too easy but she had never had one, so it was a treasure.

Then it was her stern father who brought her home, in the flatbed Ford truck. But that day he wasn't stern; he acted friendly. "So there's my girl," he said at first. He'd always lumped the four youngest together as 'the girls' — "get the girls to be helping you more in here," he would say to Mother; "they aren't much use outside" — and even to any of them, the four youngest, he had usually just said things like, "bring the book over here, girl, so I can see what you're talking about," or "you two girls be quiet now."

But today her father acted like he knew who she really was. "Annie," — he said her name as he helped her up into the passenger seat of the truck — "we piled up the seat for you because it's going to be a rough ride in this old truck. The freeze is already giving way in spots that're making holes." Annie had heard her father and brothers talk about how "you could sink an axle in some of these chuckholes in April, even by the end of March, when you couldn't see it comin'." They agreed that the ground softened fastest where melting snow water was only seeping before you could see it running or hear it trickling. Which Annie knew too, but never connected to machines. To Annie, the problems of managing a car or truck, or any other machine, were a mystery but one she was hardly even curious about. She had her mother's attitude toward machines, that some might be necessary but they were still, even the seeming necessary ones, like some kind of evil. But today she felt a secret delight that her father confided something to her that he usually shared only with his sons. And that he called her by her name when she hadn't even done something to get into trouble. She sat up high in the truck, on the old cushion and some blankets that he helped to settle her on, and for the rest of her life she never encountered a bumpy, rutty road without thinking of her father.

Along the way, that day, where the road went round the southwest edge of the homestead, her father stopped the truck and talked to old man Losey who was walking home from somewhere. They talked about April right around the corner and the end-of-March weather and about fixing up Mr. Losey's tractor, while Annie half absorbed their talk and half dreamed. It was a beautiful day, with the air warm and the little sound of water beginning to trickle from snowpiles along the side of the road mingling with the men sound of their chuckling voices. It felt to Annie, right then, as if the whole world had decided to celebrate her coming home.

Even that wasn't the end of Father's rare good humor. At home he actually chuckled some more, at her appendix in the jar, and then he took down the medical book and showed her where her appendix had fit into her insides. He sat with her, at the big table, explaining some of the amazing parts of the body that were so astonishing to see. He even laughed with her when she was excited about all those parts working together under your skin, while she didn't confess that she had tried to puzzle some of it out before, when she had persuaded Walter, twice, to take down the book for her. (She might have confessed it, since her father was being so friendly that day, except she knew he wouldn't be friendly about Walter, or about how she had persuaded Walter by "promising" him she wouldn't tell on him to Father about how Walter had been playing ball half the day instead of doing his work. When Walter hadn't even asked for a promise. Father would call that worse than tattling; tattling was bad enough, but Annie understood that trying to get something you shouldn't have by promising not to tattle was even worse.) So she pretended to Father that she had never gotten to look at the magical overlays. Which wasn't that hard, even with her feeling of some guilt, because they *were* magical, and she hadn't understood many of the words her father was now explaining. Most of all, she had almost never had Father's attention just for herself. Had never been bold enough even to ask him questions but this day finding herself asking, and him not only answering but explaining. Talking to her. Laughing with her.

Old man Losey still farmed, all by himself with his old tractor, even after the colonists came, but he sold some land to them when they started wanting land to build up a town. "He would have been near eighty by then," Annie's mother told her years later in some of their talks over tea, "I was pretty surprised myself when I figured out he might have been near sixty when he first helped us. He worked from dawn far past dusk like all of us did that spring, wiry and strong and never ending." (Still later, far from the Valley, Annie heard that Mr. Losey had died and people thought he must have been about a hundred years old though no one was sure.)

The town was named Hammond, after some man, and grew up next to the spur railroad line and right up next to the homestead. What had been wilderness with a dozen homesteaded farms before Annie was born had turned into a town with hundreds of farms by the time she was seven years old. It was a project of the United States Government, she learned, to send hundreds of people called the colonists to the Valley when she had been a baby. Annie's older brothers and sisters buzzed about it, infecting Annie's babyhood with an excitement of the unknown, and then telling their tales over and over about meeting so many new kids at once, and about how, when they knew the colonists were coming, Mary and Walter skipped school to go down and watch the train come in, wanting to see what a colonist looked like. They were disappointed to see that colonists were only people, that their kids just looked like kids. Walter, brash and good-natured nearing eleven, made friends with some of the new boys pretty fast. And Mary, after beating up on some of the kids who called her and her sisters "squaw" and her brothers "dirty Indians," began to make friends too.

"Feisty Mary," Father would sometimes say, "you'd better watch out being so quick about everything. Life's going to make you slow down." But Father liked Mary better than he liked any of the other girls, Annie could tell.

The United States government had given the colonists land, and the money to build homes and buy farm machinery, so Annie learned. There was a picture of the government in the post office, a great man in a wheel chair in a far-off big place with a white dome behind him and an eagle over his head. Annie heard it was long term loans and she heard, but was slow to comprehend, a bitterness among some of the old settlers and a definite dividing line that took shape between settlers and colonists, began to understand that the old settlers had nothing but the land they had proved up on and a struggle through hard labor to have any farm machinery at all, or to keep it running, while they saw that the government handed everything to the colonists, so they said, "on a silver platter."

But her father had quickly had work. He had been a sheet metal man and had worked on the Copper River railroad before deciding to take an already growing family to stake out a homestead in near-wilderness in the Valley.

"It was a surprise to me when it turned out I'd married a farmer," Mother said. "I might have known the other, if I'd stopped to think about it — you don't stop to think if you're in love — but I might have guessed that he had the railroad in his blood and what that meant, that it meant something about distances. But there's no way I could have known the other side, what it was that made him want to be *settled*. What made him want a farm."

Father seemed to understand any sort of machine. Almost like he was a machine himself. He came to be more and more in demand for that, seemed to know and be known by everyone; he made friends everywhere even though at home he was not a friendly man. They needed their machines, the new people did, and needed their machines to keep running. They were something like a flock, Annie felt, all sticking together and wanting the same things. But there was something puzzling about their sticking together because it was about a lot more than their machines. It seemed to be about almost everything, so that they seemed different, somehow, from her and from her family. And they had a flock judgment against Natives; they didn't accept that Mother was a wonderful person, or a real person at all. It set in with Annie, from an early age, to be deeply angry about that. Although she loved puzzling over mysteries, this one made her more angry than puzzled. Her oldest sister, Margaret, just a year younger than Walter, seemed more and more to be going over to the colonists' "side"; she acted ashamed of their mother, made friends among the new people and shunned the family.

Father was deserting the family too, tending to the needs of all the new people. Annie sensed that this somehow must be the reason for her mother's attitude toward the colonists; Mother never shared in the bitterness of some of the old settlers but kept her solitary silence about both parties.

Mother didn't seem to care that the colonists had more things. Annie decided that even making a whole town that shut her out may not have been enough to turn Mother against these new people. She had a rightness of her own that didn't depend on them. But they made such a dividing line between her and the man that she had married; they liked him while they wouldn't even look at her straight, and — this was the terribly worst — he seemed day-by-day to be buying into the way they looked at things. He was acting ashamed of having married an "Indian" — and she wasn't an Indian but proudly an Aleut. Mother and Father already had their troubles with each other, and this made it worse; it was doing something like wearing down her mother's soul. Mother didn't seem to have a well-defended soul. She didn't come up with "reasons" for being right, as their father did and everybody else did, including Annie and her sisters. Whatever way it was, Annie wanted Mother better defended, wanted herself to be able to defend her. Mother didn't try to defend herself. She cared and she worked. She worked and she cared. She was always there; she never left the farm.

Mother seemed to enjoy endless work; humming to herself or crooning to the newest baby as she cooked, as she scrubbed, as she fed the chickens, tended her pansies and her beloved raspberry bushes, washed the clothes and put them through the wringers, hung them to dry and gathered and folded them, went back to more cleaning and cooking and directing the older girls and trying to direct Martin and get the garden and animals cared for. With always the littlest girls, Elizabeth and little Jeannie, to listen to and care for.

Life is a work, life is endless doing, is what Annie was learning from her mother. And from her father: you keep up your responsibilities, do what needs to be done, no complaining or tattling. But Mother was the one who really never did complain, while Annie was sure she heard her father doing it. He complained at Mother, more and more, and Annie heard it sometimes from him when he was with the "cronies."

"It's just their way," Mother said, "men are always trying to work against nature instead of going along with the ways of it.

"Nature has its deep ways," Mother said, "but men don't like that."

But life shouldn't be constantly interrupted by the likes of her brother Martin, his taunts and teasing and endless daredevil pranks,

Annie was learning for herself and from both parents, and she developed an impatience too like her father's for her own comfort. She longed to be calm and patient and present like her mother but she wanted to be left alone; she wanted to read instead of endlessly working. She liked to ramble and think and be left undisturbed by the constant calls to get back to work, or by Martin's ceaseless pestering. She was not enough like either parent, not hard-working enough, she knew. She knew she was lacking.

She didn't make much of a connection to her brothers. All four of them were older. William and James, the toddler and the baby kept warm by Mother's and Father's labor and Mother's fires when the family had first come to the homestead, were near teenagers when Annie was born and grown men by the time Annie knew them. They often worked long days at home or away from home during Annie's earliest years. The next brother, Walter — born years later, after Margaret — Annie remembered Walter as usually at work on trying to fix up some old car. If Walter wasn't doing that, or working outdoors on the farm, he was off with his friends. "Hell-raising around," people said. Mary was close to Walter; she was only two years younger and always with him, always covering for him to keep him out of trouble with Father, but Annie didn't feel close to him at all.

Her older brothers hardly lived in the cabin anyway; they came there for meals and often on winter evenings, but when they were home they spent most of their time up the hill in the Boys' House where they had their own shortwave radio equipment, and model airplanes built from kits. The younger children were not allowed in the Boys' House; it was worth your life to touch any of their special things. They had those kits and radio parts only because they sometimes worked for money. Money was something that Annie understood was scarce, and valuable, but she never could feel it was really precious, like so many of the colonists seemed to think. Like her oldest sister Margaret thought. "She really likes having money," Ellen said about Margaret. "She would like our family if we had more money." Margaret lived in town, where she had a job as accountant at Valley Electric. She was smart and had always been good at math; she bought herself beautiful clothes in Anchorage.

When Ellen was eleven (and Annie eight) Ellen heard that Margaret had been telling new people in town that she was an only child. This was so astonishing to Annie that she couldn't even *think* it — imagine denying so many brothers and sisters! — but Ellen believed the people who had told her about it. And the story tickled Ellen so much — Ellen being like that, tickled by so many things while Annie was surprised at her, so often feeling nervous or narrow compared to her — it tickled Ellen so much that she cooked up a scheme. The next time the girls were allowed to be in town, the two of them went, taking six-year-old Elizabeth with them, to find Margaret at her lunch hour at Deb's restaurant. And the three of them ran up to her, crying, "Sis, sis, we haven't seen you for so long. Sis, we miss you; why don't we ever see you any more?"

"Sis," proclaimed Ellen, loudly, "you haven't been to the farm since the old sow had piglets."

Margaret ignored them but Ellen kept going on, "do you remember, sis, the first time I got to go with you and Walter to feed the pigs and you were supposed to help teach me? And I found out that you had this deal with Walter? You did his math at school while you stayed out of sight at home — sat out on the hill in the sun on a nice day — and let Walter tend to the pigs so you wouldn't get dirty?"

Margaret, after at first trying to ignore them, gave Ellen a furious glare. Then Ellen turned to the other people at Margaret's table — the "young set" that Margaret hung out with — and said, serious and round-eyed: "Margaret had our brother Walter wrapped around her finger. Like all our brothers, Daddy says. She always wraps the males around her fingers, he says."

But this was a bit later, after the war came.

Martin was the youngest of Annie's brothers but still five years older than her. He was banned from the Boys' House too, until he was past twelve. He was ever more the bane of Annie's existence as he kept growing older, because his teasing then sometimes became mean. Annie couldn't handle it as easily as her sisters did. She hated being the object of Martin's relentless taunts and pestering; it could make her wild. If she hadn't adored her oldest brother James, who she hardly got to see very much, she would have grown up even more intimidated and irritated by males. As it was, half afraid of her father and near to hatred of the one brother who was a constant part of her family world, she developed an attitude that came to express itself in spatial relations. She worked it out: that since males were so big, with longer arms and legs, they were always taking up more space than they should be entitled to, and she felt, strongly, that that difference meant that they should be limited to a certain circumference and required to keep a distance. Not only that, but their very being, the souls or spirits of most males, were weightier than women's and girls'. They were oppressive. She didn't understand why boys and men were allowed to impose that weight on women and children so freely. It was unjust. There was something so wrong in it. But since the world let it happen, Annie could only think how to try to make some space, keep some needed distance for herself. When inside the crowded cabin she struggled to keep up her own walls.

But living with Martin toughened her up. No longer the helplessly angry or weeping five-year-old, she was becoming a tough little cookie by the time she was eight. She came to see that the troubles with Martin were partly because Mother couldn't control him. Their father was gone long days, for days or even sometimes weeks at a time, working for the railroad or for other people, fixing machines, building coal washers for the mines at Jonesville. The word about him had kept spreading, as a man who could fix any machinery, fashion parts to keep a Caterpillar or plow or engine running during the long wait for parts to come from the world Outside. When Father was at home he did keep Martin in line, put a stop to Walter's teenage wildness. But he was often not at home. And their mother had the fault of so many Native women — if it was a fault. Among Aleuts, Annie learned later, children did not "belong" to a particular family; they were raised communally. In traditional Aleut culture, by the time a boy was six years old he would become more and more the responsibility of the men of the village, spending his time with the men and the older boys learning the art of building the kayak and carving its special long paddle, catching fish, hunting seals, all the other duties of the male. Learning where the baby seals were overabundant in one year but protecting them, taking few, in any season when the seals had a poor year without so many babies. Then the Aleuts, Annie learned, would have a bad year along with the seals having a bad year.

"You would get skinny," a very old Aleut man told Annie many years later when she was searching for her mother's family. "But that's what the old gods said — and even the Russian god said: you get skinny or fat. You can't always be fat. Because that's not nature. That's what the old gods said and that's what the newfangled Russian god said.

"You had to stick together in bad times. We could always chew on something the women had put back and hope for a whale that the young men took — I was a young man too, and I helped to surround a whale three times in my life, and bring it down. Then we could eat for days. But you never took a whale either, unless you talked to the gods about it and knew the whales could go on. The old gods never wanted for either you or the whales or seals to die off and I guess the new Russian god didn't need that either."

Those years later Annie met Native women from the villages who, even two and three generations removed from her own mother's generation and living in a world where the Native way of life had virtually fallen apart, still found themselves unable to control a son with much spirit. They seemed baffled by the task. In spite of having so much wisdom about so many other things, they had hardly learned what to do with a son beyond tending and coddling him in his early years.

Annie never blamed her mother, though Father did. Annie deeply loved her small and gentle mother. Humming while she worked and always working, always there. She wasn't always patient, would give you a look if she felt you were pestering but she lost her patience only with Martin, who could drive her nearly to distraction. He delighted in it, in making somebody angry. And then he still wouldn't stop, seemed incapable of calm. He was afraid of nothing and nobody, hardly even afraid of their father. Not that he was ill-natured; in fact the opposite: he was always laughing, delighted with everything he could do in the world and do *to* anything in it. Seeming puzzled that people were so easily upset. At least that was his way when young. He was remarkably competent. By the age of eleven he had built a merry-go-round that sailed smoothly on its ball bearings and he would push it around for his little sisters, at first as pleased to be doing that as to be pestering. Within a year after being allowed in the Boys' House, he built a motorized toboggan that could be driven back up the hill behind the cabin that they'd long ago turned into a sled run. Like their father, he loved machines. He spent hours with the *Popular Mechanics* magazines that someone passed on to the boys, always tinkering with building something. When he was sixteen he built a "flying" boat of the kind he had read about being used in the Everglades, to take out onto lakes.

By that time though, Martin lived in Kenai and Annie was free of him. Life had changed.

Father seemed a world unto himself. "Father Almighty" Annie thought of him, from some Christian connection she heard about but took no comfort in. She went to Sunday school for a time because some neighbors wanted to take her there, with her sisters, and they were allowed to go if they had done their chores and cleaned themselves up, brushed their own hair — Mother wasn't going to fuss with four daughters' hair an extra day for the benefit of white man's nonsense. Annie wasn't at all sure she could like God. And, for some reason, Jesus seemed remote too. But she loved the fact that they had pencils and crayons and a chalkboard at the Sunday school. And scissors; she wasn't allowed to touch the only family scissors at home. But her interest in Sunday school faded once she went to real school, with books to read and her own pair of scissors, marked with her name. But her attitude toward God didn't change; he was too remote, unlikeable. And he disrespected her mother.

It set in as a rankling from an early age, that her beloved mother was somehow not good enough. Annie couldn't understand it but she took against the attitude before she ever entered school. By the time she knew, in first grade, that it was because her mother was a "squaw," a "Siwash," a "dirty Indian" — names that Annie and her sisters were also called — her own antipathy was set. And it included her father, who was angry that he had such a wife. He'd married a beautiful little Native girl of seventeen — Annie loved the only picture she saw of her pretty, dark-haired mother so young — but now he blamed her, criticized her. Annie wouldn't forgive him. It was years and years before she understood that her unyielding father, who had seemed to her capable of overriding anything, mastering anybody, had let the general prejudice sway him, that it fed into his own frustration and inability to understand their mother, her view of life so different from his own Midwestern Protestant roots.

Annie was intensely surprised when Almighty Father showed a gentle side. One night she had earaches she cried over, and it was her father who got up and who stayed up with her in the night. Putting warm drops in her ears. When she began to hurt less, feel better, she danced around the big hand-hewn table where the two of them had sat alone with everyone else asleep. She danced wanting to woo him, this stranger her father had turned into, and he smiled as she acted silly. She was maybe five years old. Another time she and her sister Ellen brushed the longish hair around his balding head when he'd fallen asleep by the fire, Ellen trying to put it into little braids because, three years older than Annie, she knew how to braid. Six-year-old Annie was afraid of the sleeping giant, though she had an edge of daring even without a conspirator, but he wasn't angry when he woke up. She almost loved him the day he brought her home from the hospital.

He did everything right, her almighty father, had no weaknesses. He would do whatever was necessary and do it without fuss or hesitation. When Annie tore the back of her leg open, throwing herself too carelessly under the barbed wire fence bordering the south field, he stitched it up, all the while eyeing the medical book open beside her on the kitchen table and eyeing her leg like a thing, a thing neither he or Annie seemed to believe was part of her. He congratulated her on being a brave girl; he said it like he assumed it, took it for granted, but Annie couldn't move afterward, so stiff with the effort not to cry, not to show she felt anything. She felt proud of herself because she couldn't help it, being praised, but she was hiding anger, and hopelessness. She felt the other side of that terrible strength, felt how deeply and strongly this man held to his own unwavering passion, a passion without passion, a passion for a life that seemed to be without feeling.

Which meant he made his own silent war upon their mother, who was the embodiment, by difference, of all that was vulnerable, weak or foolish. His hard will made itself felt at the core of existence; there was no contradicting his rightness. He didn't hear it. Annie felt his impatience, and a near contempt for her lesser being, even when he was trying to teach or help.

And he was big, much bigger than her mother, taller than most men.

But he made everything work: they had lights because he kept the generator working. Annie had to read by wavering, hissing kerosene lamp, extinguished far too early, if the generator failed while he and her big brothers were gone. They had water in the house because he had laid the pipes and kept the pump going. The rain barrels for baths and hair rinsing were clean when he was home; the animals were fed on time; everything was orderly.

But it was changing; he was gone more and more. He built a sawmill a few miles on the other side of town and was gone for long hours even when he was no longer riding the railroad to other places. He leased out the west field, then the north field; it was the neighbors who began to control most of the homestead. There was marvelous freedom with him away but there was growing confusion, Martin out of control and the other brothers gone, most of the animals sold: no more cows in the pasture, Old Smoke long gone and the collie Maggie beginning to limp, moving slowly; only some calves and the chickens left to care for, and four little girls and a pesky brother barely helping their mother to keep a life together.

The War had come and soon behind it came the soldiers, suddenly flooding the Valley.

Chapter Three

"How can you be working in town when you've got Martin and these four little girls to look after and all the work here?" their father demanded of Mother. Annie agreed with him this time; she hated seeing her mother go to work for Rusty Crown.

"I take Little Jeannie with me and the others are all in school now. Mary will be here until I get home," Mother was stubborn in her reply. She was not even five feet tall, and usually gentle, but about some things, where her mind was made up, you couldn't move her.

Mary was past fifteen and she didn't like staying on the homestead much any more. She had her friends in town and, besides, she had joined in the craze for going to the USO dances and meeting soldiers, running around in cars with her high school buddies. Mary was popular, the best jitterbugger in the Valley, and there was a whole gang she ran around with, boys and girls together, mostly a year or two older. She resisted staying home after school, sneaked off half the time leaving eleven-year-old Ellen in charge. Annie had turned eight. Their father grumbled, frustrated and angry, and took thirteen-year-old Martin to the sawmill with him most of the time. James and William were gone, joined the Air Force, and Walter was hardly home either, just marking down the last days to his seventeenth birthday, to leave for the Navy.

Annie would have liked to hate Rusty Crown but she couldn't. She was a big bosomy woman, friendly and full of life; as soon as you heard her laugh, throwing back her head of thick red hair, you had to like her. She had just the right name, Annie thought. But she was coaxing their mother away, persuaded her to come to work for her at the laundry in town. Other women had never come to the farm to visit Mother — she was an outcast, still the only Native in the Valley — but now with new people coming in because of the war and the soldiers, Mother was making a few friends. She and Rusty Crown were as different as cat and dog; Mother looked tiny beside the woman with the big voice, big hair, big laugh, but they became fast friends until Rusty left town a year later to drive a supply truck between Anchorage and Fairbanks.

Annie didn't like rambling the homestead much any more. The empty barn, even the calf barn empty now, the fence of their old pasture along the driveway losing its rusty nails, these things made her sad. Mother not being home, going to work in town, was the worst sadness; the homestead was lonely without her. After school Annie and her sisters went to the laundry, right across from the school building, trying to pester Mother, got in trouble for missing the bus. As the weather got better in spring they'd always been allowed to walk home, not much more than a half-mile to their south field by shortcuts, but now they hung about town looking for Mary and her friends. Looking to pester Margaret. Mary was more and more running around with her friends and young soldiers, through spring and into summer. The town began to see that the children were untended.

They stuck together, the four girls, Ellen oldest at eleven and little Jeannie only four, because life had grown scary. The town and the countryside that had been so quiet burst into new life almost overnight. Fort Richardson and Elmendorf Air Force Base were only fifty miles from the Valley even by the first, old road which was soon straightened, and soldiers poured in, an occupying army. There were parties and the USO, a dance every Friday night, dances and parties all weekend; convoys full of soldiers up and down the road right past the homestead, coming or going from Fairbanks — long parades of dirty, brown-green trucks with dusty-looking men under canvas tops waving at the girls. Margaret, the sister who had been living and working in town for two years, was dating soldiers. Walter left for the Navy in the spring.

It all happened so fast. The little girls had repeated warnings not to trust them, our own boys in uniform, not to be out at night, not to accept rides. They had always walked everywhere and always been happy for a ride if a neighbor stopped, but now they didn't know who was a neighbor because new people appeared all the time and soldiers weren't always in uniform. It was confusing because Mary was sneaking out to run around, meeting soldiers hardly older than she was, and the town celebrated them, praised them in speeches and on the radio. Their own brothers were soldiers now. But the girls were taught to fear them, not to even go berry picking that summer without a grown-up. It was strange, Annie thought, how her brothers and other local boys were sent away to be soldiers somewhere else while all these strange boys from far away places were sent here. They popped up everywhere, soldiers and other men. And some of them, the sisters told each other, were so nice.

Annie did already know that men got drunk, wearing silly grins and acting like they shouldn't, could start leering and become frightening; how even the good ones changed if they started fighting, how they could terrify. Or try to get you alone and get under your clothes, even the good men. But the girls had known names; not just old Witze, a neighbor Mother had told them to stay away from (but Margaret and Mary had long since taught the younger girls how to get the candy and still get away). There had been other men; they knew it was a thing about some men, especially if they were drinking.

Now there were terrible stories, some on the radio and newspapers and some not. "My aunt was right next door," Donny Wilkins bragged on the school playground, "and she ran over and they were stabbing each other. She said everybody was bloody and there was blood spattering in the frying pan." That was three men, soldiers.

The stories kept growing in the schoolyard: Wilma's friend's mother was murdered and Wilma, in fifth grade, didn't come back to school. It was Wilma, visiting her friend in Anchorage, who first saw her friend's mother's body, her legs hanging out of a dumpster. It was after an all-night party with soldiers and her husband got jealous and went berserk, they said. Wilma's sister said Wilma had nightmares. Annie could never quite remember in which school year she heard these things; couldn't separate in her mind those three worst of the bad years.

Bobby Wyrksaw's tiny sister Anna, four years old and skinny, died in a fire when some brawling soldiers knocked over the kerosene lamps in an outside shed where they had been told, by the young couple of the house, that they could stay overnight because they were drunk and AWOL. That was right in the Valley, near town. Annie heard old John Marsh and young John Marsh, volunteer firemen down town, talking to some other men about the fire which had burned down house and shed and all, the talk of the town. Old John Marsh said, "awfullest thing I ever saw. That little thing, looked like she hid behind a twenty pound sack of potatoes and they were all burned to a crisp, her and the potatoes melted and crisped up together." The rest of the family got out. And the soldiers.

That one, in the newspaper, said that there would be a court martial. The AWOL men in the shed were all young, the same ages as William and Walter.

Kids on the playground talked about brawls and knifings, learned new words: assault, robberies with violence, manslaughter, rape. Murder.

Big MPs in stiff-looking uniforms and white-starred, hard helmets had started running everywhere in jeeps, with clubs on their belts along with guns. "A second army trying to control the first," said Father.

Then came the dance that night, the height of summer, the night Rudy followed Mother.

Annie had nightmares about the man Rudy for years. In her dreaming eye, strangely, she hardly saw the uniform; instead she saw a looming dark shape with a terrible gleaming face the color of dark honey. He was not a hairy monster; he was smooth, oily-ripply smooth. In her nightmares he was following Annie or following her Mother. Annie wanted, from looming dread, to stop him. But she was so afraid she needed to keep getting away, needed to hide. Then the awful paralysis set in: Over and over, in every dream, he reached for her and for her Mother and Annie was frozen, unable to move. Suddenly then she would wake, feeling such horror that her veins were icy cold. She would lie stiff in the bunk next to sleeping Ellen, afraid even to breathe, feeling her heart pound her frozen body.

He was a soldier from Fort Richardson who had come to the USO dance in town. Mother had gone to the dance — was it Rusty Crown who had encouraged her to do such a thing? — and was walking home alone, hardly more than a mile even by the road, near midnight but still dusk in the long Alaska day that hardly turned to night. He caught up to her just before she reached the south field and left her raped and beaten in the grassy ditch by the side of the gravel road.

It was Father's terrible anger that woke half the girls when Mother got herself home. But when he sternly ordered Annie back to bed Annie didn't go, in spite of seeing in her father the worst anger yet. Because she couldn't move. Seeing her mother's utter stillness lying on the sofa she knew that her mother was dead, murdered. And her own heart stopped. She stared, not wanting to see them, at swellings turning purple in her mother's face, the long scratches or gashes on the bare legs and feet, the torn filthiness of Mother's only good dress, until her father pushed her back to the bedroom.

It was Elizabeth, six years old, who was also awake. And crying. But at least then, because of Elizabeth's crying, Annie heard her mother's voice from the other room (there was no door to the little bedroom, only a wide arch that let the heat from the big heater in the main room circulate through the cabin). Mother had never been able to hear one of her little ones cry, especially Elizabeth, without some murmur of consolation and Annie began, with a depth of gratefulness, to hear those murmurs, recognized them and hushed Elizabeth from crying so that Elizabeth could hear them too where the two of them huddled together in the bottom bunk of the three tiers in what was now entirely the girls' room.

Ellen and little Jeannie didn't wake and Martin had been sent to the Boys' House (where he pretty much lived, with his brothers gone). Mary wasn't home herself yet, still out running around after the dance, and there would be more trouble, more anger when she came in, Annie knew. She was awake for what felt like a long time after Elizabeth cried herself to sleep, heard the renewed anger when Mary did finally come home, heard Mary trying some of her back talk, but half-heartedly and half-cowed. And then, as if Mary's attitude was some sort of signal of normalcy, finally some tight hold on Annie's body loosened enough that she herself fell asleep.

Everyone soon told stories about the rape; it was all over town. Annie realized that it must be Father who had reported it. Certainly their mother didn't and Annie thought she was right. Mother let you know she didn't want you even thinking about it; she gave you the look that meant she knew what was in your mind and you'd better just get busy and do something useful. Her face healed up without scars and she was her old self again and staying home; she gave up the job at the laundry.

Annie thought the rape should be hidden, that people shouldn't talk about it, shouldn't even know about it. She herself tried to bury it, forget the sight of her mother battered, but Rudy came back night after night in her fright-filled dreams. She knew his name because there was a story in the newspaper. She heard the other stories too: That Mother had gone to a dance without her husband was enough by itself to cause gossip because the women of the Valley who were the good women wouldn't do such a thing. Some believed even dancing was a sin. But the good women thought the rape was a wonderful scandal. They made up stories to suit themselves and they enjoyed making them up; you could hear the glee in their voices. Some of them maybe thought that little girls wouldn't hear the glee, but some knew and took pleasure in hurting. They clucked sometimes to sound sympathetic but it was false. It was Mother's own fault, they clearly meant to say; she had it coming. There were stories that Mother danced all night with Rudy; stories that she was drunk, that she danced with dozens of soldiers, a different one each time; stories that Father went down and dragged her from the arms of some soldier.

In all that smoke, what does a child know of whether there was fire? The imagining burns in memory. It made Annie squirm, made her stomach sick, to think of her mother showing any fire, any passion, in public.

The newspaper story said that there would be a court martial. The Army wanted the man identified, but Mother wanted nothing to do with it. So there was a standoff: Mother dug in her heels and wouldn't go. It was just like what Father said: "wild horses can't move you, Teresa," he'd thundered once. Annie loved that in her mother, secretly: that, small as Mother was, and quiet as she usually was, Mother saw things just the way she saw them — saw things her own way and seemed to see right through people and their talk, that she had her own unspoken way of "putting her foot down."

But the Army was stubborn too; it wouldn't take no for an answer. So the Army did an astonishing thing: Mother wouldn't go to the Army, so the Army came to Mother. With a convoy truck full of soldiers and four jeeps full of MPs — two jeeps in front and two following the truck — the Army came in a procession up the long driveway onto the farm raising the summer dust and unloaded them all, MPs guarding soldiers, right there in front of the old cabin.

Tough-looking MPs in stern faces and hard helmets with their heavy sticks and guns, the parade of dusty-dirty machines bearing the stars of The Army, the rank of soldiers unloaded from the truck, all in uniform. In dread Annie knew, when she was in the yard and first saw them coming, there had to be the enemy. But the white stars on the shining MP helmets and the same white stars, dirty, on all the vehicles, said that these were "our own boys," the United States Army. The dogs went crazy.

Father, coming from the calf barn, calmed the dogs and talked to the MPs, talked to a big wiry man, dark-haired, sharp-eyed, who looked and acted like he was in charge. Then Father came in and talked to Mother, who was trying to deal with all of the children who had run indoors, stunned by the invasion, variously huddled or alone. Martin, now thirteen, the oldest, soon went out and swaggered around on the porch showing he was not afraid.

No one explained why the Army had invaded the farm. Even Mother hadn't explained rape, wouldn't talk about it, and Father wouldn't talk about such a thing to girls.

Father went out again and talked some more to the big MP. Only slowly did Annie begin to realize, half-realize, what was happening: the Army wanted to line up some men, and have Mother identify the man who had attacked her. They had brought some "suspects," and some other soldiers who supposedly looked like them — or who had been at the dance; they had many soldiers there. Back and forth Father went, from the big MP and dirty truck and drab uniforms of the men in line, and back to Mother who looked so little. And finally talked Mother into it, since the Army wouldn't leave.

So Mother went out.

This was the picture Annie saw from her corner of window, the picture that stayed with her: her little mother walking slowly alone down the line of uniformed soldiers, they standing stiffly in a row in the dust with an army of MPs at attention around them. Some chickens scratching in the foreground. The collie Maggie at attention too, sitting tightly on her haunches near two brown chickens and, for all that Father had been saying Maggie might be losing her sight, intently watching Mother. The other two dogs had been shut in the house with the children.

And Mother stopped when she came to him — to Rudy. She stopped both times, on her way down the row the first time, and again on her way back. And Annie saw the way he looked at her, with that dark flash from sideways eyes in shiny honey skin.

It was years before Annie wondered about others looking at this picture, how the world might view it. There had been so many other pictures, so many people who drew pictures in their stories, their gossipy talk. Blaming Mother.

And Rudy: what was Rudy seeing then?

At the time, Annie was stone quiet, struck dumb, but crazed like all the other smaller creatures closed in the house. At first she knew the

Army had come to punish them all, especially herself, for their shame, for their guilts. She had stolen candy once. She hated Martin. Above all, she hadn't protected her mother. Like sobbing Elizabeth and littlest sister Jeannie, and the dogs shut in with them, she was out of her mind. She'd been mean, even to Mother; she was a mean child. She didn't even like her scary father, though she had courted him, quietly and fiercely. It was she, not her mother, who deserved the punishment of the invading army.

She thought they were after *her*. Her mother. Father had been so furious. At Mother, at everything. Martin hated him, hated Rudy, but Martin despised Mother for going to the dance. Even Mary had been cowed. The shame. The shame.

But some relief, deep relief, when they blamed Rudy. The testimony at the court martial was that Mother was at the dance for several hours, that she spent most of that time talking to her friend Rusty Crown and only tried to dance some schottische dances, watching until late the heightening revelry at the peak of the dance — the whirling foxtrots and jitterbugs — before going home alone. Annie absorbed every word of the Anchorage newspaper that she took — stole — from a table at Deb's on a trip with her sisters to town with Father. Father was never at the dance, the newspaper said, by his account or any account.

He was there in fantasy, in a macabre dance of his own inside Annie's head, competing with the shifting shape of Rudy: night after night she would have the dreams of the two of them: the huge shape of her father's grim anger and the sneaking gleam from Rudy's eye as they both stalked Mother. She was terrified that she couldn't tell them apart, her father from Rudy. But, sometimes, when she woke in awful panic, she found Elizabeth or little Jeannie having a nightmare too, and she learned, especially from Ellen, that in trying to soothe her little sisters she would feel better herself. Ellen slept better than anybody but sometimes she would be awake too and she and Annie would take turns telling their little sisters a story. A story could always take you away from the bad stuff.

Sometimes Father killed someone and Annie woke, again terrified, not knowing who he had killed in her dream. In the daytime she fantasized that he would kill the gossiping women because she wanted him to: He could rend them, tear them to pieces; in her daytime fantasies she let him kill them all. She wanted him to. But never *her*. Never Mother. He rescued her, or none of it ever happened.

In real life Almighty Father was never violent anyway; Annie was surprised to look back later on his awful violence in those bad dreams. But he was so angry.

The court martial did blame Rudy. It appeared that Rudy of the rippling skin — Rudy, aka horrible shape of dreams — had followed Mother from the dance, and for that and his other acts he got fifteen years at hard labor with a dishonorable discharge. A hard penalty, as Annie saw much later. As a child it meant to her only deepest relief that they didn't blame *her*. Or Annie. Or the family.

Still, the family was pulling itself apart: Martin growing mean, Father home more than ever but more grim than ever, and Mother's quietness different, heavy with a weight Annie had never before felt in her.

Annie was afraid of anger, of anger felt in her father. Her own anger, the angers of little Annie as she used to be, had seemed innocent. But she knew now that things were changed. Some hidden thing infected them all, and she hid her own self more than ever, held down her own angers. She had been used to hiding — in fact she had liked hiding, finding her own secret spots around the homestead or her own special time away from the endless work and away from Martin, or being absorbed in a book away from everything. But now something hard, cold, was threatening and she clung close to home, close to her mother.

She wanted to blame Rudy, the Rudy named in the newspaper. But sometimes, into her worst dreams or trying to enter her daytime thoughts, there intruded a hint, a suggestion, of an awful notion: that the family was to blame, that they had brought it on themselves. And she would get a glimpse, in those awful moments — because something in her saw, briefly, past the vehicles and the uniforms of the soldiers lined up in the dust, and the guns and hard slick helmets of the MPs surrounding them and her Almighty Father talking to the tough, dark man in charge of them — sometimes she would get a glimpse of something that really scared her: that the soldiers looked sort of weak and cowed in the middle, in the middle of all the threat surrounding them. And they looked too much like her own brothers. That old monster Rudy, horrible Rudy of her nightmares, was one of them: not an old monster but a frightened and droopy-looking soldier as young as the rest.

She shut out any such notion. She wanted to blame Rudy for what was happening to her family and she did blame him. But she shut him away too, along with other bad things, as soon as the nightmares lessened. He became a nobody, a blurry unrecognizable picture in some Anchorage newspaper if she ever thought of him at all. For years she didn't even remember his name.

Chapter Four

Mother took the girls away after this, to Anchorage, to a little white house with dark-paneled rooms near downtown, with funny-smelling closets, and went to work at another laundry. But their escape from the homestead was short-lived. Father came and loaded the four girls into the flatbed truck, behind its bars, and took them home and Mother soon came back too.

It was a hard year then that followed, the family wrenched apart, their father grim when he was home, almost daily now for short spells, usually angry but mostly living out at the sawmill where he fixed up a room and a stove for him and Martin. Sleeping in the Boys' House with Martin if he did stay over night at home. Mother increasingly stubborn, more and more inclined to speak her mind, not putting up with criticism. She would simply leave sometimes, go to Anchorage with friends.

Christmas of that long winter was a barren thing, Mother not at home on Christmas eve, Father mostly ignoring the holiday as he always had, no hard candy in the plump or curlicued shapes that their parents had always ordered in a big can from Sears Roebuck and doled out to the children over the rest of the winter. No popcorn, the once-a-year treat that, always before, came in another big can that they could keep eating as Mother — and sometimes even Father in a rare expansive humor — would be popping it in evenings so that there was enough, even with eating it, for Mother and the girls to string the white balls on Mother's bright red thread. Enough so that, even with all the mistakes, over and over, of breaking or crumbling the balls, you could finally have a pretty string. Which you then, so carefully, with tongue between your teeth, helped to drape over each window, trying to arrange each string neatly, trying to be sure that Father wouldn't call it a sloppy job.

There had never been a decorated tree; why would you cut down and drag in from out-of-doors a tree that had been living on its own? There wasn't room for it in the cabin anyway. When Annie first read about such a thing it seemed strange. But then she began to see that the colonists had houses big enough to do it and their decorated trees were beautiful with colored lights, shining colored balls and other pretty things. So it was another thing to puzzle over.

There had never been gifts. Or that Annie thought you could be given any special thing, any gift, that was for yourself alone. A gift was like one of those good things you discovered when you didn't expect it, or a blessing that came to everybody, like the rain coming at the right time or good weather for the harvest. Even if things went better for your own family than for some others, you couldn't believe you were supposed to be blessed beyond those other people. Mother said that and Father seemed to believe it, always going off to help somebody else. Except when Annie was in the hospital, there were no times in her childhood when she was given anything just for herself. And while she treasured those gifts — and the wonderful aftermath of being treated like someone special after the pain and sickness — she never quite trusted those feelings. She had safeguarded the teddy bear for awhile as her own but then she gave it to little Jeannie and gave the jigsaw puzzle to Elizabeth. Only the book remained her own possession, that she was quietly proud to see sitting up on the shelf by the Books of Knowledge and know that it belonged to *her*. (It was strange that years later she couldn't even remember what the book was. She had been thinking for a long time in those early years that, if she ever got any money, she would order *Heidi* from the Sears catalog, but this book from her brother wasn't anything like that. It was by Pearl S. Buck, maybe, and hard to understand.)

The U.S. marshal came to the house one early evening in spring. The marshal was practically a neighbor but he was wearing his uniform that evening and he spoke solemnly to her parents, the rest of them banished from the house while the three sat around the kitchen table. Then Martin was called in. Annie was horrified as she learned what he'd done — the word spread among those outside as fast as wildfire — and Annie walked and walked around the yard, went deep into the woods. Thinking without thinking, wanting escape from thoughts of terrible punishment. But she had to come back, had to know the worst.

Martin had stolen from the Farmer's Co-op. The only store in town. The store of the whole town, with more than things to buy: everybody's hopes and future were stored there, where they all took their crops, got them shipped to sell, got what they needed and credit for when they needed more. It was stealing from everybody, worse than stealing from the family — which Martin had never done. Worse than anything Annie had ever imagined. (You couldn't even touch anything that was important to somebody else, but Annie knew, guiltily, that she had done that, more than once. That was why she knew how bad it was, how it made you feel sneaky and wrong even to be touching something precious to somebody else or needed by them. It was wrong unless you asked, unless they let you touch. And how bad everyone would know you were if they found out you did it anyway.)

This was so much worse, worse beyond thinking. And what people owed to each other was kept at the Co-op — Annie had learned that much, that there was a record written there about how much you could have, how much you had to pay back and how much you hadn't paid back yet. Annie had heard Father explaining that to Mother when he said he was going to do some work for the Co-op to help build coolers and storage lockers in an extension. "Then you'll have credit there," Father said to Mother, "to get what we need. And they get the price to sell our grain and extra potatoes, so people won't just be trading things around so much on their own. Or letting anything go to waste like it sometimes has with the grain."

Mother had seemed suspicious about all of it but Annie was fascinated by the idea. When she was maybe six or seven years old, in love with learning numbers and learning to spell, liking lists and orderly pages, she had begun making little lists of her own that made sense out of things: 'reasons to stay away from Martin' was one such list — 'never trust unless he's really hurt and not pretending,' was at the top of that list. She slyly took Martin's spelling book, that he never opened and never missed, and labored over her pages about him. She struggled to put down the times, and the ways, to stand up to Martin instead of just avoiding him. Then her father's talk to her mother about the Co-op opened a whole wide world in her imagination: people all over the Valley could list what they really wanted, could put it down, neatly, onto pages, and everyone could know what you *didn't* want, so they would leave you alone about those things. And help you with the things that you *did* want. She pictured the big book at the Co-op; she thought it should include what you owed back to people if you had been hurting them or pestering them all the time. She made another list, of what Martin owed to her: "days of being gone," was the first thing on that list, but then she put it second to "never bothering Mother."

Would it throw the whole book into confusion, now that Martin had taken things that didn't belong to him? And he owed for guns? — a staggering thing, and a staggering price — on top of what he owed for messing up the book. And what could you owe for being a thief?

Annie could not imagine it. She knew that Martin would be taken away, would be terribly punished. She couldn't think how her parents would bear the shame: The worst kind of thief in their own family. And Martin: Much as she thought she hated him, she dreaded what would have to be awful punishment.

She was shocked when she saw the marshal leaving. Without Martin. She hurried into the yard but then was terrified again, when she saw her father and Martin near the Boys' House. Their father was more frightening than the marshal and he had Martin by the arm, shaking him, his face dark with fury.

Martin lost all his freedom. For weeks he couldn't go anywhere without Father. He had to work right beside Father, maybe at home but mostly at the sawmill, working for dimes or a rare quarter until he paid back the Co-op. He had joined some older boys in the theft and they were the ones who had taken the two guns. Martin had taken ammunition. And a jacket — which he had to return along with the last of a cache of bananas and candy which he had hidden in the basement, what was left after the boys had gorged themselves, and what was left of the ammunition after the boys had been on a shooting spree in a far woods above the Riley farm.

"Bananas were so expensive, remember?" Annie was saying to her sister Mary years later. "And do you know what I thought? I'd just about forgotten this," and she told Mary, both of them laughing about her childhood fantasy of the "big book" at the Co-op. "I thought it was a record of what everybody owed every other person. And I wondered if it included what you *didn't* want. And I made all these lists of what I wanted and didn't want. I thought kids should be able to list those things in town too, like the grown-ups did."

"Maybe not such a bad idea," Mary said. "Maybe there is some 'big book' in the sky like that."

"Sounds like karma to me," said another friend when Annie described her childhood fantasy.

Spring came round again, and then summer. Long lovely days and lingering twilights. This time when Mother took the girls away, as soon as school was out, they moved to Mountain View, near Anchorage and the Army base at Fort Richardson, and their father didn't come to get them. They had to fend for themselves, mostly, because Mother went to work in the laundry at Fort Richardson, working from four to midnight or after. And she had discovered Alcohol. Annie and Ellen decided it was true what they'd heard, that Natives couldn't drink. Mother turned into a completely different person when she drank, sloppy and careless, laughing about even disgusting things. Unless someone tried to cross her, then she became loud and cantankerous, had a bad temper.

She had met this man named Kiley somewhere and it was his house they lived in, on the edge of Mountain View close to the base, a house not as big as their cabin at home, with a wide deck but with only one tiny bedroom. The girls slept together there, Ellen and Jeannie at one end of a bed that took up almost the whole room, and Elizabeth with Annie at the other end. There was a little window over the bed and, to one side, just enough space for a wooden dresser. By the door were two rows of rods where Kiley hung his neat shirts and uniforms. There was a bigger bed in the bigger front room, where Kiley slept, if he slept at all. Annie could never decide if the man really slept; he seemed like a cat, sort of awake even if it looked like he might be sleeping. He and Mother often partied half the night and Mother would be snoring softly in the girls' room through the daytime.

Kiley was a staff sergeant living off base though he was on duty some nights. He was old, though not as old as their father, and a strange type, one they'd never met before. He said he had a wife and son in Missoula, Montana but he didn't seem to think anything wrong with living with another woman in Mountain View. He was a party man, Annie decided, liked his liquor, liked to party, was always inviting other soldiers to come by.

He left the girls alone; mostly he seemed amused that they even existed. He made no move to protect them or to correct them or to bother them in any way. He seemed mostly amused by Mother too, laughed a lot even when she was drunk, especially when she was drunk. He never seemed really drunk himself, though he was often drinking. Even when he acted angry at Ellen and Annie for stealing some of his cigarettes, Annie had some suspicion he didn't really feel it, was putting on.

Mother didn't stay really drunk during the week; she had to go to work, but she didn't go to bed right after work either, often did drink and laugh or loudly argue with Kiley half the night. Cranky if you woke her up before noon. The only good hours were afternoon, sometimes, after she'd had enough of her tea and might talk occasionally instead of chasing everybody out while she cleaned and cleaned the whole place. On her days off it was one long party time. You couldn't trust her at all then; they had to look out for themselves.

As it happened, they were well trained for such a life, as strange and different as it was from their lives on a farm with brothers and father to protect them. They soon realized that "their house" was close to the head of what was called "the sneak trail," the back trail through woods and a canyon, that soldiers used for sneaking off the base or when trying to sneak back onto base when AWOL. There was a lot of sneaking along that trail and, whether coming or going, half the sneakers were frightening: ready to party or already drunk and, no matter which, looking for girls. They didn't act like Natives were really human; there were stories all the time in Anchorage about Native girls and women being raped. A story that a young Native girl was hauled around town for a day or two by a gang of soldiers like a captive while they all used her for sex. But Ellen and Annie, at least, had been well-taught in independence and in looking out for themselves and they protected Elizabeth and little Jeannie and taught them in turn. They knew not to let men take advantage of them and they knew how to rustle up food and how to cook. What Annie didn't know how to do, what made her heart sore in her aloneness at night and heartsick whenever she watched her getting drunk, was how to take care of Mother.

Help against the rest of the world appeared in a most unexpected way. Though they had been as much afraid of the MPs as of other soldiers, the girls soon realized that they shouldn't fear the two MPs who often came patrolling the sneak trail. As young as William and Walter, one of them as serious as William, the two MPs became friends and protectors.

The serious one, called Bud, came close to putting into words what they had worried over and been afraid of from men without any adult really telling them the words for their fears. "If they try to get you alone, or get in bed with you," Bud said, bold as could be, "they'll likely do things they shouldn't do to girls. They shouldn't even touch you and don't ever let them touch you where you'll have breasts, or below the waist." The girls did know that much from Margaret and Mary but had never heard it from a man; they were surprised that a man admitted it. They had no clear idea of what was to be feared anyway, only that there was this cloud of hints and suggestions and warnings, and odd "facts" gleaned from peoples' stories that Ellen and Annie talked about, trying to figure out what it really was that a man might "get up to." They felt that a girl just had to live a guessing game trying to figure out for herself who to trust and whether the same man could be trusted all the time. Whether to trust any of them all the time. Why it was that women, and girls, were always marrying men and maybe doing those things that were bad, that you were supposed to be afraid of.

They went further, the two MPs, Bud and Wilson. They drilled it into the little girls that they had a right to stand up against adult men, even men wearing the uniform of authority. The girls had been half intimidated by the uniforms and by the sympathy of knowing their own brothers were now like these men, must be wearing uniforms too. But the MPs, especially Bud, didn't want them to sympathize, insisted the girls shouldn't trust any man who got too close even if he was kindly, even if he was good to them. "Especially if he offers fruit or candy," Bud said. Fruit or candy that Annie and her sisters so seldom had.

Bud and Wilson made a game of it, Wilson helping the four girls to fashion weapons, telling them to stick together and to use their weapons, all together, if they couldn't get away from a man bothering them. They marched the girls up and down the broad outside deck like a little army. Annie's weapon was a stout stick sharpened at one end. "Aim for his gut," Bud said, "the middle of him. Right here," he pointed to his own lower belly. "Or trip him with it. If he won't leave you alone, poke at his face, his eyes even. . . ."

"Wait a minute," said Wilson, "let's not teach them to be blood thirsty. . . ."

But Bud must have had something in him like the anger Annie carried in her soul since her mother's rape. Because he had no sympathy for men like the one Ellen and Elizabeth told him about, who had grabbed Ellen on the sneak trail and tried to chase Elizabeth away. Elizabeth had set up a screaming holler and, by the time Annie came running, Ellen herself had kicked and kicked the man's shins while

Elizabeth had run back up and bit his one hand holding onto Ellen, so that the man was swearing and then running away.

"But he was drunk, I could smell it," Ellen told the MPs. "And he wasn't very coordinated." She was sort of sticking up for the guy.

But Bud wasn't: "Don't ever talk that way," he told Ellen sternly, "he's a soldier. He's not supposed to be drunk, or grabbing girls."

Bud and Wilson had some disagreements and that was one of the days they went aside to talk to each other. Wilson sounded a little tougher after that, though still full of remarks that had the girls laughing. "Why not a child's army?" he called out as they marched up and down across the deck: "one, two, I'm as smart as you. Three, four, you don't know what you've bargained for."

Little Jeannie's weapon as they marched was a woman's high-heeled shoe, the long heel very pointed. Ellen had a piece of metal pipe. "Careful with it," Bud said, but he knew by now that Ellen was inclined toward sympathy, maybe too much so. Annie couldn't later remember what was Elizabeth's weapon but that was because Elizabeth didn't like it, was always putting down or forgetting whatever it was, would rather appease anyone older or bigger than to fight. Elizabeth at age seven was as roly-poly as ever, with dimpled cheeks and a winning smile; Annie, skinny and standoffish, had long resented how so many people cooed over Elizabeth while they acted like Annie didn't exist. But the sisters were in it together now for real; Ellen and Annie had to protect Elizabeth along with little Jeannie, and Elizabeth usually went along. Little Jeannie, as they always called her, was easier to train than Elizabeth. Unflinching like Ellen and as self-contained as Annie, little Jeannie nearing six took to the drills happily.

Ellen was the most good-natured one and the strongest as well as oldest. Taking things as they came, sturdy as a birch tree. Annie adored her, tried to be like her. But Ellen laughed the most too, and Annie couldn't emulate that; she just didn't get such a kick out of life and people as Ellen did.

They did use their weapons that summer, more than once. One night when Mother was passed out and a man kept insisting on getting into the bed where the four girls slept together, while Ellen and Annie were unsuccessfully trying to beat him off, unable to reach their weapons under the bed, little Jeannie rose up from the foot of the bed and almost put out the man's eye with the high heel of her weapon-shoe. He retreated, bleating, holding his face while the older girls with their stick and pipe forced him out the door. Another night while they were alone, a man kept trying to crawl through the window over their bed. The girls pushed and pushed at him but he leered and wriggled back every time they got him part way out. Finally Ellen picked up her metal pipe and hit him over the head. He went limp and they pushed him out.

Ellen had nightmares about that for long after. "I thought Bud and Wilson said they took him back to Base next morning," Annie said when they talked about it. She was shocked that Ellen still worried about it as a grown woman with a family. "They said he was fine, just another drunk passed out along the sneak trail. That's what they reported to the base, they said."

"I never believed them," Ellen said. "They were just protecting me. I'm sure he *was* drunk. But I'm sure they did believe *me* about that crunch I heard when I hit him; didn't you hear it?"

Annie didn't remember. And she didn't want to realize what a terrible thing it could be on your conscience, that you may have killed a man. She had never pointed her sharpened stick at a man's face or throat, couldn't bring herself to do it, in spite of Bud's instructions, used it as a beating stick instead. And in that old time she had believed the MPs, Bud and Wilson, that they had found Ellen's "killed" man and reported him as a drunk passed out along the sneak trail. *(More hiding from herself, over the years, things that she knew?)*

They came by the house often that summer, Bud and Wilson, drove out partying men when they found them, even tangled with Mother in some of her belligerent, drunken states. Not that they could do anything with her. Kiley never argued with them; if he was home he simply tossed up his hands, laughed, told them to get on with it. Didn't care if they were driving his drunken pals away. Life was just one thing after another to Kiley. Ellen was sort of like that too, just taking whatever came along with a good humor, but she was caring through all of it and Kiley was not. Not at all. Annie kept wanting to be like Ellen, but never like Kiley; she wanted not to be so tense or unhappy or worried, and she followed Ellen's lead all the time, trying to learn.

There were neighbors who gave the girls even more of an education in some of the ways of the world. A woman with two daughters lived close by, daughters only a little older than Ellen and Annie. The daughters knew all about sex, had a dildo they called a "wiener" and talked about its delights, how they used it for each other. They offered it to Ellen and Annie but Ellen turned up her nose. Annie was shocked and a little sick to her stomach, but on the way home Ellen giggled and laughed: "Silly, stupid girls," she said. The girls' mother, a blonde with thick long hair who was beautiful, had soldiers at her house too, though she never seemed drunk and wouldn't let the men touch her daughters. The daughters seemed sort of mean talking about their mother. "They're jealous of her," Ellen said. Another puzzle, and Ellen couldn't explain it either.

Annie and her sisters roamed the neighborhood and all through Mountain View that summer, sneaked into an empty cabin looking to see if there might be pennies to take or anything just interesting to see, but there was nothing except dust and some chairs. They made friends with a skinny girl who lived with her grandmother in a little house that was shining clean but had a very odd, heavy smell. People said they were Finnish. The grandmother cooked things they'd never heard of that didn't sound good, and she didn't talk much in English. She wasn't either friendly or unfriendly, just kept a close eye when they came to play with her granddaughter, wanted them to stay mostly outside, offered them some strange, crunchy bread with something on it that didn't taste like butter, though the girl said it was. "From our goat," she said. And, to Annie's fascination, because she had never seen one, they did have two goats in their back yard. But the girl didn't seem to know how to play and the sisters stopped going back much.

Sometimes they played down into the canyon of the sneak trail, eating the little orange-red clusters of berries from what they called ground dogwood, but they never ventured far in that direction, stuck close together and kept their weapons handy. They walked down to the Mountain View store and bought candy, having pennies or nickels from Mother or even a rare dime that Kiley gave them. They stole pennies or a nickel from Mother's purse when she was passed out, once even a quarter.

Annie felt two ways about the stealing. She knew it was bad, but did it matter so much when you took only little things, things that didn't seem to matter much to the person you took it from? Still, they were adding up; she used to keep track in her mind: paper from the Sunday school — was it six pieces, or only five? — a candy bar once, but she had been punished for that, by Father, so did it really count? Six pennies. But it was twenty-seven pennies by now and two dimes, one quarter. That was getting close to a whole dollar and she knew it would be bad to take a dollar from anyone. But they hadn't taken it from one person, so maybe it wasn't so awful as it seemed when she first realized how it added up? The newspaper about Rudy, but hadn't somebody just left that newspaper there, not caring whether somebody else took it. And she was sure Kiley didn't really care about the two cigarettes either.

But it struck her, as she was lying awake in the night after taking Mother's quarter, as she saw the risen moon out the little window over the bed and heard an animal cry — it struck her in remembering Mother's look, Mother's look before Alcohol, the look that knew who you were, and she saw that she had been denying, had stopped counting. But no . . . no, that wasn't true either; her mind had been counting but she had been ignoring. It was eighty-three things stolen by now. Eighty-three. A horrific number.

She vowed, vowed fervently in the night, that she would never let the number grow larger.

Mary came to Mountain View a few times, with friends in a car or on the new bus service, but she always fought with Mother if Mother was home, whether Mother was drinking or not. Mary had always been one to talk back and now at sixteen she was worse than full of sass; she tried to boss Mother around. If Mother was drinking the fight became terrible. The younger girls simply stayed out of Mother's way when she drank and didn't cross her, it only made things worse. Annie couldn't understand Mary, why Mary didn't see that.

One early morning the summer came to an abrupt end. Cold that morning even with the sun out, when leaves had already been falling. It was the beginning of September and there was snow moving down from the tops of the mountains.

Father drove into the dusty yard in the flatbed truck.

Annie was outside near the deck, could never remember if she was actually, physically alone there, because she *felt* so suddenly alone, stricken. Could never remember, although she did know that she had come out of the house by herself very early in the quiet and then kept following the sunnier spots among the birches around the cabin, trying to sit in the sun and think about what she had read in a *Book of Knowledge* about sunny Florida, trying not to think about Mother passed out and sprawling, naked, with Kiley half on top of her: it was the sight of the two of them that had driven her out of the house, feeling sick and trying not to look at them tangled together on the big bed right inside the front room as she passed. But hadn't Ellen come out after awhile, and made light of things before she went back in?

Annie was sick all over again, the moment Father drove up, so afraid for Almighty Father to see Mother spread naked like that under Kiley's naked body and hairy legs, that she actually tried to stop him from going inside. But after a quick, hardly noticeable nod to Annie, he took the few steps up to the deck in one stride and entered the door.

Annie waited, terrified, for the explosion, the furious fight. For that anger of his to break out. She knew to her bones that it must break out, how long it had wanted to.

But there was silence, long moments of silence. Then Father Almighty reappeared, looking like a thundercloud. Herding Elizabeth and little Jeannie, hardly dressed, with hair uncombed, before him and up over the slats of the truck bed. Ellen called to Annie from the door: "we have to get our things together; we have to go." So Annie went in and they quickly found what clothes and treasures they could carry to the truck, went back for more after begging their father to wait and he barked at them to take no more than two minutes.

Mother roused up, sleepily. But belligerent. She muttered about "old B.A.," her epithet more and more commonly used for their father, using his initials in contempt. Kiley had rolled off her and sat on the edge of the bed calmly lighting a cigarette, naked as a jaybird. He gave a lazy wave of his cigarette and one of his devil-may-care grins at the two girls as they hurried for the door.

Mother didn't come back to the homestead this time. And Father didn't give up what had now become his habit, of living at the sawmill rather than at home. Instead he forced Mary, sixteen now, to move back to the homestead. Or perhaps he thought he succeeded at that. In later years, trying to give him his due, Annie wondered how much he'd believed Mary's half-truths and the girls' evasions. Because Mary didn't move back; she brought some of her things, as a pretense, but she had an after-school job at the soda fountain in town and a room with a family there, had her own life apart from the family. She came to the homestead cabin sometimes after school, most usually by supper time, and helped to get potatoes from the root cellar — a poor lot of potatoes, a year old — and brought other food because Father gave her money. Mary called him 'Dad,' not 'father,' and stood up to him as big as you please. She'd gotten to know him, Annie saw, in a way that Annie never would. But

Mary didn't tell him the truth, that she was really still living in town, and the girls didn't tattle on her. And Father didn't press for the real truth as he had always done. Ellen threatened Mary with the truth at times — Ellen stood up to Mary too; she had always said Mary was bossy and they quarreled often — but Annie was never anything but grateful to Mary for coming at all. She appreciated that Mary had always taken her side against Elizabeth who was coddled by everyone. Elizabeth with her dimples and winning smiles, past seven now, had long been able to cozen even their father, wrapped Mother around her little fingers while Annie felt left out in the cold. "Getting more proud and standoffish by the day" Mother had said to Annie. "You didn't want to be cuddled even as a baby. You pay a price for aloneness." But by the time Annie knew that was true she couldn't stop the aloneness. And she had long been glad for Mary, who'd defended her, even though Mary herself was bossy.

Ellen and Annie were becoming adult-like. Back on the homestead there were fewer long days of playing, less of Ellen's giggling about the foibles and hypocrisy of people around them, more of Annie's secret worrying and anxiety to get things done right. They were all in school, of course, and for the first time they took it seriously. Because they had to get Elizabeth and Jeannie fed and clothed, and everybody off to school on time. The weather was getting colder by the day, Father saying he would be coming by in the mornings to start the fire, though Ellen and Mary knew how to do that, and Annie had been learning. Father was delivering wood and they spent some after-school hours moving the wood from the piles where he dumped them to stack it neatly close to the cabin near the chute.

But they didn't do it fast enough. They hadn't moved any of the wood to the basement. The big round drum that warmed the cabin was heated from sheet metal pipe that came up from an even bigger drum in the basement, the basement that had been dug into the hillside. To get to the basement where you kept the fire going, you had to go down the slope around the house, but to get the wood into the basement you had to keep pushing it through a chute while someone below kept moving the pieces to a pile. The person above couldn't work too fast or there would be smashed fingers or even a bruised head down below. There was an art to pushing the wood through properly so pieces didn't get crosswise and stuck, and doing it at the proper pace. Ellen and Annie hadn't gotten it done. And they hadn't fastened the tarps over either their neat stack or the newer piles outside. Maybe they were fooled by lingering good weather but more likely, Annie thought as they blamed themselves for years afterward, more likely they still weren't careful enough, prudent enough, weren't paying attention, still playing too much after school.

They did know the first snows came in October, earlier or later. "I knew that," Ellen must have said dozens of times later. But this time, the snow suddenly sneaked up on them and when the snow came one evening, it didn't stop. In the thickly falling stuff, they shoved some wood into the basement, knocking off snow, and then waited for the storm to let up. They didn't think to rescue the tarps from where they had left them lying beside the dumped pile or the too-slowly growing stack they had begun to build by the chute into the basement. Since the furnace was in the basement they had to go down there, and get the wood down there, in order to have the fire that would warm the house.

The snow came and came, overnight burying everything under three feet that was wet and thick and heavy. Next day as they struggled to get more wood from under it, with snow still falling, they still forgot the tarps. Ellen built a fire in the furnace with what wood they had pushed down there.

Father didn't come and Mary didn't come. "They probably got snowed in some place" Ellen said, "but they'll get here." By now the girls had grown used to the fact that they had to spend whole evenings alone, even without Mary, cooking for themselves, relying on no one but themselves. But it still left a loneliness, a longing for family, especially that October day as the day turned early to night and they kept hoping.

It took a while before they began to be frightened. At first it was a lark to be snowed in — it meant no school — but by evening the generator failed and they were in the dark. Annie didn't admit to the loneliness growing in her, that had been already growing for days, for weeks, for over many weeks. They knew what to do, she and Ellen, and she prided herself that she could be like a grown-up, like Ellen. She didn't admit to the awfulness of the alone feeling that kept growing, in spite of their hardiness, through that second day.

In spite of their early laughing fun in the snow, that day changed from careless delight in new snow into darkness, with not enough wood to burn and no light and no help coming. First Elizabeth and then little Jeannie began to cry. And even Ellen, Annie could tell, was getting worried, though she hid it so well from her younger sisters, joking and telling stories. That night, as they scrounged for candles and kerosene —

finding no candle but finding one lamp that did have enough kerosene to burn for an hour — even that night they blamed only themselves for being careless. It was their litany through high school into adulthood: "I should have known then," Ellen said so many times, every time they talked about it.

"*We* should have known better," Annie would correct her; "I knew too."

"You were only nine," Ellen would say, "but I was supposed to be the one watching out for all of you. I was twelve; I knew about all of it, the early snows, the fact we should be sure of kerosene and being sure there was wood in the basement."

"You can't keep blaming yourself," Annie would say. It was probably thirty years before they stopped going over this litany when they came together.

As that day waned past suppertime and they used a bit of their wood in the cookstove to half-fry some potatoes, and opened cans of corn and tomatoes, and then huddled in the dark telling stories, Annie became quite frightened. For years afterward she found herself waiting, just waiting, when dark was approaching, even when she expected no one. And she learned it was worse for Elizabeth, the roly-poly child who had always captured hearts. "I have a hole in my heart," Elizabeth told her when they came back to knowing each other as adults, "that no one can fill."

"But someone else can't fill it for you," Annie said, "it's up to you to know what it is and try to fill it for yourself." Elizabeth had so long seemed to count on getting her being from Mother or from being part of others that Annie thought she had no sense of how to fill her own heart. Elizabeth turned to Jesus before she was forty and after Annie thought some about that, she was not surprised. Elizabeth seemed to need someone who showed love and approval for her almost every minute and Annie thought that she herself had escaped that fate. *(What an arrogant shit I was, even past forty, to think so.)*

The first blizzard came that night after the snows. In her sleep Annie half heard it begin its moaning and grow into a determined battering. It was dying off to a steady chill wind by morning, but the drifts almost covered the windows and they couldn't get the door open. When Ellen and Annie, with the little girls helping by pushing them from behind, finally got a crack open wide enough for skinny Annie to get through, she scraped at the hard-packed, icy snow outside until Ellen could come through too. It was bitterly cold. They tried to fight some wood out of the frozen mountains that were the wood pile and the pitifully small wood stack by the chute. Sliding back inside often through the narrowly-opened door to rub their hands over and over, trying to keep them from frost bite, they kept fighting wood out from the two piles, managed to break loose some pieces from the edges to burn in the cook stove. But each piece was a struggle and their little fire each time would burn down, leaving the house as cold as the outdoors, icily cold. They used all but the last of their kindling.

That's when little Jeannie, usually as brave as a little soldier, really began to cry and couldn't seem to stop. They put her in the big bed, Mother and Father's bed, and covered her with their eiderdown, and with blankets, and still she cried. Elizabeth was suddenly brave, and talked to her, lay down with her and sang to her.

The awful cold, their desperation for the wood, for fire, little Jeannie's relentless crying and the knowing that everyone had abandoned them — these were forever after that in Annie's mind and soul the same one thing: There was no Mother, no Father; there was no Mary. No big brothers or sisters. No family. No help. There was terrible cold, and aloneness and strife and War. There was a bitter battle, a desperation to save little Jeannie from freezing to death.

Annie could never remember how long this nightmarish misery had gone on, the fighting of the wood pile, the icy cold, the stinging wind, her frozen hands, little Jeannie's crying that wouldn't stop. In her memory they were all in the house at a certain moment, trying to get warm though there was no warmth, trying to console Jeannie, knowing they had to have the wood somehow.

"We need the axe," Ellen was saying, again, "so I can chop into the pile and so I can break the basement door open." She had already slid down around the cabin to find that the door to the basement — where the axe should be, or at least the hatchet for chopping kindling — that the basement door was deeply drifted and frozen shut, then having to struggle to get back up the slope. While it seemed to Annie that it had begun to be forever that they were left here, with no help in a steadily darkening house, Ellen was saying it now for the fourth or fifth time — the insistence on getting the axe — with something new in her voice, something close to the despair that Annie was afraid of as that despair kept growing in herself.

They had slid down around the house again, Ellen and Annie together, and yet a third time and yet again, struggling with the frozen basement door and struggling back up again to worry over little Jeannie.

Elizabeth at least wasn't giving in. The roly-poly seven-year-old turned into a sturdy little mother, soaking more oatmeal in canned peaches on the warmed cookstove, feeding and consoling little Jeannie, running for tools if Ellen asked her to find something, rubbing Ellen's hands and Annie's, to help warm them; trying to dry their soaked gloves or mittens and finding more. Back and forth, to the bedroom to cuddle Jeannie and sing to her (Elizabeth couldn't carry a tune but that didn't daunt her; she loved to sing and knew all the words to dozens of happy or kooky songs); then back to the kitchen, tidying up, washing the table, picking up their two days' mess; finding Jeannie's rag doll and looking for anything her sisters asked for; washing the bowls and cups and spoons.

At least they had plenty of water. Father had deeply buried the pipe that came from the well — and none of the girls realized at the time that the part of the pipe that came up through the basement into the house would freeze if they continued to be unable to heat the place.

"You know," Annie said to Ellen in high school, "that piece of the pipe would likely have been already freezing that day if Elizabeth hadn't been running water so often. . . ."

"The water was running slow that morning already, I think I remember that . . . probably already beginning to freeze up in that pipe. And if we hadn't kept running it we might have been S-O-L. As Walter liked to say. Even if we did soak our best gloves right off the bat so they were freezing too.

"And turn the porch into an ice rink . . ." and Ellen and Annie both started to giggle over how they had skated around trying to get in and out once they *did* get the door further open by pouring water around, but then causing the door to get even more frozen up so that they couldn't get it shut again to save what little indoor heat they were managing to produce. Until they whacked at the frozen door with every tool they could find.

"I'll bet we could have conquered the basement door too, between us," Annie said, "if I'd gotten down there. . . ."

"If I take off almost everything," Annie said in a moment that she afterwards kept remembering as the moment of her eyes meeting Ellen's eyes and she, Annie, knowing that Ellen changed from big sister protectiveness into accepting Annie as an equal, "if I do that, I'll bet I can still slide down the chute and shove the hatchet or axe back up to you." They had all taken their turns sliding the chute when younger but skinny Annie was the only one who might still hope to do it without getting stuck. Except for little Jeannie who couldn't possibly shove even a hatchet up the chute (and they wouldn't have taken a chance, anyway, of putting Jeannie into the basement).

"But if you can't scrape your way back up through the chute," Ellen said with that new look, "what will we do? If I can't chop that door open down there?"

"We have to have the axe," Annie said, shutting out the other fear that neither she nor Ellen would admit to, that they agreed, now as equals, not to admit to. The fear that the axe might not be there. It *had* to be there. "I'll be working on the door down there," Annie said, "from the inside. Father's sledge hammer is probably still there; I think I saw it." She had never been able to lift that sledge more than four or five inches but that would be enough for her to beat at the bottom of the door.

"Someone has to be down there," Annie insisted. She and Ellen stared at each other again a long moment. There would be no fire unless someone was in the basement to build it. That's what they both knew. "It won't be colder there, anyway," Annie said, "than it is up here without a fire. It's even warmer usually, and there's kindling chips all over."

But that was when, suddenly, a dark shadow appeared looking ominous above the drifted snow over the kitchen window and turned into a face. Then a pounding at the door.

It was Mr. Gearhart, the neighbor from over the hill. He had somehow come through the drifts across the north field, Annie thought; no one came or went to Gearhart's place except by the path across that field. "But he had to have used his plow, come up the driveway," Ellen said later, and Annie agreed that must be the truth. But the truth was, they could not remember how he took them out of there, whether all together in his pickup with the plow on the front or not. It was a blank in their collective memories, because it was the last time they saw the homestead, except as passersby, for years. They went to foster homes.

"Isn't it strange," Ellen said once, "that we all have that very same "loss of memory?" All four of us? We remember so many things — so many details — even about the bad things. Along with the good things and just little things. Even though our memories about a lot of them are different. . . ."

"I remember how you pointed out that my heifer Bluebell had one lop ear. Which I never noticed. And how Elizabeth loved the pigs, and I loved something about them, but you. . . .

"I never really connected with any of the pigs, not like I did the other animals. . . ."

"You actually talked to the rooster, Cocky, and I almost hated him. But you're right, we all remember things about all of them, the cows and pigs and chickens and heifers, and the rooster. Even Jeannie remembers them, remembers crying and tearing up something because both the pigs and the cows were being hauled away. When she must have been only four or so. And we talk about memories of the bad stuff too: Mother not home for Christmas Eve; us walking home scared after the war started when we'd never been much scared before, by anything but our own imagination. . . ."

"And all the bad stuff in Mountain View," Ellen said. "We all remember a lot about that."

Chapter Five

Everything happened at once. Their father, Almighty Father, was dead of a heart attack. That was why he hadn't come to the homestead.

It was Martin, Annie learned, fourteen-year-old Martin, who had fought his way through the deep snow of the long road out of Father's sawmill driving the old truck, by rigging pieces of rope to serve as a fan belt. He had discovered the broken fan belt after bawling — "bawling like a baby, and then just sitting there," he was telling Ellen and Annie when they talked much later "— bawling over finding Father. Just sitting there; in a stupor-like for a long time. Half the day, maybe, just watchin' the snow keep comin' down. I couldn't seem to move, not even stir a finger. I wouldn't look at Dad, just looked at the snow. I don't know what woke *me* up.

"I'd found him half out of his bunk, middle of the night, one foot turned ice-cold on the floor, and tried to wake him up. Then I finally put him back to bed, tucked him in and built up the fire in the pot-bellied stove and just sat there." Finally, he put Father in the truck and, hooking the snow scraper to the front, stopping repeatedly to replace each piece of frayed out "fan belt" rope with another, made his way out the road from the sawmill and the three miles into town.

Martin drove around then, in town, in a white world, with Father's body in the truck, and couldn't decide where to go. Almost nobody was out in the deep snow, which was still falling, except some colonists he didn't know or trust, shoveling at their doorsteps. So he kept driving around, he said. He didn't want to give Father up to anybody. He got gas at Hamm's Garage where old Hamm had been running the snow scraper on his pickup along his street. And old Hamm gave Martin a fan belt, because Martin only had thirty-three cents over the amount for a tank of gas. Old Hamm let him have the fan belt for free when Martin told him about using the pieces of rope. "He congratulated me," Martin said; "'the durndest cleverest thing I ever heard, to get here without one,' he told me when I told him I needed a fan belt. You know the way old Hamm talks, with everything being the 'durndest funniest' or 'durndest meanest' or durndest something. 'That's something worth at least a fan belt,' he said." And he wanted to come look in the engine to see for himself how Martin had fitted the pieces of rope to get him into town.

"I'd done this pretty mean thing to Dad when I was pulling into town," Martin said. "I pushed him down so people wouldn't see him and wonder. Cause I wasn't going to give him up until I knew where to go. So I kept old Hamm from going near the passenger side and I showed him where I was pulling the last piece of rope off the . . . off the grooves. And he stayed yabbing to me the longest time while I put on the new fan belt and checked the antifreeze and everything. There was nobody else comin' around and he was full of talk. I thought I'd never get away from him while all the time I wanted to get away but didn't know where to go."

Then Martin drove all the way to Anchorage, stopped twice to pull out people stuck in the snow, covering Father with the old gray wool blanket kept in the truck. In Anchorage then, he drove around, hunting for Mary, who he was sure had come to Anchorage with friends and was probably staying there until the roads were cleared. He hunted through the early dusk and then into the dark, until he was afraid he was using up too much of his precious gasoline.

When he had been hunting for Mary for hours, he fell asleep, he said, unexpectedly, in the truck outside the dark house of some people Mary knew. And they woke him up, startled and confused, bone-cold and shivering, when they came roistering back on foot from some neighbors' house down the road. "It was right after that it started to blow, I guess," he said "the blizzard coming up."

Mary wasn't with them, the friends. Martin fell asleep again there, on their sofa, forgetting Father and forgetting Mary. Forgetting everything. "I slept like the dead," he said, "and that's a bad thing to say, because of Dad, except I kept dreamin' about tracking Mary. But when I woke up — right out of a sound sleep and it was already morning, early morning — what woke me up was, I was hit with this awful feeling that I'd left him alone. Because then I knew he really *was* dead. But I still needed to be with him. More than ever. So I got out of there, scared of the drifts too and I don't know how I got through 'em till I hit the main road, and got back to Palmer before I used up all my gas. Followed a snow plow all the way.

"Dad was stone cold, frozen cold, all curled up where I'd pushed him down almost below the seat, all cramped up. It scared the hell out of me that I'd left him like that, left him to freeze. I was to blame for everything anyway, for him dying — I was such a shithead to him — and in all that drivin' around I wasn't letting him die even though I finally knew it had happened. I kept trying to find somebody to tell me it hadn't happened."

Getting back to Palmer with half the roads in town not yet cleared after the blizzard, struggling through heavy drifts or fighting his way out of them after getting stuck when the snow scraper wouldn't cut into the frozen stuff and fought him back, he finally went to the marshal's house when he arrived in the Valley. He'd stopped at Beanie's house first, out of town, he said (Beanie was his friend of many years, his friend of the harnessed flies), but "they were hardly movin' around there. Beanie just stared at me like a dumb shit and not even awake, not even when I told him my dad had died. So I just drove away."

Then Martin finally remembered, he said, when he saw the marshal, that his little sisters might be alone on the homestead.

Chapter Six

It was the end of the world. Annie was in a strange home, a foster home. She was alone there; Ellen went to a different home and Elizabeth and little Jeannie together were living in yet another. They saw each other only at school. Martin went to some people in Kenai.

Before that, there had been hope: Mother would come back. If they were good enough, could be careful enough, could stop being careless and little, Mother and Father could be together again. They would have family again. But now Father was gone and Mother didn't come.

Annie didn't cry when she heard Father was gone and she didn't cry at the funeral. She had a mighty anger building but she held it in, pushed it down, repressed it, hard. There was nothing left in the world now except keeping control of herself. She was practiced at doing that and now she absolutely had to do it — everything else was gone. She saw her mother at the funeral but wouldn't let herself run to her or sob like Elizabeth did. Mother had gone on living in Anchorage, or Mountain View or wherever she was: "Nothin' but a drunk now like all them Indians" was what Annie heard repeated at school. She knew it was the good people, the adults, who were saying that, overheard by their children. She was proud of herself that she didn't let any of it bother her that much. She decided to make people call her by her given name, persuaded her sisters to call her Anne. Which they didn't remember to do for quite a while, and Annie would sometimes herself forget.

Besides seeing her mother, what Anne remembered of the funeral was that everybody was wearing winter coats although there was a fire in a wood stove at the back of the hall. It was a small white church with a long name and the minister had been something of a friend of their father though their father had never gone to church. There were a lot of people there; everyone had known their father, "Hard-Working Birney" they'd called him. Reverend Felton was the name of the minister and he sang a song in a big mellow voice, a song about how life was like a mountain railroad and it seemed, in the song, that her father had been the engineer. Which he never had been an engineer except on the spur line that ran into the Jonesville coal mines. But he'd repaired snow plows for the Alaska Railroad — "cow catchers" they called them — and helped repair track and rode up the line often toward Fairbanks and on the spur lines into mines to get to jobs. He knew almost everybody who worked on the Alaska Railroad.

The song stayed in Anne's mind though it was a hillbilly sort of song; she remembered some words. Years later, nearing forty and a world away in New York City where she heard a blue grass group playing — three lively young guys and a bearded old guy on a banjo they called "Pappy" — she asked Pappy if he knew that song. He was surprised to be asked and seemed reluctant to sing it. "Not the thing for this crowd," said one of the young ones, meaning the rowdy bunch in the East Side Irish tavern; "it's a mournful tune." He was a lively, blue-eyed young man probably in the middle of his twenties. Anne almost pleaded: "I've never heard it since my father's funeral." So the young man sang it after all, Pappy accompanying on the banjo, drawing out some of the long vowels just as Reverend Felton had done, so that they sounded like a distant train whistle.

But in the foster home at age nine Annie tried to forget everything about the funeral. There was a lamp downstairs in the living room of this house, and soft chairs, but they didn't mean much to her. Or maybe they did, because the house and the family were good to her. But she lay awake at night in a room alone hearing the moan of the cold Matanuska wind around the house, a big frame house like all the colonists had, hearing the rattle and scratching of dead branches against the wall and window of the upstairs bedroom they gave her, a room that had belonged to their oldest son, that they cleared out for Anne. She tried to cling to good things she remembered from the *Books of Knowledge*, anything to keep her out of the pit of cold dread that she felt in the middle of her, anything to keep her from falling into it. She had tried desperately for awhile to withdraw into herself, forget the pain of abandonment and Death. But the inside of her was a wasteland of pain, of unwilling grief and anger. So there was no place to go, inside or out. She was afraid to go to sleep; her sleep was filled with dark dreams, dreams of being lost in a maze of big buildings, searching through empty old rooms and halls and stairs that led on to other buildings, searching for someone, or something. When there were other people in those dreams they didn't notice her; they were intent on their own direction in coming or going, sometimes talking to each other and always leaving Anne alone in the dusty light already fading to dark. Then, in every dream, she would be suddenly seized by a feeling of utter terror, struggling to get away as she realized that she shouldn't be searching. That *something awful* was searching for *her*, trying to find *her*, and that she had no place to turn to get away.

Or sometimes, she dreamed she was in a dark field and she would see, far off, a glimmer that came from Rudy's oily face and gleaming sideways eye. And she would hide herself in the dirt of the field so that he wouldn't be able to see that her own eyes had a light in them too.

And, over and over, another nightmare: that she was high up, on some ledge or railroad trestle, and was losing her footing, about to fall and fall and fall into yawning black or black water far below. Knowing she would fall for a long time.

Every night she was in dread, knowing only that she had to hang on. She clung to memories, pages, from the *Books of Knowledge*. She wasn't used to sleeping alone, without the body of at least one of her sisters pressed close. On the homestead she had shared the middle bunk with Ellen after Martin moved to the Boys' House and, before that, with one or both of her little sisters. She discovered that Molly, the teenaged daughter of the new house, would put up with her if Anne, trying hard not to be Annie, went creeping into Molly's room across the hall and into her warm bed with her.

They were good to her, this foster family, the Walkers, and she survived the winter, got some spirit back. There was an okay boy her own age, their son, and he and Annie swung beside each other on swings in the dark yard with light shining on them out the kitchen window. But still Anne, trying not to be Annie, was mostly numb, her feelings frozen up inside. To her this family — the okay son; Molly the teenager; an abstracted, benevolent, plump, talkative mother; a near-silent mild father in the background — to her it felt as though this family existed in a pleasant pale world that in her nighttime dreads and daytime numbness Anne couldn't feel as quite real, couldn't feel a part of. Like a nice picture in a book. She felt a great distance, with no sense how to even begin to cross it. She felt, later, that they gave her every chance, that they reached as far across the distance as they were able. They tried to jolly her out of herself but she continued to feel them as far away.

Mr. and Mrs. Walker gave her a book for Christmas, *The Secret Garden*. She read it far into the night and fell asleep beginning a complicated dream of a home, and of gardening amidst a riot of unknown flowers in a warm, exotic place. She could hardly wait through breakfast and the dishwashing next morning to get back to the book to finish it. Then she started from the beginning and read it over again. Through Christmas vacation she read it over and over falling asleep with it night after night staying in her own bed and having strange but not unhappy dreams.

At school Elizabeth and little Jeannie were telling tales of quite a different family. They were afraid of the foster mother where they lived. "She's mean," Elizabeth said; "she uses a switch that stings something awful." Her name was Mrs. Binch. Elizabeth and Jeannie came to school in new clothes, looking scrubbed, with their hair pulled tightly back into tight braids. Bright ribbons tied to the braids. Anne learned, in the small world of the school, that their teachers praised how they looked but seemed to care nothing for how cowed and scared they felt. Her sisters kept calling her "Annie" and, whatever her name should be, she felt more and more a fierce protectiveness for them coming up in her, her first real feeling for months. She began to think she could go to live with them. She could protect them; they needed her and she would have family again.

She told Mrs. Walker she wanted to go live with her sisters. Mrs. Walker was reluctant, so that over time Annie began to beg. She didn't give a thought to why Mrs. Walker didn't want her to go; she wasn't curious about it.

And it came about; one day Mrs. Walker delivered her, with all her things and with a big enveloping hug in saying good-bye, to the Binches. Who lived in the same kind of big white frame house as the Walkers, as all the colonists did, with bedrooms upstairs. Mrs. Binch had a smile for Mrs. Walker and smiled at Annie but Annie knew from the first moment that the smiles were false. She knew women like that; the girls had long known them: they were the good women. Still, Annie — Anne — was happy to be with her sisters, excited. And suddenly, as Mrs. Walker drove away, she twirled around and around in the middle of the floor, in the big kitchen that all the colonists seemed to have. And the smile Mrs. Binch had kept on her face became more false, became scary. When little

Jeannie began a twirl with Annie too, the smile disappeared and Annie saw what was really under it.

"Take Annie's things up to your room," Mrs. Binch said sharply, abruptly mean, and sat herself down in a big brown easy chair. She was fat and filled the chair completely. It was a living room sort of chair but in the kitchen.

The girls went up the stairs, giggling, struggling with Annie's two boxes and a bag. The room upstairs was big, with twin beds. "You can have a bed to yourself," Elizabeth said, "because Jeannie and me sleep together."

"She tried to make us sleep alone," Jeannie said, "in each bed."

"But we just snuck back together," Elizabeth finished. "Now I guess she doesn't care."

The girls giggled and talked, all in one bed, and after Mrs. Binch hollered up the stairs they turned to whispering, for a long time into the night. They were usually safe upstairs, Anne began to learn, because Mrs. Binch was lazy as well as fat and seldom climbed the stairs except to creak up every few days checking for cleanliness. When she tried, not often, to sneak up on the girls after bedtime, her weight gave her away as she couldn't keep from creaking some of the steps. But they seldom had time to be upstairs, weren't allowed to be there until bedtime. Mrs. Binch didn't like Anne's habit of reading at bed time — or reading at all, "wasting her time" — and insisted on lights out. They were allowed a flashlight for upstairs like she had had at Walkers. The colonists seemed to have lots of flashlights; they had electricity without a generator but the power would go out in wind storms. Anne tried reading by flashlight under the covers but that didn't work, as the batteries burned out too fast.

The Binches' own children were grown, two boys gone into the service, a daughter already married. They had let their farm go to seed; Mr. Binch worked in town, at the Rural Electric plant — people called it the power plant — and Mrs. Binch seemed to have no interest in anything except gossip and a clean house. She did indeed have a cruel streak, heaved herself out of her brown chair to take a willow switch to little Jeannie over the slightest thing or, if she was already on her feet, found some reason to do it. Elizabeth cried and tattled to avoid the switch, tried to curry favor and Mrs. Binch gave her a cookie or a piece of candy when she tattled. It made Anne sick and she began to take every switch Mrs. Binch turned up and break it, throwing away the pieces. She was ten now, nearing eleven, and her toughness and independence hadn't deserted her; the one time Mrs. Binch tried to take the switch to Anne herself, Anne set her feet, refusing to turn around, put up her hands and grasped the piece of willow. Then she stood, holding on for dear life; wild horses couldn't have broken her grip and she stared the woman down.

But the worst was not the switch. It was the way Mrs. Binch was devious, twisted things, even your own words. When Anne tried to say that she had to read, study at home because her fifth grade teacher Miss White demanded a lot of homework — which she did — Mrs. Binch said, "are you complaining about that fine teacher? Let me tell you, young lady, you should be ashamed!" When Elizabeth said a boy was mean at school, Mrs. Binch praised his family and washed Elizabeth's mouth out with soap for "speaking against good people." But Anne heard Mrs. Binch within a week gossiping to a neighbor woman over the road and telling her, in almost Elizabeth's exact words, what a mean little boy those people had.

One of Mrs. Binch's favorite ploys was to promise the girls that they could go to the Disney movie that was coming — or to the school picnic, or that she would let them go with the neighbors who had offered to take them to some of the school basketball games — but then, at the last minute, to find some excuse not to let them go. Usually by blaming them for something. They learned not to trust Mrs. Binch about anything. They were never allowed to go anywhere except to school. Anne persuaded her little sisters to become stoic, not to believe Mrs. Binch, not to have hopes from her false promises only to be caved in by disappointments. Anne hated having her hair braided too, pulled so tight that it hurt, which is what Mrs. Binch liked to do. After a month Anne began simply taking the braids back out, first at school and then, more boldly, at home. Mrs. Binch decided not to fight some battles.

But they were her slaves. They had nowhere to go, no one to turn to. And Mrs. Binch turned to other means to keep them cowed. She was not only cruel, but petty, vindictive. Deceptive. She told lies about them to other people, how they were lazy and she had to slave to care for them. In fact they did almost all the work. Like a big toad Mrs. Binch sat watching them with unblinking eyes from her faded-plush brown chair or another like it in the living room, watched them scrub the floors on hands and knees, pushed herself up to inspect every corner, and every corner of the stairs, and make them do the entire job over if she found the least wisp of dirt. Watched them out the windows; watched them in the kitchen doing dishes, scrubbing the bathroom. Anne soon ran the wringer-washing machine on Saturdays and with her sisters hung out the clothes; she did the ironing on Sunday, almost all of it. It took her fifteen minutes to iron one of the big shapeless house dresses Mrs. Binch always wore and Annie, still Annie to her sisters but trying to be Anne, would look at Mrs. Binch hulking in her ugly brown chair, wearing one of those dresses, and wish she had burned holes in it.

When Mr. Binch was due home from his city maintenance job, Mrs. Binch would heave herself out of the chair to boil the potatoes that the girls peeled after school, fry some meat. Then she would retail gossip to her husband through supper — of course wanting the girls to hear though she told them to shut their ears — while Mr. Binch grunted, good-natured enough. Then after supper Mrs. Binch lowered herself back into her imprint in that big brown chair and watched the girls clean up the kitchen, do the dishes, sweep the floor, use oil to scour the cast iron skillet and waxed paper to polish the top of the big black cook stove whenever it wasn't kept hot. She watched all the time.

Mr. Binch didn't say much, occasionally interrupted Mrs. Binch, sort of mildly, in the middle of one of her tirades against the girls, but usually he went back outside, doing anything, except in bad weather when he sat smoking a pipe before going to bed early.

People seldom came to the farm and when a rare person did come, the girls heard Mrs. Binch telling them half-truths and lies about other people. She got her gossip by going to town once or twice a week. In Anne's first months at the Binches, Mrs. Binch would take the girls, rarely, to town on a Saturday, where they sat in the Ford sedan or stood silently around the Co-op store or Deb's café waiting to carry anything she bought while Mrs. Binch shopped and talked, talked to almost everyone she met. After Anne turned eleven Mrs. Binch left them home. In summer the girls watched her make up her fat face and drive away after threatening them with a home for juveniles if they didn't behave while she was away; she liked to threaten that, it became a staple. And the sisters began to agree they would rather go to such a home, however awful Mrs. Binch made it out to be.

Mary came to see them a few times. Mrs. Binch was falsely friendly and Mary preferred to believe her false front instead of the things the girls tried to tell her about the meanness. Mary seemed a different person now, a grown-up and thoughtless like so many grown-ups. She talked of leaving school, before graduation, and getting married to an MP she'd met in Anchorage. Anne was astonished that anybody would give up that golden goal of graduation.

Mother came, a few times, to the Binches that first summer and in the spring and early summer following. She was sober and nicely dressed. The first time, Anne couldn't talk to her, just looked a long time at her across the kitchen, stiffly put up with a hug, watched Elizabeth and Jeannie cuddling up to her, both talking at once. Mrs. Binch didn't offer coffee or anything, though she'd put on her smarmy smile, and she didn't invite Mother beyond the kitchen while she sat there in her brown chair, watching. Mother didn't stay long. There was no way to have a real visit in that woman's house, Anne knew. She knew Mother had an even sharper sense for falsehood than Anne; they both knew what Mrs. Binch was.

One day later that summer while Anne was hanging out the laundry, Elizabeth, who was supposed to be collecting wood chips for kindling with Jeannie from around the chopping block, came running to Anne, whispering: "Mother's at the fence. By the road." Anne looked down the short driveway and could just see, through some bushes and the fence boards, that there was someone there.

"She wants to see us," said Elizabeth, turning to run that way.

"Wait," hissed Anne and caught Elizabeth's arm, "Mrs. Binch is looking out the window.

"Pretend I'm disgusted with you," she said into Elizabeth's uncomprehending face and shaking her arm, "and then start back toward the chopping block. But *walk*. Just walk, until you're past the kitchen window. Then sneak around the blind side of the house while I keep Mrs. Binch from noticing. *Go*. But *walk*."

Anne turned toward the back door, the kitchen door, just as Mrs. Binch was stepping out onto the porch. Fortunately, Mrs. Binch could hardly see much of the yard at all from the enclosed porch. "They're just afraid of a spider," Anne lied boldly, "I'm going to go take care of it."

"Well, see they fill that whole box with chips; there are plenty of wood chips out there. No playing until that's done. And no noise with bringing in the box. Leave it on the porch by the door and keep those girls outside."

Anne knew that was a signal that Mrs. Binch was going to move herself into her big brown chair in the living room — the match of her chair in the kitchen — and listen to the Something-Hour on the radio. The woman's afternoon habit. And once she settled there she wouldn't be able to see either the driveway or the wood pile; she would have to get out of her chair and go stand by the far windows of the living room and crane her neck, which Anne guessed she wouldn't do with that special program of hers coming on the radio. It was the one hour of the day when the girls might have some freedom outside — unless they hadn't done all their assigned work and then would have been forced to stay in the kitchen and be utterly silent for that hour. But Anne had figured out that Mrs. Binch would rather have that one hour to herself without the girls even being in the house, as long as she had threatened them enough beforehand.

So Anne went down the driveway herself after spending some minutes pretending to look for a spider at the chopping block in case Mrs. Binch was still watching.

Mother had brought them each a Mars bar — amazing treat — which they hid in the pockets of their overalls so that Mrs. Binch wouldn't know. (Or rather, Anne hid her whole bar; little Jeannie hid hers after some bites and Elizabeth hid what was left of hers after she immediately ate more than half.) Anne was still standoffish with Mother, stood back while Jeannie and Elizabeth spilled out everything from school games to Mrs. Binch's meanness, talked very little herself. Mother didn't try to hug Anne, like she did her sisters.

"You weren't easy to understand," Mother said to Anne those years later when Anne finally told her she'd thought Mother always favored Elizabeth. "Elizabeth was easy to satisfy. But you, even as a baby I never knew whether you would *act* like a baby, never knew what you wanted when you wouldn't nurse, or squirmed right out of a lap. And then you would drive me a little crazy later, when you were four and five, following me around, clinging like glue and always wanting something. But then I would find you by yourself ignoring everybody and perfectly happy."

"I think it was stories I wanted," Anne said, "I loved stories."

"Well, that was what happened. Ellen started teaching you to read — you weren't even five — and after that you didn't even seem to need me any more. Always wanting a book and had your nose in one of them whenever you weren't squabbling with Martin."

"I used to hang around the edges whenever Father had men around that he would talk to. Even if he made me go away — or thought he had — I would hide to listen because that's when he told stories. And I always wanted to hear the stories about you and him, about what you did before I was born. That's what I think I remember about why I was following you around."

"Well, I was no storyteller," Mother said. "Too much work for that. No time for talk.

"And too much to tell," she added, with a short laugh. And Anne laughed. And then they were laughing together because of both knowing at once how much — how ironically, painfully, wonderfully much — had never been said from either side between them and how words could anyway never capture more than pieces of it.

After that later day, some of those moments of laughter with her mother, a sort of miracle began to occur as Anne was more and more redeemed from her littleness and meanness of childhood and came to freely love her Mother. But that was far in the future from those few days by the fence where Mother gave candy bars or gum but no explanations and Anne didn't forgive.

The first day that Mother came to the fence Anne did tell her that she had come at the right time (and learned that Mother had come other times, without finding the girls outside and unwilling to come to the house) and Anne stayed ready to make whatever excuses or lies to Mrs. Binch that were necessary to let little Jeannie and Elizabeth visit Mother out by the fence whenever she came.

Which wasn't often after the following summer was underway. Because Mr. Binch had been clearing land and then building, with the help of friends, a new, smaller house over the hill. And then the Binches sold all but that one piece of their land where the new house was built. And Mr. Binch had tucked the new house away, with a long driveway and almost out of sight of the road. Once they moved into the new house, Mother didn't reappear. Unfortunately, Mr. Binch had put in a row of windows not only facing the driveway but around the corner toward the road. ("Tired of that old house plan where you don't get the light," he said.) The new kitchen wasn't big enough for Mrs. Binch's old chair, so she sat it squarely between kitchen and living room with a view out of all those new windows. Which meant there were almost no places in the new yard to be out of her sight since another window, the kitchen window, faced the little vegetable garden and the woodshed, the two main places the girls were sent to do their work. Anne knew the man hadn't done it deliberately to put the girls more constantly under the eyes of his wife, but she hated the new house: how small it was, how Mrs. Binch no longer had to climb squeaking stairs but only walk down the hall to spy on them or stand outside their bedroom door. And Anne was sure Mr. Binch didn't know how his wife liked to practice little sly tortures on the girls because she didn't do that in front of him. If Mother did come to the new place, which the girls had described to her, she didn't come down the long drive or manage to get the girls' attention from the far-off road. Elizabeth got in trouble for repeatedly going out the driveway and hanging out by the road instead of doing her chores, making Mrs. Binch suspicious. But Mother didn't appear.

Anne came to regret that Mother had visited at all, because Mrs. Binch somehow learned from it Anne's own terrible weakness; the woman in her meanness seemed to home right in on anything weak. Anne had defied her in so many little ways and refused physical punishment, tried to unite her sisters in the stoic attitude of just doing the work and keeping their thoughts and feelings hidden so that Mrs. Binch couldn't get at them. But now Mrs. Binch began coming home with tales of their mother, how Mother reeled drunk around town. She sat behind Anne while Anne ironed, to practice this new torture. One day Mrs. Binch said, clucking, that Mother had shit herself in public, standing on a Hammond street talking to old John Marsh. That day Annie knew she was Anne, as she turned the ironing board around to face Mrs. Binch with the hot iron and Mrs. Binch was afraid to force her to go back to the original position. Mrs. Binch knew when to back off; she felt Anne's overwhelming rage. So she stopped the predictable taunting. But then she would slip in a remark about their mother here or there, slyly, when she herself was not in a vulnerable position. She would be remembering how Anne, newly arrived at Binches, had furiously flung in her direction the last bit of coffee, hot from the coffee pot grabbed from the stove, the first time Anne heard Mrs. Binch coaxing Elizabeth into a lie. Anne herself only vaguely remembered the event, but her little sisters spoke of it later with awe. "You scared her," Little Jeannie said proudly.

There came a time when Anne wanted to do a good deal more than scare the woman. Elizabeth came over to Anne's separate bed one night after little Jeannie had fallen asleep and whispered to Anne: "You know what Mrs. Binch said to us in the kitchen when you were outside? She said Mother was lying off the street right near downtown, right off the street, almost in the ditch, and some soldiers were lined up like . . . like they were waiting a turn to . . . to, you know. 'To do what shouldn't be done,' is what Mrs. Binch said. And Mother was waiting for them to do it."

"I don't think Jeannie heard it all," Elizabeth whispered. "I rattled some pans so she wouldn't hear. I don't think Jeannie knew what she was really talking about."

Anne and Elizabeth knew Mrs. Binch had to be telling lies. They heard plenty of whispers but never a whisper of Mother hanging around town or drinking anywhere near the Valley. Only of rumors carried back from Anchorage. It was stupid to think Mother cared to come back here anyway, that there was anyone she cared to see now that Rusty Crown was gone. "If I ever get shut of this Valley and these holier-than-Jesus people," the girls had heard her say to Father toward the end with a frightening coldness in her voice, "believe me, I won't be shaking the dust off fast enough."

Anne began to have serious fantasies of killing Mrs. Binch.

It was an odd twist in her life that Anne now had some pretty clothes — dresses and skirts — and would gladly have given them up to be free of Mrs. Binch. One thing Mrs. Binch did, almost the only thing she did in their sight beyond watching the girls all the time, was sewing. People would give her their own daughters' used clothes and she altered them to fit Anne and her sisters. She was good at it and proud of herself. The only time Anne saw on Mrs. Binch's fat face a smile that was completely genuine was when people congratulated her on how "nice" the girls looked. Then Mrs. Binch would beam, basking in the praise. But often then, too, she and the people, if the people were women, would be looking askance at the girls and saying things in near whispers. The implication was clear to Anne: Mrs. Binch was such a "good" woman to have taken in these half-wild, hooligan children of an outcast mother and be sending them to school looking well-dressed with their hair neatly tied in braids. The same women often had high words of praise for their father — "your father was such a hard-working man," one of them would brightly say to the girls, talking down at them; "he helped us with our baler." Or with their tractor, or with their seeder or with whatever. They liked to repeat what a good man Father was and how much he did for people and how he had worked so hard, how he was called "Hard-Working Birney." The implication of that was clear too, that it was a shame their father had married an Indian, that he had spawned all these unchristian children because of her.

It made Anne ever more set in her own mind against their father, more defiantly determined to cherish the memories of her sweet mother before Kiley, before Alcohol and the dreadful party scenes in Mountain View. She virtually forgot that Mother had sometimes grown wild before Alcohol, that Anne had seen her in a fury twice with Martin — once when she actually hit him with a stick of stove wood she had started to put in the kitchen stove, though Mother had pulled back her hand at the last moment and barely grazed his shoulder — and how Mother had been throwing more and more angry words at their father in that last year before Mountain View.

In Anne's mind it was the rape that had split life in two. Before that, things were still understandable, in spite of the war and her growing realization that her parents had such deep differences. Mother was still home then, home even after work at the laundry, cooking supper, and Father had always been away a lot anyway. But the rape changed everybody; it changed even Mother. She was moody, more often silent than humming at her work and, when Father came around, usually angry at him. He had come almost every day once he wasn't traveling much, living out at the sawmill but coming by the homestead most days to check on things and keep the generator and pump running. He wasn't just stern then, like he had been through Annie's early years; he was grim. There had been a little edge of an opening in him in those early years, a possibility of getting to know the Almighty Father. But the man who had tended her earache, the man who had brought her home from the hospital on a sunny day at the end of March soon after she had proudly turned eight — even the distant man who had sewn up her leg two years before that — that man disappeared after the rape. In his place was a stranger, cold, angry and unapproachable, who got things done and went away, having words along the way with her mother, tight and angry words.

Martin was the worst in that last year. From the time of the rape, and long before he stole from the Co-op in the following spring, Martin changed. He had always been open and cheerful, through all his endless pranks and teasings. Delighted. Delighted with himself and the world and everything in it. Trying and testing and experimenting with everything, seeming to wonder why people didn't share his joy in turning things upside down. But after the rape, Martin became more and more mean, especially to Mother. He disrespected her, taunted her with the fact that he was so much taller now than she was. He laughed at Mother, in a tone that made Annie sick; he made sly remarks to her. And then one day, dancing around, staying out of range of Mother and of Ellen who was defending Mother, determinedly keeping him away, Martin called Mother a whore.

That was when Mother turned with the stick of stove wood in her hand and Annie saw, in a horrifying, sickening moment, that Martin could be killed. That Ellen hadn't managed to keep him away, to drive him away, far enough away, and that she, Annie, was useless, that she had done nothing, was doing nothing, paralyzed to stop what was coming.

Anne had buried that memory and she quickly buried it again.

For Mrs. Binch, Anne developed a steady warm flame of hate. She grew sane again. She felt herself grow stronger year by year while Mrs. Binch seemed to shrink in her laziness, in her shabby brown chair. For all her cold meanness Mrs. Binch had a warm stink, of kitchen grease and unwashed fat flesh under covering sweet powder. Anne came to despise her more than hate her.

She couldn't help feeling secretly pleased, though, to be looking nice, wearing pretty clothes, even though she felt disloyal to care about such things. She could feel the approval of the other kids at school, the way they were taking her for granted as though she was one of them. She had become an exceptionally good student. School was the one place where she could get praise and attention and besides, she had a lot to prove. She wanted to show she was better than the little minds around her who liked to put down her mother and, by extension, her sisters and herself. She proved that she could get the best grades in any subject and win the spelling bees, and she kept proving it. She had some friends at school by now, prejudices seeming to have faded away among classmates. Some of them called her Anne and some not; she was still half Annie. They called her a "brain" but it wasn't mean, asking for her help with math and English. In seventh grade she loved parsing sentences, such a neat, orderly exercise. Her free period came to be filled up with helping classmates at it, which meant she had to take more of her own work home with her but she liked that too, having something so justifiable to do in evenings after work and supper and cleanup that let her utterly ignore Mrs. Binch. She was learning that Mrs. Binch could be cowed, knowing it by intuition, only slowly beginning to consciously understand the woman.

Her teachers gave Anne a pass to use the high school library — the high school classes met in the same big school building as the elementary classes, on the top floor of the long two-storied place, with their own library — and Anne read everything interesting in it before she was out of the seventh grade. The librarian, Miss Gorman, who seemed at first intimidating — so thin and perfectly neat, with sharp eyes behind little glasses — followed Anne around one day among the shelves, asking quick, pointed questions, making Anne so nervous she couldn't talk, but then for some reason causing her to spill out what she wanted: "I just . . . I was looking, I wanted to find . . . any more tales of history, like more Greek myths or early history or . . . or I don't know, whatever isn't dumb. Maybe mostly about people coming into some new place . . ." then Anne learned the woman would order books for Anne from bigger libraries, even seemed to approve of Anne's choices, suggesting more, from Greek myths to historical novels. Anne would watch as the woman pulled big tomes from behind the polished wood counter, looking up titles and subjects and writing out slips in tidy handwriting. Then Miss Gorman would say — what Anne became used to hearing — "of course it will take at least six weeks. Often longer." Anne knew that trucks were more and more coming up the Alcan Highway, bringing things faster and more often than the barges that used to bring everything to Alaska from Seattle. It was nothing, in the old days, to wait three months or more for something you ordered from Outside. (Mother and Father had always ordered winter clothes from Sears at the end of the last winter and sent their order for the big tins of Christmas candy and popping corn in September.)

But now Anne's books would magically appear usually within two months, more and more books. Miss Gorman always acted so pleased to be able to tell Anne of the arrival of even one, though Anne and Miss Gorman quickly learned to order many at a time. Miss Gorman would then slip quietly into Mr. Holcomb's eighth grade class, or later, into high school study hall, to give to Anne a note of some new arrival. Anne devoured them, reading defiantly but calmly at home in the evenings when her work was done. Careful with them and loath to send back her favorites.

In the spring, near the end of eighth grade, Anne took her first venture back into freedom. Though it became painful, the pain had little to do with Mrs. Binch, and Anne learned that much from it.

The Binches' now-neglected farm was three miles from town or school and the girls had been pretty much captives there, strictly required to ride the bus home, never allowed to go anywhere. Anne's best friend this year in eighth grade was Brenda Zibota, star of the junior high girls' basketball team. Anne herself was becoming a quick and determined little guard at basketball, sticking to her opponent like glue, becoming smarter all the time about tracking moves, making up for lack of height by an ability to spring straight into the air to capture the ball. She was very fast at track too and carried off blue ribbons every spring.

A sunny day in May, when she and Brenda had been giggling together at every break, walking with wrapped arms at recess, Brenda suddenly said, "Come home with me on the bus and stay over night. We can talk about Tommy." And she poked Anne when she slyly added, "and Miles too." A high school sophomore and basketball star named Tommy had been making eyes at Brenda while she had been demurely fluttering her own eyes at him in turn. Anne's best friend in seventh grade had been lanky, a runner with hair lanky too, and no more interested in boys or giggling with the girls than Anne was, but Brenda was different, with full breasts in eighth grade and a pretty bob in her shining, wavy dark hair. She flirted with the high school boys and she laughed a lot, though she turned into a passionately determined sort of demon on the basketball court. She looked so graceful out there on the court, sometimes, even when fighting for the ball, that it was fascinating to watch when Anne was able to just watch her. Anne couldn't help but feel flattered when Brenda, by the middle of winter of that eighth-grade year, started making up to her. Brenda was the one who first called her Anne all the time; even insisted on it to the other kids who had been saying "Annie" since first grade.

After a winter was ending, in the time from Anne's own birthday in March and through the spring, was when she herself blossomed every year. She carried off the blue ribbons for every race she entered, brought her relay team through by flying through her own part of the race no matter what position the coach put her in, flying while knowing who the next girl was more exactly than she could ever know her in any other way, knowing how to pass the baton to her, whoever she was this time, without a fumble. It was the most exhilarating thing in the world, to know like that and then to follow up your knowing into something that arrived, finally, at perfection.

This was new. It was new in an important way different from winning races by herself. There was something fine in every basketball game in which she had done her utmost, whatever the final score, but there was something especially and more deeply, wonderfully new in a relay race when she helped to bring a whole group first to the finish line. She felt proud but that wasn't really it; she was celebrating something beyond herself.

What an unlikely pair she and Brenda were, Anne thought later: the long-legged, budding beauty about to become high school star and cheerleader and skinny, backward Annie still running from devils she wouldn't look at. But that day in May while Brenda teased her about Anne getting shy around Miles Thorson, Anne's archrival for grades in math, they were best friends. And Brenda was guessing — probably correctly — that Anne, hardly interested in boys, was fascinated by their one classmate named Miles.

Anne made up her mind in a sudden burst of excitement: *Why not go home with Brenda?* She knew exactly what to say to Mrs. Binch in a note sent with her sisters after school. She knew the poor, stupid woman was intimidated by the sort of people like Brenda's parents, upright, church-going people with a thriving dairy farm; Mrs. Binch wouldn't risk coming to try to drag her home if she thought Anne was invited there. There would be some consequences later, of course, but *so what, Mrs. Binch can't kill me*, Anne thought. She felt bold, from her own daring and from Brenda's invitation.

All the way to Brenda's on the bus going two miles in the opposite direction from Binches, in the same direction where Anne's father had had his sawmill, she and Brenda giggled or laughed together, calling out gay or silly good-byes to other kids at the many stops the bus made along the way. Past the Butte, the great marker on the south side of the Valley, growing green now but gray or white according to the seasons, they hopped off the bus themselves to a chorus of teasing or gay good-byes. The air was warm, delicate new leaves on the birches around them quivering in a light breeze as they laughed and chattered up the driveway to the Zibota's neat white frame house.

To be met with a crashing disappointment. Helen Zibota came out of the kitchen door before they arrived at it, a tall woman with a frown as heavy as her thick dark hair. She gestured Brenda aside and spoke to her in quick, sharp sentences that were too low for Anne to hear, but Anne heard the sound, like hissing. Then the woman turned to go back into the house, pulled open the screen door to enter. But then she did stop, after all, and looked at Anne. It was a look in which Anne could read volumes combining much of what she had been reading in volumes from the libraries. First she saw that the look had a hint of something almost like apology: I'm a good Christian woman, the look seemed to say, and I have a little worry whether I should just turn my back without . . . without something like noticing that you must be human. So the look had that little, reluctant edge of doubt, of worry. But it was mostly a sharply defending look, with firm lips, with anger in it, and it conveyed to Anne a clear message about generation: her classmates may have been outgrowing prejudice, exchanging prejudice for familiarity and friendship, but their parents hadn't changed. To Mrs. Zibota Anne was still the child of an outcast. And worse, an outcast who was a drunk. Mrs. Zibota, for all her neat house and modern farm, was like those ancient people Anne had been reading about who lived in fear that their own uprightness could be contaminated by even the slightest contact with other than their own tribe. They killed every last man, woman and child of an enemy tribe, Anne had read, even burned all their possessions, every vestige of their possessions, to avoid any possibility of an alien influence creeping into their lives. Some tribes, like the ancient Israelites, had even killed every one of an enemy's livestock, down to newborn lambs and nestling doves, out of fear that even those little animal lives had come into being through the power of some god or gods that belonged to those other people and might be powerful enough to disrupt their own lives, upset their own god. Mrs. Zibota, standing there in the sunlight of a May afternoon in the middle of the twentieth century, was afraid that letting a skinny eighth-grade girl into her house would be letting in some unknown and awful influence.

Anne felt the day destructing as she turned away. She hardly heard Brenda's stammering apology. There was nothing Brenda could do; Anne knew that and she should at least have acknowledged it. But she was suddenly so furiously angry that in her first fury of marching back out the driveway, she blamed Brenda too. She blamed them all, all the idiot people of the Valley. Marching along, head high, roiling with violent thoughts, knowing she had almost six miles to go but hardly thinking of that, she renewed all of her hate from her early years. All the "good" people who put down her mother, all the nasty little remarks of people blaming her mother for her own rape and terrible beating, all the brats who had called her and her sisters names in first and second grade

— all the people in the world and their God too — she hated them with a steady, pounding beat of hate along the road.

There were moments she would have screamed, wanted so furiously and fiercely to scream that she almost did it, screaming about an awful and impossible world and an awful and impossible God. But she didn't scream. And somewhere along the way, having left Zibotas' farm far behind in her mindless fight with humiliation and hate, she began to learn something about herself: she wasn't a screamer. No matter how awful the world, no matter how painfully she could be rejected, left alone — again — no matter how it hurt, she didn't scream. She had never screamed.

She slowed to ponder this. Even Mary screamed, and of course Elizabeth and little Jeannie. Anne idled along, wondering if she had ever heard Ellen scream, Ellen her idol. She didn't think so. She had plucked a willow branch from the side of the road somewhere without knowing it and she swished it around, thinking of Ellen and wondering if Ellen ever screamed, whether she ever furiously told the world what she really felt.

Our Father, she thought. Almighty Father. Her steps picked up. You don't complain. You mind your own business; you do what needs to be done and you don't complain, you don't worry about what the rest of the world thinks. She swished the willow branch harder, walked faster.

But wasn't that Mother too? Anne laughed out loud at the idea of either her mother or her father screaming. Even when Mother was drunk, she never screamed. She could get loud, be ornery, but that wasn't her mother, that was Alcohol. Mother was the opposite of someone who screamed; Mother was the one who *really did* what needed to be done and had never complained about it until Father put her down so far and so badly, just for being Aleut, just for being different, that she took to Alcohol.

Anne was suddenly surprised to discover that she was almost in town. She'd covered two miles without even noticing it and was halfway across Hogworth's field. Old Hogworth had long since given up trying to keep people from cutting across that field into town, had left a real public path and planted the side nearest his house only in vegetables instead of trying to keep the whole field in grain. Anne looked ahead across town; there was no place to go except back to Binches, back to her sisters, and she picked her best shortcuts: over the tracks near Hamm's garage and rising up behind the houses on the other side, up to the beginning of the first real hill on the road to Binches. Then she forgot about her path, pursuing her own thoughts about life. About the teachings of her lost mother and the preachings of her lost father.

Soon she was on the other side of town; she would have been looking back down on the town if she had turned, if she hadn't been wrapped in thoughts far from this day, from this year. But at the next hill she did stop and turn back, at first without seeing. Still only thinking. But gradually the Valley that spread before her in glorious spring sunshine grew in her consciousness: it was such a beautiful valley that you couldn't help but see it, and keep seeing, keep looking. Off to the left, beyond the town and the new-plowed spaces around the nearest farms, rose the Lazy Mountain, the only foothill. And from the direction she had just come after Mrs. Zibota's rejection, the Butte almost due south. She was at a height almost equal to the Butte rising so abruptly from its low land and she could see the delicacy, the shimmer of new green color up there as it trembled and clung to life. She loved the Butte in that moment, its long, familiar steadiness, its being a landmark. She could have swum in the warmth of sun between herself and it, the warmth that had it gently trembling, blurring and beckoning across distance.

She looked a long time. Across the Valley, around the Valley, before her eyes rose beyond it and beyond the Butte. Beyond all of it to where, encircling her world, the range of real mountains grew higher and higher, each one more snow-covered than the last, until you saw the tops of the ones that wouldn't lose their dazzling white even in the height of summer.

But all the near valley was growing green, the willows beside Anne opening into full leaf, the green growing up Lazy Mountain. She could see the line where the fresh color was creeping up there. White birches shimmered in every bit of woods, some very close in a patch of woods just off the east side of the road. The sparkle of their trunks was as alive in the still-bright western sun as their whispering leaves.

She knew what had made her stop. But she stood looking a long time out over the beautiful valley before she went to satisfy herself that she was right about the scent. She knew they went together, the greening of the Valley and the delicate fragrance of bluebells. Turning, finally, from the Valley spread below her, she parted some willows beside the gravel road and looked into the thickening grass. And there they were: clumps of them among the grass, holding up their gently nodding heads of perfect little lavender blue bells. Only some blooms opened yet, toward

84

the tops of stems, many still tight in little buds more pink than blue. She breathed in the scent. And then, clearing a space in the grass beyond them, she sat, screened from the road by the burgeoning willows, where she could continue to breathe in the fragrance of the bluebells along with the other smells of the earth now fully warmed after the long Alaska winter. Deep smells. The smell of animal lives. Remembering Bluebell, her heifer, the calf barn, the pasture. How she had named Bluebell in spite of admonitions not to name or coddle the animals. How she had sneaked to talk to Bluebell, patting her warm neck through the fence while Bluebell tried to nuzzle in return, bending that beautiful sleek neck with its gentle pulse to put her nose through the fence, breathing over Anne.

Immediate memories, some bittersweet, but the bitter was fading into the sweetness of the spring air. It was her favorite time of year and her favorite time of day, the Valley about to enter the long spring evening when the light was soft like no other time.

She sat and dreamed, remembering the laughter-filled evenings of childhood and the joy of rambling quietly alone around the fringes of driveway and plowed or growing fields on the homestead, eating wild raspberries, finding again the places where wild currants grew, searching with her sisters after a rain for morel mushrooms. Thinking of the dewy mornings, of playing through long twilight evenings. Remembering the crunch of peas fresh from the vine in her mouth, gasping over the tart, first taste of red rhubarb stalk pulled from the bunches growing near the old cabin but immediately wanting more — trying it with salt, the way Mary liked it. Margaret turning up her nose but sometimes helping Annie to spell words. Ellen laughing. Martin in summer evening pushing the merry-go-round he built for his little sisters. James and William still at home, around the big wood table at suppertime, James so kindly, William quiet.

Father roasting slices of moose meat on an iron rack over the bonfire at grain harvest time, the mouth-watering smell of the roasting meat; Father sliding pile after pile of the smoking meat onto the platter held by William, who then doled it out and wouldn't let the little girls touch their part until it cooled off some. Eating until you were stuffed with moose meat and Mother's fresh-baked bread and smoked salmon and juicy-crisp slices of raw turnip. James or Walter turning and turning the handle to make the rare treat of ice cream. Raspberry ice cream, rhubarb and strawberry ice cream. Falling asleep on the blanket by the fire that night, hearing big brothers and sisters and Father all laughing and talking around the fire with Mother softly crooning to little Jeannie on her shoulder. Allowed to sleep out all night — Anne had forgotten that — remembering now that even Ellen hadn't known it until waking next morning when James said, "because Martin and I stayed here too, to keep away the bears and the mosquitoes." Anne had wakened looking through a strange hatchwork of dark lines at something like the sky, and then at some dark lumps of forms beyond the hatchwork. It turned out Father and brothers had rigged their big pieces of mosquito netting over planks and sawhorses after the fire died down, to protect the little ones through the night.

"*You* didn't stay awake to keep off the bears," Anne accused Martin after one of the lumpy forms turned into her brother waking up. But she didn't accuse James, who was already stirring, or Mary, who turned out to be the other dark lump, who finally woke up last.

In her memory Anne saw chubby Elizabeth rolling and tumbling around beside her as soon as she woke — Elizabeth usually happy and especially happy that morning to discover she had slept outside with the big kids. *She must have been about four*, Anne thought, *so I would have been six*. On the other side of Elizabeth — Elizabeth wedged between them — Ellen stretched and yawned and then suddenly leaped right out of the makeshift tent, almost collapsing the netting over Annie and Elizabeth, to go chasing after Martin who had begun poking her feet with a stick. Then Annie chased too and Elizabeth tried to chase and they all came back laughing, panting, barefoot when Father called from the door to come in to the cabin for breakfast. Hot cakes with cranberry syrup, a bit of bacon, and lots of eggs flipped out of the hot cast iron skillet by Father while Mother kept dishing up the pancakes. Annie didn't like fried eggs — "yucky," she agreed with Elizabeth — but Ellen did, and the brothers devoured them.

Sitting among the bluebells, remembering many big breakfasts, thinking of Martin eating eggs across the table from her that long ago morning, and his having two pieces of bacon instead of the one piece Ellen and Annie got, she remembered how much more subdued Martin had been whenever James and William were at home, how he copied his big brothers all through that harvest time. Then she thought of him giving all of his sisters rides — especially Mary — down the big hill in his motorized toboggan that last winter on the homestead. Sometimes almost kind, like James. Martin always made them climb back up the hill, all the way to the top, if they wanted the long ride, while he took his own less steep route round the hill driving the toboggan up alone and flying back down again at speed, sometimes many times in between offering rides.

Thinking of her brothers as she sat by the bluebells, Anne was glad that they were all coming back safe from the war. But not to the Valley, not to see Anne and her little sisters, except occasionally William, who newly lived in Anchorage but seemed intimidated by Mrs. Binch. So that he hadn't pressed to take the girls on a promised outing after Mrs. Binch met him at his car and gave him her dishonest reasons, in that familiar smarmy voice: that "the girls know they can't have outings if they haven't been doing their work: Not that I expect much, but they can't just let it slide. Or talk back about it. You know that isn't the way to train children."

But Anne didn't want to think of Mrs. Binch, or of sorry William going away like a wimp without challenging Mrs. Binch. No other adult seemed to see through the woman except Mother, so why should William be any different? He was starting his own family, already had a little girl, and Anne had refused to be sad when she watched him drive away. He brought apples the first time he came — the rarest sort of treat before the war and not common even yet — and Mrs. Binch did let Anne and Elizabeth and Jeannie each have an apple.

Anne was putting that memory aside without much thinking about it. She was thinking of winter, of Martin on his toboggan, of his giving to Ellen the ice skates he was outgrowing, the only pair of real skates they ever had, that Martin had somehow badgered or traded out of some other boy. That Ellen sometimes gave to Annie to try out that last winter, Annie stuffing the toes and wearing extra socks and finding she could actually glide across the ice on the low end of the south field.

She was thinking, as she sat in spring sunshine, of romping in the snow. Of the great fun of sledding, of wobbly skating, memorable snowball fights — of how friendly was the dark in those days, because it was always dark when they played before or after school in winter. She smiled, and then was suddenly laughing out loud at the forgotten memory of chasing after Ellen the minute they bounced out of bed in winter mornings and flew out the door, racing Martin around the cabin in bare feet in the snow. Back to the cabin door, hot and panting and laughing, feet not the least bit cold until they were back indoors and being scolded for doing it. It was a game Martin started; Ellen and Annie had become determined to beat him at it, to outrace him, but they never did.

So long, Anne thought; how have I forgotten so much, so many good things, for so long? She touched her breasts, each one, that had been tender and growing for awhile. She knew she had to have a bra but she had been refusing to say anything to Mrs. Binch; she wouldn't ask the woman for anything. She plotted, briefly, how she would ask the right friend for hand-me-downs (Ellen and Brenda were already too big), as she had traded her help with school work for Kotex starting a few months ago — far better to do that than to ask Mrs. Binch for anything. But those were passing thoughts; her mind didn't linger on them. Something as gentle as the scent of bluebells was settling inside of her and she was wrapped in memory. She wouldn't let annoyance at anyone or anything, not even Mrs. Binch, intrude upon it. She lay back and stared at the blue sky through willow branches. She heard cows begin lowing in the fenced field behind her; they would be starting back toward their familiar barn, for milking time.

It seemed perfect, just then, to know that cows knew their milking time and their own barn, that bluebells knew when to bloom, that even winter knew its time and would come back just as this marvelous spring would always come back.

When she roused herself at last and began the final two-mile walk to Binches, she was still the same girl turned away from Zibotas. But she was very much again the same girl, the often happy girl she had half-buried under cold and hate for four long years. And she was a new girl in whom feelings of hate had almost worn themselves out, leaving her ready for something new.

Chapter Seven

In high school Anne's life began to open. She couldn't believe the freedom of walking off the school grounds to eat her lunch sandwich with Ellen or Brenda or other girls at Deb's, a combination soda fountain and café that welcomed the school crowd at noon. (Where Margaret had once worked and where Mary used to work after school before she married her MP and got pregnant and went off to live in Oregon.) The freedom to sit outside on nice days and talk to Ellen for most of an hour at lunch, instead of seeing her only in passing in the halls.

For four years under the thumb of teachers or Mrs. Binch every hour and a watched slave at home, Anne had been learning to repress feeling even more strongly than she had done around her father. With no softening mother to balance the growth of toughness, with a petty and sadistic female in Mother's place and unable to bring her mother back, she had grown by now an even stronger protection around her real thoughts and feelings. But her life has been expanding, too, at school. And now she is rediscovering freedom, supported by having known the same Valley kids for a dozen years. She is one of them. She sings at school assemblies with Brenda and three other girls, having a clear and quietly yearning soprano voice although she can't hit the notes precisely without practice and having the other sopranos beside her. She doesn't have an ear for making music, only a growing love for it, a strong desire to get it perfectly right. She is a starting guard on the second string basketball team. She writes little pieces for the school paper. Her classmates elect her to the student council. She finds herself chatting away as never before, realizing she does have friends — or that at least a lot of the kids like her well enough. For days at a time she would forget that she was supposed to be some sort of pariah.

It made her bold. One day she simply walked right past Deb's and several blocks further along to the post office to see the postmistress, who was the wife of the magistrate. For some time she had known that it was the local magistrate who was responsible for sending her and her sisters to foster homes. And that, contrary to Mrs. Binch's lies that she was keeping the girls out of "the goodness of her heart" — *what goodness?* (But Anne didn't like the contempt she felt for the woman and her lies, would rather forget her) — Anne knew by now, through her brother William, that Mrs. Binch had been paid, was being paid, through the court, forty dollars each month for each child she tried to victimize.

Anne wanted to put a stop to all that. She couldn't begin to think of going to the magistrate himself. Bold as she felt that day, tough as she could be in a pinch, she wasn't up to approaching that man with the unapproachable title. People around town called him "the judge" and even though she knew that most of them said it in ignorance, knew she was smarter than they were (she'd known since second grade that Alaska wasn't a state but a territory and didn't rate a federal judge either, had won spelling bees in which she spelled "magistrate" among other words) it was another one of those things she didn't like in herself, the feeling that people were ignorant compared to herself. Not even half the adults around the Valley had finished high school, some of them had never even gotten close. They'd worked on family farms instead, in the upper Midwest, before coming to Alaska. They *were* ignorant. And sometimes Anne indulged in a feeling of her own superiority, felt a pride in it, but she was ashamed of it too. It was too close to being like Margaret, who Ellen said was a snob. "She was a snob from the time I remember her at all," Ellen said. Ellen was six years younger than Margaret, which made Anne nine years younger and Anne hardly remembered Margaret being at home. "That's because she wasn't home," Ellen said. "She was out of the house all the time, hanging out at the Bogles or someplace by the time she was twelve or so. The Bogles had lost their only son and were disappointed in their daughter running off with a boy when she was only fifteen or something. So they made a big fuss over Margaret and Mother let her stay over there a lot. Mrs. Bogle made clothes for her; she was the only one who ever had dresses.

"You know the first thing I remember Margaret telling me?" Ellen said. "When I was only five or six? She told me she was the daughter of some Russian prince or king and had gotten transplanted into our poor family by mistake. But that the son of the prince, or son of the king or whatever, was going to come to woo her and rescue her any day.

"Fancy that," Ellen laughed, "she's the daughter and he's the son, and the son is going to come wooing her? She got really mad at me and tried to get me in trouble at school and with Dad because I told her she must have things 'down-side up' — as Martin used to say. She hated the way Martin sometimes said things like that when he was little — always trying to correct him — and she hated it that I had gotten onto her games. She didn't like being part of our family. And she insisted on having the upper bunk all to herself that last couple years, so I had to sleep with bossy Mary, and you three younger girls were all crowded together in the bottom bunk after little Jeannie was out of the crib and Martin went to the Boys' House."

Anne didn't have more than vague notions about any of that. But she remembered, to her bones, that acting superior was not allowed in her own growing-up years (*how had Margaret gotten away with it?*) and that Ellen despised it.

Anne couldn't have approached the magistrate, didn't know how. She'd heard about him, seen him at a distance around town and he didn't look like someone you could talk to. But the magistrate's wife, Mrs. Harbison, who was the postmistress, had always seemed a kindly woman. The day that Anne walked right over to see her, Mrs. Harbison took some time, listened to her as Anne began to try to tell how life was miserable with Mrs. Binch: "She tells lies about everyone. Likes to tell us bad things about our mother. And she tries to find willow switches to use on my littlest sister, the kind to really sting but not leave bruises."

Then, squirming about it but desperate to get Mrs. Harbison to understand, Anne suddenly blurted: "She tries to make my sister Elizabeth beg to have Kotex since she started her periods. I would have had to do the same, except that I bum from friends: I do homework for them in exchange." You didn't talk about "periods" except to close girlfriends and Anne blushed, hot and red, over mentioning such a thing to a grown woman she didn't even know, a woman so respectable and married to a magistrate.

"Can you see whether Elizabeth can go to live with our brother William in Anchorage, and find a better place for little Jeannie and for me?" Anne pleaded.

"I can work for my room and board," she told Mrs. Harbison earnestly, serious in every word, "I can do almost anything; I'm good at cooking, cleaning, ironing, and any garden jobs; I even bake bread, and pies. And I don't need much. No one would have to be paid to keep me."

Walking back to school, Anne was surprised at herself; she could hardly believe that she had gone through with it, said everything she had planned to say and then even embarrassingly more. But Mrs. Harbison had been a good listener: she never interrupted and she didn't give those looks of so many adults, the looks that said they weren't really hearing and didn't care to hear you. *Maybe there are some people who aren't taken in by Mrs. Binch*, Anne desperately, hopefully thought. *And Mrs. Harbison seems smart, maybe she could be one of them.*

By this time the War was two years over and Anne's three oldest brothers had come home safe. But not "come home," all married by now, and raising their own families elsewhere, only William settling anywhere near by, in Anchorage. On another of his rare visits to see the girls at Binches, William had half-heartedly said that one of the girls could come to live with him and his wife and baby girl. "But only one." William seems different to Anne since the war, not only a man now instead of a teenage brother, but even quieter than before. Unlike her favorite, oldest brother James, William had never been outgoing or warm anyway, but now he seems almost solemn. He had been a radioman in the Air Force — and he did love radio — and never left the ground although he had wanted so much to fly.

Anne wouldn't see Martin for years; he had gone south to Texas, some unremembered time before, with the Kenai family that he'd been living with after Father died.

Mother has stayed away. Part of Anne knows that Mother feels too much shame and pain to face her children; Anne saw that in her mother's eyes the one day that Mother did come inside at Binches' house, and she knows her mother's fierce pride because she shares it. Deeply beyond that, Anne loves her mother just as proudly, just as fiercely, defending her in her mind against all critics, including the voice inside herself that sounds wounded, abandoned, rejected. Anne — little Annie and now Anne — considers that hidden voice to be a whiner and, if it creeps into her mind, she puts it down. Hard. She will not let it grieve; she refuses to let it whine at her.

Mary and Margaret were gone by now too, everyone moving to the States and starting families of their own, some already well along at it: Anne has nieces and nephews coming along that she's never seen and she can't keep their names straight, not knowing them. In Anne herself there is some aversion to starting a family; it seemed such a huge and foreign idea. She wanted out of this little town, this summer-dusty, windy and winter-frozen town, with its prejudices and its narrow ways. But not by getting married. She wanted to get to the States, like all of her brothers and sisters, but she wanted to see so much more of the world. She dreams of college. Wanted college. Very badly.

Ellen, like the rest of the younger girls, had been in a foster home for four years, a home where she had never felt wanted or liked. She said that the woman, the mother, was smarmy, "false-goody-good," and that the man had been trying to catch Ellen alone. Ellen would soon be graduating from high school, less than nine months away now, and she and Anne talked, many times, about living together as soon as Ellen turned eighteen next summer and got a job. But lately their talk had been less excited, had slowed to where Anne knew that Ellen was losing interest. As Anne was. What sort of life was left for them here, where Ellen might be a waitress at Deb's or Morton's Restaurant, or add her name to a list to work at the post office or one of few other offices? Where Anne already felt that every good thing, except for Brenda and the beauty of the Valley itself and maybe a few friends, was gone. Where Anne was close to despising more than half of the people inhabiting the place and hated that feeling in herself. None of her classmates talked of going on to college or even knowing more of the world, and Anne couldn't see what they could be thinking of as a future. Beautiful as was the Valley, its horizons were closed, filled with mountains and glaciers except along the road to Anchorage and the Outside. All of Anne's own best memories were wrapped around pain, around parents and homestead gone.

The changes came suddenly. Mrs. Harbison hadn't made any promises but it was no time, it seemed, before Anne got a note at school to come and see her again. "This is where the couple named Watkins live," Mrs. Harbison said. "You must know who they are? They want someone to live there, help out with the young children, and Elaine Watkins will see you right after school tomorrow. Shall I tell her you can come?" Anne did know who they were, a young couple with two kids, living close to town. "Your sister Elizabeth is going to live with your brother William in Anchorage by the end of the month," Mrs. Harbison was going on, "and your oldest brother James in Colorado is sending money for your littlest sister Jeannie to go to live with him and his wife."

Anne was surprised, and more than surprised, that Mrs. Binch might be giving in so easily: She had expected some sort of struggle with the woman, had thought Mrs. Binch had an awful grip on all of them and that there might be a real fight, even in the court. Though she didn't understand such things, Anne had been preparing herself, for weeks, for weeks even before she had walked to the post office that fateful day, had rehearsed over and over in her mind every argument she could think of to get her little sisters away from Mrs. Binch. Had pondered plans for her own freedom, prepared to advertise herself to work for room and board as soon as her sisters were safely out from under Mrs. Binch's iron hand.

And now it was all so easy. Except that now Anne was alone, her little sisters gone elsewhere; Anne living in a strange new place, among strangers, walking the seven blocks to school in the blowing cold that was turning into another winter. Seeing Ellen only at school, Ellen who was beginning to talk of leaving town herself as soon as she graduated, getting a job in Anchorage and saving to take the Alaska Steamship to Seattle and a bus to Oregon to live awhile with Margaret or Mary until she got a start on a life of her own.

The Watkins treated Anne well enough and she had new freedom, though she was very slow to feel it, didn't explore it. And she didn't like them. Bruce Watkins was big and slow and seemed dumb, sprawling after work with his beer, dirty from his mechanic's job and drinking himself stupid. Margie Watkins was restless, well-meaning enough but always tapping her toes or fingers, often out of the house as soon as supper was done, leaving with women friends to play cards or play Bingo, leaving Anne with the cleanup — which she didn't mind — but also with the job of getting a bumptious six-year-old boy and a clingy three-year-old girl off to bed. Before their father got stuporous he usually cleaned himself up and went off too, apparently to drink more beer with buddies, and then come rambling noisily home after everyone had settled down.

The house was tiny and Anne slept in an alcove with only a curtain and their thin bedroom door to separate her from the night sounds of the

Watkins: his snoring, his pleadings for sex or the worse sounds of the rhythmic pumping and breathing and groaning when it happened.

The Watkins were being paid, after all, to keep her, and Margie Watkins gave Anne two dollars each week. "Pocket money," she called it. It was exciting to have it though Anne hardly knew where to spend it, it was such a lot of money. She was startled when Margie Watkins suggested the first time that Anne should go to a Friday night movie (a movie theater had opened in town) or on a weekend outing with friends. She bought a book, *Anne of Green Gables*, and two used records, one of Strauss waltzes and one of Sousa marches, that she could play in evenings on the Watkins' record player — which wasn't even a wind-up like the one from home. The freedom of doing such things, of buying things, of walking around with freedom and money in her pocket was delicious, but Anne couldn't believe in it; she kept waiting for something. "Waiting for the other shoe to drop." She remembered old Mr. Losey saying that, about something, on that long-ago sunny March day when he'd been talking to her father. That memory came back to Anne one crisp, cold winter day so clearly that she heard her father's voice. His friendly voice after they had left old man Losey, explaining what Mr. Losey meant by the peculiar words about another shoe to drop: "What comes next can be either bad or good," Father said; "that's what he meant. And sometimes life likes to hand you something bad soon after it gives you something good. That's the other shoe dropping. But don't you worry," and he had patted Annie's knee, so unlike himself that day: "You've had enough bad for awhile, with that appendix and that hospital. You don't have to worry about such things until you're a grown-up. It's the grown-ups who are supposed to worry and take care of anything bad coming your way."

Well, they hadn't taken care of a lot of it. There had definitely been another shoe to drop. And another and another. But Anne always squelched such thoughts. Life wasn't that bad at the Watkins.

She was at a loss with the two children; they were so different from her own brothers and sisters. Instead of putting up with anything, they whined or acted out when they couldn't have their own way, the little girl hanging onto Anne, the boy throwing things and yelling. Every night was a trial until they finally stayed in bed and Anne had to learn to do all homework in study hall and in every spare minute at school because there was no quiet at home. For years afterward she felt guilty that she hadn't done better by those children, hadn't understood or sympathized that there can be deprivations as bad, though different, as those she'd grown accustomed to in her own life. Those children at the time seemed to her to have everything: parents who stayed together, a father who laughed at their antics, plenty of toys, no onerous chores, a mother who came home every night, was there every morning when they woke up. Their little lives seemed so easy and so safe, yet they acted like they were entitled to more.

Anne couldn't later remember whether she asked to leave the Watkins' home when she talked to Mrs. Harbison now sometimes at the post office. She didn't think she had: she wasn't used to asking for anything; you made the best of whatever came along. But Mrs. Harbison suggested, after some months, that Anne come to live with her own family. "Since Jeffrey's moved out we have a spare room and it would be good to have your help around the house." Jeffrey was their grown son going off to college.

In some ways Anne got out of the latest frying pan into a new kind of fire. The "judge" had roving hands and a very canny awareness of how to avoid the eyes of his wife. Anne had to become equally devious to try to stay under the eyes of Mrs. Harbison or near the twelve-year-old daughter Caroline. After the first time the judge caught her in the drying room and tried to get his arms around her, bringing his jowly, sour-smelling face close to her own while she ducked away, Anne learned to listen with the keenness of animal's ears to the sound of footsteps around the house, keeping track of everyone's movements. She soon learned that the judge never came upstairs so she was safe in her upstairs bedroom next to Caroline's. A good thing, as there was no escape route. Probably the reason the judge never came up either, as he couldn't have slipped away from his wife or daughter from there or easily explained himself. Or maybe (trying to give him some credit) maybe he was decent enough that the girls' bedrooms, his daughter's next to Anne's, were off-limits in his own mind. Still, she never felt safe from him even there unless the family was home.

She was calling him "the judge" herself now, as he was judgmental, self-righteous except on that slippery side of him that had him creeping after her. She was repulsed by him physically, with his usually grim mouth, lowering thick gray eyebrows and gray hairs growing from his nose. He was either bossy or silently cranky around the house a lot of the time while his wife quietly put up with it. *Such secrets everyone has,*

Annie thought, people so different at home from what you see of them out in public. She could never have guessed what Mrs. Harbison was putting up with. Mrs. Harbison didn't act any different at home than she did anywhere else. She was slender and upright, still dark-haired — "handsome" in the word of books — with understanding in her eyes and in her listening, calmly tending to things and to everyone.

Anne was carried off to church with the family twice on Sunday and again on Wednesday evening for prayer meeting. This was a new experience, partly interesting but mostly just strange. Mother had never said much but little Annie had known, even before the rape, that her mother had wanted no truck with the kind of people who went to this kind of church, dressed up on Sunday but thin-lipped about life. These were the "good" people, the ones who looked down on anybody not like themselves. It was interesting to have them acting false-friendly to her now, so many of the women the same ones or like the ones who had shunned her mother and crowed over the rape. Now, supposedly, Anne herself was respectable, living with the judge's family and known as an outstanding student and track star. She wondered about Mrs. Harbison's attitude: was she just staying quiet, like Anne, about these people's hypocrisy? She wasn't like them; she had a kindliness that showed in her eyes through all her calm and reserve and orderliness.

Anne mused about that phrase "having no truck with" that came to her mind: It was Father who had explained it to Ellen and Annie. Ellen had heard Father laughing with old man Losey and Mr. Riley, saying that they had "no truck with" some church-going colonists. Annie was glad, at age four or five, to be there when Ellen asked Father the meaning of those odd words, to be included on any rare day when she might hear Father explain something. She had loved to hear him when he took time to explain things, especially words. "What did you mean about having no truck with the Harcheks?" Ellen asked when Father sat down on the high porch that was like a deck, for some rare quiet minutes before supper. Curious herself, and loving words from the earliest time she could remember, Annie had never known of any truck except the flatbed that her father and big brothers worked at and nursed along, something so important to them that working on it took priority over everything important to Annie or her mother. They talked about it so often, Father and brothers, about keeping that truck going, about working on it — and about the generator and the pump and the tractor and any other machinery and the Model T.

Anne remembered how, on that long-ago day as she sat listening, the long late sun was making everything look golden. As it did so often in spring and summer. In the windy cold of another March, walking home from school to Harbisons, she was remembering how peaceful might be times like that summer day, especially in the lull that came when outside chores were done, before inside chores and arguments and studying began.

It would have been summer, because Anne remembered how she was swinging her bare feet back and forth off the edge of the high wooden porch while she listened to Father and could see Martin messing around with some sticks out by the henhouse. And beyond Martin the growing grain of the south field rippling in the sun. She was on one side, Ellen on the other side of Father sitting solidly in one of his two biggest handmade wooden chairs between them.

Father didn't answer Ellen, looking off as though he hadn't heard, so Ellen repeated herself: "You were fixing their truck; weren't they the ones you were laughing with Mr. Riley about while you helped him fix their truck? The Harcheks who never give back? How come you said you have no truck with them? While you were fixing their truck."

"Little pitchers have big ears," Father first responded, another saying of his that interested Annie. But then he patiently explained. "A lot of words can mean more than one thing — the same word can mean different things. . . ."

"Like when you said that Margaret putting on the dog didn't have anything to do with real dogs?"

"Yes, that's right. But sometimes the word might mean something *like* the other thing. Having truck and having *a* truck might mean close to the same thing. Having a truck is a way of getting back and forth, dealing with other people, trading with them. Trade means getting what you don't have from somewhere else and trading off your own extra things like our extra grain or potatoes to somebody who doesn't grow their own. It's a back-and-forth thing, getting and giving. And you couldn't carry on trade without something big enough to haul the stuff around. Like a truck. Or the train. . . ."

"Or the big boat that brings all the clothes and the fancy stuff up to Alaska, from Sears Roebuck," said Annie, proud of understanding things. "Because Sears Roebuck is in the Lower Forty-Eight and you can only get there on a big boat. And they don't send the stuff just because you want it. You have to send them the dollars from the sweat of your brow, like Mother said."

"You're pretty smart, both you girls," Father said. And Annie kicked her feet, swelling with more pride but wishing she wasn't always lumped in with "you girls." "That's exactly what I'm talking about," Father was saying, "having truck with somebody means the back-and-forth between you, getting along, having things to share. But there are some people you don't have much truck with. You can always do them a favor, like I did helping to fix Harcheks' truck, but you don't have other back-and-forth. . . ."

"Because they don't share," Ellen said, "the Harcheks don't."

"You're certainly getting so smart you'd better be learning the next lesson," Father said. "You remember what I told you about that?"

"Yes," said Ellen, and Annie turned to her, fascinated to find out what could be the next lesson. But then disappointed as she began to hear a message that sounded more and more familiar even if in some different words. "Don't get too big for your britches," Ellen was reciting, "being smarter doesn't mean better. Doing it right doesn't mean anything except you can feel good about yourself; it doesn't mean you get to blame somebody else for not being able to do it as well as you."

When Anne described the Harbison family to Ellen, sitting outside the high school eating their lunch together on the first warm day of April, they giggled about "churchy" people, as Ellen called them. "But they don't have to be going to church," Ellen said, "it's the same as Mrs. Binch — 'putting on a good face to the world,'" as Dad used to say, 'and hiding what skeletons they have in the closet, even the lively skeletons.' Remember him saying that? I loved the idea of lively skeletons."

Anne didn't remember she'd ever heard that. But she noticed how familiarly Ellen said 'Dad' while Anne herself still thought of him as 'Father.' Or Father Almighty. How long had Ellen been saying "Dad"? Hadn't she always said "Father" when they were children on the homestead? Only the older kids, somehow magically transformed by age or high school, had dared to get so familiar with Almighty Father as to call him Dad.

Anne put down a feeling she didn't recognize as jealousy but she felt a little hurt that her beloved Ellen, her compatriot in all struggles against the world, had gone over to the other side.

"The Brenders are that way too," Ellen was saying. The Brenders were the couple she'd been living with for over four years now. "They don't go to church any more. I guess they did when their kids were growing up but now they don't bother."

Anne told Ellen about the judge trying to get her alone.

"Oh, no, what *is* it about men? Mr. Brender's sneaky too, though he doesn't sound as bad as the judge. In all the time I've been there, he didn't start bothering me till last fall. I think she knows it but they both pretend like it isn't happening. At least Mrs. Harbison sounds smart and sounds like she pays attention. Mrs. Brender isn't very smart; she just moves around from one thing to another and sort of gets things done while she seems to be sort of talking to herself. She reminds me," and Ellen giggled some more, "she reminds me of one of the old cows in the pasture, the ones too old to give much milk any more? Just chewing their cud and plodding from one place to another. Not that she's a bad person. . . ." Ellen always seemed to like people, no matter what. She had liked the old cows and she had the same liking in her voice even as she giggled about Mrs. Brender.

"I don't remember cows like that," Anne said.

"Probably Dad and James butchered those when you were four or five. . . ."

"I thought they sold all the cows, when I was seven or so. Except some heifers."

"They did sell what cows were left, then. But what I was saying is, Mrs. Brender isn't a bad person. And I guess he isn't either. But he's been sneaking after me just like the judge is sneaking after you. Even came into my room one night, late, and pretended he'd just made a mistake when I woke up with him right beside my bed, when I jumped out of it and said I'd holler to his wife."

"Made a mistake?"

"Right. Picture that, since their room is downstairs and mine is the only bedroom upstairs. See what I mean, that he isn't smart?" And Anne giggled with her this time.

"It does sound like your judge is smarter. So it's a good thing his wife seems smart too. Mr. Brender's been so slow that he didn't do anything over the winter after I scared him that night last fall. So I was able to figure it out when I was sure he started plotting something awhile back. Planning to fool us, I think — his wife and me — while pretending to go to his night out with the guys on Thursdays. He always took Mrs.

Brender to her sewing circle on Thursday night, always takes her, and then meets the other husbands and some guys . . . but I'll tell you later; we're going to be late for the bell. . . ."

"We have almost ten minutes. . . ."

"Okay, I'll tell you what I wanted to get to. It's about being smart, in looking out for yourself. Be smart about it. So okay, I figured out that Mr. Brender was probably going to come back home after taking her to the sewing circle. When I'd usually had Thursday nights to myself, to wash my hair and catch up on anything, like math or washing my underwear. So I outsmarted him. I told them we were starting rehearsals for the play and I would be staying after school on Thursdays and Hilda would bring me home. Since I'm a senior, what could they do? And it wasn't totally a lie, because Hilda desperately wanted to be Rebecca, the doctor's daughter in the play, and wanted me to help her with lines, for the tryouts. And I didn't think she could make it without help, because she didn't really understand the play, how Rebecca fits. . . ."

"And she isn't Rebecca, didn't get the part," Anne said. Everybody in the school knew who was in the play, *Our Town*, which was going to be put on in a couple of weeks, near the end of April. Put on mostly by the seniors, their tradition.

"She's going to be helping me backstage," Ellen said, "she couldn't have been Rebecca, she's not . . . well anyway I'm trying to get to the point. I was interested in the play — you know it takes place mostly in the cemetery, you said you read it — and Miss Dickson asked me if I would try out for the narrator, who's supposedly stage manager too but he's a main character. Miss Dickson thought it would be interesting for a girl — me — to play that part. But George was perfect for the onstage parts of that and I didn't want to be on stage. So . . . anyway, you know I really *am* stage manager and Hilda's helping me back stage.

"Now," said Ellen, and she pushed Anne's arm down when Anne started to pick up their lunch things off the bench where they had been eating their sandwiches together, "this is the point I've been trying to get to. And we must have another five minutes anyway. I don't care if we're late for the bell: I know you worry about that more than me. And I know you blame Dad a lot — I do too, for some things — but some things he said to me a few times help me a lot. And I want to tell you what he said to me one day when I was the most hurt and mad I think I've ever been. I'm telling you because it can help you with the judge. It's about looking out for yourself, protecting yourself, like from the judge. Dad told me, that day, to walk with him. And do you know where we walked? You may not remember Maggie's mother, our first border collie. Trudy. She was old when I was little and we buried her out under a birch tree when I was four or so. And remember that's where the raspberries grew thick and extra juicy around there after we buried her?" Anne did know that story, and how big and perfect were the raspberries in that spot. "I was maybe nine when I came off the bus that one day," Ellen went on, "and started bawling all the way up the driveway. Janet was my only real friend; it was fourth grade and I remember it was a pretty day right after school started that fall, but I kept kicking my spelling book in the dust after I dropped it coming along the driveway. Even Martin was scared and ran ahead because he'd never seen me do such a thing. I don't even remember exactly what Janet did; it was that kind of kid stuff where your best friend has turned against you.

"Anyway, then I was making a mess of my chores, bringing in the water and the wood with Martin. And I was the one to collect the eggs, because I was the careful one with them. But that day I dropped the basket and some broke. So then I did this thing you'd think would get you half-killed; I kicked the hen when she started cackling around my feet. And just then Dad was coming past the henhouse on his way from the barn or pasture — I didn't even know he was home. And I knew for sure when I saw his face looking in, that I would be half-killed."

Anne had forgotten about the school bell. Never had she heard of Ellen acting like this. Hurting an animal? A little bit mad sometimes, yes, usually at Martin. And a few times, in Mountain View and afterward on the homestead with no family, Anne thought she had heard Ellen maybe crying quietly in the night. But to think of Almighty Father catching you kicking an animal! Bad enough to be messing up at doing your chores. Even to be bawling or complaining. Anne couldn't believe Ellen did those things, but she suddenly pictured it clearly: the henhouse enclosed with plywood on three sides but with only chicken wire on the side by the path, so that you could look in on the chickens from there. Almighty Father peering in to see that you had broken the eggs — but far worse — that you were kicking a hen!!

"But he didn't punish me at all. Instead he talked to me a long time." Anne didn't truly hear in Ellen's words what, some years later, she wished she had understood. She did listen to Ellen; she had tried to put aside her own worry that the second bell would catch them outside of class. She remembered Ellen leaning toward her and sounding so seriously unlike her usual self. No giggling, no laughing. She remembered, vaguely, that she had been late, after all, to her history class and that Mr. Rich had graciously overlooked it. She thought she had been listening to what Ellen said.

So why hadn't she understood it? Why did it take another seventeen years or more before she began to want to know what Ellen meant? And more years after that, of memories, of talks with Ellen about all the implications of differences and misunderstandings among her siblings, before Anne actually perhaps understood the message that impressed Ellen so deeply at age nine. What Ellen said that high school day, insistent while Anne tried to put down her own fear of being late to class, was after all so simple: "Anyway," Ellen was saying at the end of their noontime talk, "it just means be smart, don't let the judge catch you. He probably doesn't see how fast we can get on to their tricks. . . ."

"Could he ever guess how fast little Jeannie came up with her high-heeled shoe in Mountain View?" Anne said — thought she may have said — in a sudden burst of confident recognition that Ellen must have inspired in her.

Probably it was because I'd *heard* it so repeatedly, Anne wondered. The same message on so many occasions, in similar words. So that it had become just the stuff that, in Father's own words, "went in one ear and out the other." Anne had never been brought up short to hear it the striking way Ellen must have heard it as a nine-year-old on that fall day when she was in the most miserable state of her childhood and Father appeared in one of his rare kindly moods to comfort her.

"So tell me, can you remember what he was saying?" But it was those seventeen years later that Anne was asking Ellen if she could repeat what Almighty Father had said on his walk with her to the raspberry burial ground.

"Well, I can't remember exact words," Ellen said, "and it started with the usual stuff: 'be your own person, do what you have to do; don't worry what other people think'. All that stuff we heard over and over: 'Do your job. Keep your eye on what you're doing.'". Anne remembered all that very well. "But then he stopped me," Ellen said, "before we came to Trudy's grave, and started asking me questions: "did I know why he was telling me this? Did I understand what he really meant?

103

"I don't remember all he said, but when we sat down by Trudy's grave he started telling me she was named Trudy because 'old Trudy was so true to what she was.' The reason I keep telling you so often to look out for what you do" Dad said, "is because you can fall into not being like Trudy. There will come times when you don't have help, when you don't have me, or your mother, and you have to look out for yourself. When you have to figure out everything for yourself. And you won't be able to do it if you've got a habit of worrying what somebody else thinks or whether somebody likes you. . . ."

"*Habit*, that was it. He talked about habits. . . . And oh. Oh, how could I forget this? He thumped me, first on the head and then on the heart. Just lightly. And then he thumped me on the head again. 'This is a habit I want you to have. I want you to have a habit of keeping these two together,' he said, 'your head up here and your heart in the middle of you, keep them together. If your heart is hurting like Janet hurt it, don't lose your head and go hurt some other helpless thing like a chicken. And don't go getting off so far into your head that you don't know what your heart is telling you is right.'

"'Other people hurting you is not as bad as you hurting yourself by doing something that isn't right." he said. "Or following somebody else along into doing something that isn't right for you.'

"And of course it wasn't 'right' that I kicked the chicken or tried to make everybody else feel as bad as I did that day. We talked about that.

"And you know what? I heard Dad saying some of the same things to Martin the next spring — or no, it was another spring after that — when Martin stole from the Co-op. Remember? And Martin never afterward did another thing so far out of line; that's when he really started spending his time building things with motors. . . ."

"I thought he built that toboggan with the motor sooner . . . but anyway. . . ."

"Well, I might have some things mixed up. And I don't remember Dad's exact words either. But I know he made a big impression on me, encouraging me to be myself even if it hurt. Talking to me, just me, so long that day."

Over years Anne thought a lot about what Ellen said, what "Dad" had said to Ellen that day, what Anne had heard Almighty Father say many times through her childhood. Thought about all of it sometimes with anger, sometimes with a yearning that brought unwanted, unexpected tears.

She didn't miss the irony: who else but Almighty Father had done most to turn Anne herself into a worrying creature always trying either to get things right or to get away? Who had so put Mother down, when Mother was really the one who kept head and heart together? Who else had seemed to have so little heart, so little love, that he left Anne vulnerable with longing for at least some show of warmth — at the very least some signs of approval — from a male figure who loomed large with importance and strength and authority? Why else had Anne spent almost forty years trying to find some of that warmth? To garner, through twenty years of marriage, what bits of love and approval she could get from a husband too like Almighty Father?

She found a poem, *Dancing on the Grave of a Son of a Bitch*, and she danced and danced to that poem soon after her divorce. She found Sylvia Plath's poem, *Daddy*, but that one frightened her, frightened her so much that she stopped the dancing with any spirit.

At the Harbisons Anne never felt successful as a confidante or "big sister" to Caroline, though Caroline would come to Anne's room and want to talk. But she was full of Bible stuff. She was almost as tall as her mother and wrapped her long brown braids up around her head like her mother did. She almost sounded like her mother at times, using the same expressions and gestures, but she was prim, terribly so, which Mrs. Harbison wasn't. In her dark-framed spectacles Caroline looked more like forty years old than twelve, already had a judgmental edge like her father's. Over the summer she and Anne worked together in the vegetable garden but Caroline didn't like the work. She would disappear into the house and that was fine with Anne.

Ellen did leave town that summer for Anchorage, on her way to Oregon by fall.

Anne got saved in the fall, when a visiting evangelist stirred people up at a big meeting, playing on emotions until people began flocking to the altar to receive Jesus, some of them crying. Anne didn't cry but she was filled with hope and contrition and thought she felt the love of this icon/man Jesus for the first time. But it didn't last. In a short time she came to resent the evangelist — and all his kind — for playing upon her feelings. The preacher did it for his own ego, is what she thought: all those people coming crying and begging, even falling at his feet while he stood up there thundering or pleading, crooning, coaxing, crying out to heaven with arms out flung, filled with his own power to make even grown men and women into something like slaves. "The power of the Word," is what he called it. But when Anne began to read, carefully, the Word for herself, she saw Jesus never talked like this and she didn't think he would have condoned it. She became ashamed of having been "taken in," in her father's words, and began to decide that here was another kind of predator to watch out for, stirring up emotion to weaken you, to get at you. Not that she was able to think all of this through at the time — her thoughts and feelings were vague — but she came to feel a squirming embarrassment over the fact that she had let herself follow some of those people to the altar.

At the Harbisons it was the practice to read Scripture, aloud, taking turns at the reading, almost every night of the week (Sunday and Wednesday readings shortened because of having been to church and sometimes Saturday night off so that Mrs. Harbison could bake or sew for the latest church project and the judge and Caroline could study for their Bible classes). The family read through the entire Bible, from beginning to end, Mrs. Harbison had told Anne when she came to live with them, and then started over to read it all again. They had been in the middle of *Kings* or *Chronicles* — Anne could never keep those straight — when Anne arrived. And she had sat, bemused (and maybe amused?) thinking of Ellen and what Ellen would have said about such ultra-seriousness as the judge and Caroline put on in their reading, declaiming the words of these ancient people with their ancient way of taking themselves so seriously, listing every deed of every king (it seemed) and every little reason that their ancient god got mad at the people or the king. But when the reading came to *Ezra*, and then *Nehemiah*, Anne began to read with some feeling herself: the people sometimes came alive, as alive as people in the Greek stories of Greek gods.

Esther was interesting but *Job* was long, boring, with no answer anyway as to why he suffered so horribly. The Greeks would have given some answer, Anne thought — maybe Job was just too comfortable before the afflictions, and hard-headed on top of it like Odysseus? (Hard-headed like her own father?)

The family was making its way through *Proverbs* or *Ecclesiastes* — Anne could hardly keep those straight either — when she got briefly saved in the fall. It had been a long struggle through the pages and pages of *Psalms* in the summer, Anne's eyes glazing over from the endless repetitious wordiness even though there was something beautiful in the language and its rhythms. In high summer, after work in the garden, Anne often found — in the living room with its rugs and its lamps, all the comforts that she had once dreamed of — found that her eyes were closing over the whispery thin pages of the new Bible that had been given to her at the church. She would jerk awake suddenly and try to pretend it hadn't happened. There were times the judge did doze off himself and if he started to snore Mrs. Harbison would end the reading with a smile, whether they had gotten through the chapter or not.

Toward the end of Psalms, one night soon after she had crawled into her bed, Anne's face grew wet with tears and she lay awake with the silent tears still coming: *By the waters of Babylon we sat down and wept When we remembered Zion.*

There was another line that stayed in her mind, she hardly knew why, for years; from *Ecclesiastes*, from the time soon after she was saved: *Dead flies make the perfumer's ointment give off an evil odor.*

Meanwhile she had been skipping ahead to read the books of the New Testament for herself, curious, finally, about this man Jesus. She was fascinated by things that he said, puzzling over some of them for days. *Why did he curse the fig tree?* What did he mean telling his disciples that brother would deliver brother to death and parents and children would rise up against each to put each other to death? Because most of what he was saying was about kindness, and love. What did he mean by saying the meek shall inherit the earth? She gave up on the repetitious wordiness of Paul, even though she liked what he said about love. *If I'm going to have to sit through all this again*, she said to herself — having developed a habit of talking to herself in her own mind (but not out loud except when alone in the garden or walking to and from school) — *if I'm going to have to listen to all these preachings of Paul through the reading in evenings to come, there's no point in reading it twice. I'm getting enough of preaching as it is. Didn't these people know that repetition could simply put you to sleep?*

She came to be grateful, though, in later years — and even at the time feeling, vaguely, something pleasing in spite of repetition, in spite of boredom — something that grew into pleasurable satisfaction over the years, grateful that her head came to be filled with the cadences of King James English.

That year, as Anne began to learn that an evangelist might be another male to prey upon you, she also discovered that an evangelist could have more subtle ways of capturing a soul than he might show in public.

The Harbisons, as faithful members of the church, often took in traveling Christians or a visiting preacher or evangelist. During the year and a half that Anne lived with the family, they gave the tiny upstairs bedroom — across the landing from Anne's and Caroline's bedrooms and almost part of the attic — to harbor several such visitors. None of whom were memorable in Anne's mind except two: the first a kindly, careful, Catholic spinster who was thinking, she said, of joining the Sisters of Providence. She was a nurse, traveling Alaska by herself. Anne tried to keep herself from staring at the woman across the supper table as her mind was full of questions: if the nurse was a Catholic, what was she doing coming to this house? To the Harbisons' church? And dozens of questions about the Sisters of Providence. Anne had heard of them, nurses who had traveled Alaska by boat and through cold winter by dog team since the days of the gold rush, still traveled Alaska through every kind of weather to care for the sick among the miners and the Natives far to the north, often flying now on the little planes of the flying services that had begun to spring up all over Alaska. The Sisters of Providence, it was said, wanted to build a hospital, a big hospital, in Anchorage, to take in people from the tiniest, farthest villages, and they would even pay, if Public Health wouldn't, for sick people to be flown into Anchorage to a real hospital. And they weren't like the Baptists or Methodists who took little Native children away from their homes and families.

Anne wasn't brave enough to ask her questions. The judge dominated the supper table with his long unctuous opening prayer and then a description of his own travels, as a preacher fresh out of high school, around Missouri and then into Illinois and Indiana. (A preacher; Anne hadn't heard that before. It made sense. But how could anybody be preaching just out of high school? Not any boy Anne had known; they didn't even seem to be as smart as the girls. As so often in Anne's imagination, Ellen giggled in her ear: *Maybe the good Lord touched him with a wand or something at graduation and turned him into a preacher.*) "Getting brave enough to move north," the judge was saying, "and I met my good wife at last in Indiana when the good Lord took me there. And the good Lord told me to settle down with her there and raise a family and study, study the law."

With Ellen's voice sometimes poking at her elbow or whispering in her ear, it was in Anne's mind to wonder what the good Lord might have told Helen Wheeler (as Anne was learning Mrs. Harbison used to be) about this prospective husband approaching her. But Mrs. Harbison herself spoke up just then.

"He was so handsome," Helen Harbison said, "and ambitious. He was named magistrate in no time after he got his law degree, before we married. Then we had our children, of course, three wonderful children, though we lost our first."

"By the Lord's will," said the judge at once, and bent his head over his plate.

Anne had heard the Harbisons talk about their first born. A son named Michael, maybe five years old when he died. And often talking about their second son, Jeffrey, off at college, whose old room Anne occupied. Anne felt, suddenly, some real warmth for Caroline who sat across the table listening meekly to considerable talk about both her brothers. Anne's own father had talked about each of her brothers, and to them, by name, sometimes at length, while he lumped the little girls together, or hardly seemed to notice them.

She was distracted by Mrs. Harbison saying ". . . when the talk was all about the colonization of Alaska, some of my family were really excited and my brother in Wisconsin was going to go — to come up here, I mean."

"But they didn't," the judge broke in, sounding like he was blaming his wife. "After I saw a notice where a magistrate was needed in Alaska, we got all excited about coming up too. Then they changed their minds. But we were already signed up; I had signed on the dotted line as the magistrate for this new town and there wasn't any getting out of it.

"But I have to bless my good wife," he added, again bending over his plate (but not sounding sincere to Anne's ears) "that she and the good Lord have brought me here, even farther again into the north."

Maybe he would have been happier, was a thought that intruded upon Anne's listening, happier if he had stayed in that southern state of Missouri, the outline of which was clear in Anne's mind from the maps she memorized. She didn't have any good idea what kind of life filled in the outline but the judge's behavior kept suggesting, without his saying so, that it was a life he must have preferred in spite of the good Lord and the good wife drawing him ever farther north. Anne could sympathize with that, an affinity for the south, but Missouri was a good deal farther south than she had dreamed of going. And if the likes of the judge were happy there, she thought, then it probably wasn't her own cup of tea.

Anne's father's family had its beginnings in Missouri, she briefly remembered.

The second memorable guest was a freckled, red-faced and red-haired evangelist who called himself Pastor Bendz. From Oregon, he said, "Pastor Bendz from Bend." He seemed to think there was something humorous in saying that. He seemed young. And as peculiar a character as Anne had known. She decided, over the two days he was in the house and the one evening she was required to hear him preach, that the peculiarity came from the fact that he was actually two different people. At least two. She had known other people who were energetically alive — though none so fiery about it as this man — and she had known people, many more people, who were quiet, abstracted or even morose. Pastor Bendz was all of the above. And you had no warning of any appearance. It was almost alarming when he threw up his voice, and his arms — and even his flaming hair standing straight up in bits around his excited red face — to say the grace over supper on the first evening after he arrived carrying a beat-up brown suitcase. Guests were always asked if they would like to say the grace and it was often a tedious thing, but this man made electrifying what was almost always a quiet if sometimes a terribly long prayer over food growing cold.

The words were usually the same: thanking God for "these good people" who had taken in the traveler, sometimes with a reference to Scripture, (Jesus' praise of hospitality); thanks for the food and then thanks for this and that (sometimes droning on in thanks for whatever, for the town or the travel and even, in the words of one guest, thanks for the Territory of Alaska). Then at last the amen.

But this fiery man made even ordinary words sound primitive, like words escaping for the first time from the mouth of a wild man. He didn't just give thanks for "these good people" — or maybe he *did* precisely give thanks for these good people — but no usual words sounded usual from his mouth. He didn't add or embroider with wordiness. Whatever it was that he first said (and Anne couldn't later remember) she felt that he was comparing all of us, all people, to needy creatures in a wilderness. Fearful creatures. But madly joyous creatures. Anne had a sudden vision of both at once: strange, dark-eyed people peering from thick jungle foliage while others danced madly like the beautiful centaurs.

And then, with the hair raising on the back of her neck, Anne heard — actually heard — the voice of John the Baptist crying in the wilderness.

Did Pastor Bendz mention John the Baptist? Anne didn't remember. But she *saw* the wild man, *some* wild man, crying out like Ezra or Jeremiah or John the Baptist.

But suddenly they were supposed to be grateful for the food. Which seemed to be coming alive on the table: beets and green beans growing as she had helped to grow them in the garden last summer; and in the two roasts (leftovers to be taken afterward to the church supper) she saw the pigs her father slaughtered, saw the heifer dying. She even watched, though there was no chicken on the table, watched the chickens while Mother and Mary, and later Martin, hit them quickly over the head and then wrung their necks.

"How they all thank God!" Pastor Bendz was exclaiming. And before Anne could wonder if pigs or chickens ever thanked God, suddenly at the table they were supposed to be back in their own world, the world of people. Traveling people, people coming or going on the Alaska Steamship and people in the towns along its route. "So many souls," Pastor Bendz was almost weeping over them: "So many souls over the teeming oceans and in the dark, untamed forests rising up to the great mountains of God!" His voice grew louder: "All over the world, people making towns, people of the deeps and of the steeps, the steeps of the mountains! And their spirits rising, endlessly rising, everywhere rising, up from the deeps, up to the steeps to the Glory of God!" (something like that, Anne was sure he said, though she got a bit confused over the steeps and deeps). She peeped sideways at him from downcast eyes when she suddenly felt, had an eerie sensation, that he was rising too, up to the steeps. She saw it was only his arms, and his eyes, going up to heaven but she had thought, suddenly, and still felt, that she wouldn't have been surprised to see the whole man lifting off with the spirits.

"So many fine souls," he was going on, now lowering his voice again, and his fiery face, "so many souls who saw me on my way" (*saw* him?). "So many souls I loved," his voice became a hushed whisper, "souls I wanted to save." And Anne knew, with the hair raising now not only on the back of her neck, but on her arms and tingling all over her body, that he was seeing actual *souls*, souls without bodies. Her father's soul? Maybe her own? *Could he really see people's souls?*

"I saw them. I see them. So many on the ship, and in the towns. At their work. With their families. In their pain. On the wharves. In their little boats struggling out among the waves like the fishermen of God, the disciples of our Lord Jesus." Then Anne almost jumped out of her chair when he suddenly shouted "I say *amen!* When I say "amen" I say amen to All! To *all* God's creatures, to all men and to all women and to all little children — to all the world of God that gives us life! We must lift our voices; we must lift *ourselves*, to say Amen! To say amen, and again amen! To say amen to our everlasting days, the days we will spend with God when our earthly struggles are done. To say hallelujah and to say amen forever!"

Well . . . Anne thought, drawing breath at the end. *Well.* . . .

She felt two ways about the fact that she didn't have to go to the church to hear him preach that evening; she had an algebra test tomorrow and she wasn't expected anyway (thank goodness) to go every night of a revivalist meeting or an evangelist's preaching. "One night is enough for a schoolgirl," Mrs. Harbison always said to the judge, "and they have homework." So Anne and Caroline were both left home on Thursday night to study and would go on Friday night to hear this crazy man.

While she began to go over her algebra — which she really didn't have to study since she had a habit of careful work along the way in every class — Anne wondered about Pastor Bendz and what had happened during the grace, why such strange visions, visions so real and some so frightening, had come sprouting, one after another and tangled with each other — come sprouting from his ordinary words. How did he bring everything so alive that you actually saw how terrible some of it was? And so much of it crowding upon you — the growing, the trying, so much struggling. Traveling, killing, dancing, dying. Feeding, looking, building. Wanting.

She was too unsettled to study. How had this man wrapped death up into the middle of it all: Was it just words, as he flung them so furiously out of himself, that had stirred up all of that? *Her heifer, Bluebell, the gentle one that Anne had so loved and secretly named for her favorite flower that came into bloom in her own favorite places in the spring.* She had talked to Bluebell at the fence beside the calf barn and talked to the bluebells flowering for her in the places where she had gone alone to sit beside their fragrance or mourn that they were ending for another year. *How she had hated her father for killing Bluebell!* How she had cried,

112

and not wanted her father to know she cried. How she had refused to cry when her father died.

She couldn't see how this peculiar-looking, red-haired, red-faced man that Anne couldn't trust had brought all of this together, wonderful and frightening pieces tangled together. Made you feel so alive yourself at the table and so confused that you didn't know whether you might laugh at his wildness, or cry, not wanting to do either one in front of him or the Harbisons.

She wondered why the man was traveling Alaska in the dead of winter. He was like a flaming torch, a firebrand in the midst of the cold dark of January. She wondered if he did have some actually special mission — special to one God, or to moving people toward that one God, like supposedly the old prophets had. Or whether the old prophets had had any special mission either. Her thoughts, far from her algebra, and wandering far again from her own life, were vague. And she liked many of the Greek gods better than the stern old Hebrew god. But she did wonder.

It was a good thing she liked algebra, its neatness. She buried herself finally in the delicately perfect equations she had been writing out in her notebook in the weeks since the last exam.

Next day when she went into the drying room after school to collect some clothes from the drying racks for folding, she met another Pastor Bendz. The drying room was not that small but it was crowded, with water heater, washing machine, shelves, deep heavy sinks bolted to the wall, and with three standing wooden racks for drying as well as a clothesline strung across the room above the sinks. As Anne was pulling down two of the judge's shirts from the farthest rack — she always started from the farthest ones, and worked back toward the door — she was suddenly, utterly startled to see a hunched figure in the darkest corner. Her heart thudded right to her toes; she turned to run.

But just as she was turning to flee out the door, back into the kitchen, her eye caught the reflection of the hunched figure in the dark window to her left, and the figure at the same time was raising what looked like its head. The light was dim — she hadn't turned on the big overhead light but only the bulb over the sinks — and of course it was full dark outside — but the idea of knees and head registered in her frightened mind even in the dimness. And there was no mistaking that red hair, glimmering even in the reflection of the window.

But the face was a different face, a frightening face, drawn and gaunt. Pale, with burning eyes. Somehow so grotesque that Anne's heart was pounding again. She had fleeting thoughts of the movie *Jekyll and Hyde* as she still wanted to get away.

It's only the bad light, she said to herself, trying to stay calm and still needing to gather the clothes from the racks.

She hovered by the door. It was part of her share of work to get the clothes folded, stack them and carry hers and Caroline's upstairs to put away.

The shape, the man, mumbled something and immediately shielded those staring eyes, turning away, and bent down again into the corner, away from the window and the light. *He must be praying*, Anne thought. And immediately he said that, mumbling something about being at prayer.

"I'll just get the clothes quickly," Anne said, sounding in her own ears as though she were mumbling too, "and I'll leave you alone."

I wonder if he will be able to preach at seven o'clock, occurred to her while she was folding the piled clothes on the kitchen table. Maybe he's sick. He looked sick, pale and weak. She thought that she probably should do something for him, about him, but she didn't know what to do and she didn't want to go back into that room. It was after four o'clock, she noticed, but neither Mrs. Harbison or the judge would be home for at least an hour. Caroline had been already home when Anne came in but staying in her room — "I have to do my Bible class study," she had said when Anne checked to be sure she was there. This was a dismissal by Caroline that Anne was used to, her excuse for not helping with anything around the house unless her mother was home and directing her. Which Anne didn't mind; in this household Anne liked working alone. And to give Caroline credit (*credit?*), she did seem to be reading the Bible all the time; she prided herself on the volume of her memorized verses and there was something sweet about her when she was glowing with accomplishment and forgot her primness. It was her father she wanted to please.

She takes her good mother for granted, was one of Anne's thoughts as she carried Caroline's folded clothes up the stairs, *but she's not going to get more out of her grumpy father than the bits of attention he doles out to her now.* Such thoughts made Anne more careful and gentle with Caroline than she actually felt, and it was in such a gentle mood that she slipped into Caroline's room, after tapping on the door and hearing her "it's okay" in response.

She tapped Caroline lightly on the head, too, after setting her clothes on the bed. She didn't mention that the brilliant preacher who had captured Caroline the night before, lighted her up all through the evening so that, instead of being the staid and stodgy twelve-year-old-near-middle-age, Caroline herself had been glowing, more and more. She didn't tell Caroline that the wonderful torch that had so stirred and lighted her up the night before had turned into a dark ghost hiding in the drying room.

As she was going back down the stairs another thought came into Anne's mind: *it took me forever to get used to sleeping alone.* Now I have my own bed and a whole room to myself and I love it. Could I ever be willing to crawl into bed with prissy Caroline, like I used to sleep with my sisters or crawl into Molly's bed at the Walkers? But what did sixteen-year-old Molly think when pathetic little Annie as I used to be came creeping into her bed in the night?

I'm not like laughing, good-natured Molly or her jolly talkative mother. I'm not very helpful to people. I'm almost Molly's age now, sixteen in two months, and I'm not helpful and easy like she was. I'm not like Ellen; I don't know how to be with people.

She stopped, suddenly, near the foot of the stairs: *what would Ellen do about the strange man in the drying room? Maybe he* was *sick.*

Ellen always seemed to know whether to go to someone or to shun them.

Anne finally compromised, after mulling it over in her mind into the kitchen and through the peeling of the potatoes, setting them to soak in cold water while she did the dusting and polishing in the dining room. It was almost five o'clock when she decided, almost safe because Mrs. Harbison was soon to be home.

Anne went to the door of the drying room and after opening it part way, put in her head: "Can I get you anything?" she asked. *Too soft; my voice sounds like a whisper; how can he hear me over that moan of the wind?* Then louder, she spoke up (*too loud?*): "Do you need anything? Should I bring hot soup or. . . ." She trailed off. Then she remembered that her father had wanted a cold cloth when he once, long ago, had sat down indoors with a headache.

"Would you like anything cold? A cloth, or. . . .?" It was a pathetic offering, in the sound of a voice that was pretty pathetic, the best voice she was able to bring up.

But there was an answer. Faint at first, but then repeated: "yes, please. Cold, (or cold cloth?)." And then, fainter again but Anne thought she heard it correctly: "no light."

She closed the door on the kitchen light and, glad that the clock had almost turned to the exact hour of five, got three washcloths from the little stack that Mrs. Harbison kept in the bathroom and soaked them in cold water. She wrapped two of the cloths in a soft towel, left the third to stay cold in the cold water, and went through the drying room door, leaving it only slightly ajar and feeling her way in the near dark around the clothes racks to the corner.

He was obviously grateful. So then she went back and forth, to and from the cold water in the kitchen, changing the cloths that were so quickly warm from his forehead.

Then she became more brave: there's cold water right here, in the sinks of this room, she said to herself in the drying room, if I would be willing to stay in the same room with him. And it was the light from the kitchen that seemed to bother him, the least light.

She left the door to the kitchen only very slightly cracked, to feel safer for herself but to cut out the light for him, and she stayed in the room with him, running a very slow trickle of cold water in the wash sink, making her way to him in the dark. Near pitch dark but of course her night vision grew keen as she was no longer blurring it by going back into the light.

Back and forth, from sink to preacher and from suffering preacher to dripping sink again, getting almost comfortable with the routine of it.

But it couldn't have been long before she heard the front door of the house open and close and then the back door, the kitchen door. The judge always came and went by the front door, she knew his sound, while Mrs. Harbison usually went around the house to the kitchen door, looking for the cat Hannah along the way, waiting for Hannah to crawl out from the warmth of the basement to be let into the kitchen for her evening food and milk before being put out again after supper. Anne went to meet them.

And the ghost came out of the dark drying room just as the cat came through the door from the outside cold followed by Mrs. Harbison.

116

Very polite was the man now, greeting Mrs. Harbison — calling her "ma'am" again now, instead of by her first name, Helen, as he had begun to do the night before at her insistence. And he didn't seem sick, exactly. But he was an utterly different person from the firebrand of the evening before. Near silent, subdued all through supper and on the ride to the community hall. He had drawn into himself, was what Anne kept feeling as she rode in the family Pontiac through the cold, white night with him at the opposite end of the back seat and Caroline between them. She felt something dark in him, in the place that he had drawn into. Like the real man was hunched in some dark place just as he had been hunched down into a dark corner over his own knees in the drying room.

The community hall was overcrowded, getting stuffy and hot very quickly. Churches always used the community hall for these gatherings, as none of the three Valley churches that went in for evangelism was big enough for a crowd. There were more people here than Anne had ever seen for such a service — or maybe anywhere except at the old Friday night movies — people sitting on their coats in the aisles the way they were sitting on them on the metal folding chairs, people standing around the sides and back of the hall. There was a growing heat of anticipation in the air, and a growing buzz as the anticipation kept widening and spreading, until — long before Pastor Bendz finally appeared at the golden-oak lectern on the stage at the front of the hall — Anne began to feel, right against her face, a pressure that added to the heat of crowding bodies.

But first, before the appearance, as the ripples of sound temporarily quieted, they had to sit through a long opening prayer by the minister of the Something-Something Church of the Second Coming. Then Mrs. Jantzen, the school music teacher, stood before them to blow four tones through her voice harp, repeating each twice more for soprano, alto, tenor and bass, and then they all sang *Shall We Gather At The River*, with Mrs. Jantzen leading them. Anne always appreciated the songs; words never sounded so questionable, or sappy, when set to music. You didn't have to think about the words or think whether somebody was trying to push you into believing them.

Reverend Wolfson was next, the minister of the church Anne attended, the United Protestant Church ("it's pretty much Baptists trying to get along with Methodists," Anne had heard somebody say around town, "with the odd Lutheran or whatever thrown in").

Reverend Wolfson was mercifully short, just saying "a few words to tell those of you not here last night that Pastor Bendz hales from Oregon" and that the pastor had traveled up the coast on the Alaska Steamship. "He hoped he might bring some light from Scripture into the dark Alaska winter."

People were disappointed by Pastor Bendz tonight, Anne could soon tell. The mood of anticipation that had grown to such a high pitch before he finally appeared, looking small before them, did take some time to dull. The excited rustlings at first fell into total silence at his appearance, a kind of breathless hush taking over the entire hall. Then it did take more time before the rustlings began again.

They did give him a chance, Anne thought later. But when the rustlings did begin again, they had a different tone. Anne was hearing little whisperings here and there along with the renewed rustling. People shifted in their seats, then they fell silent and waited, then they shifted again. Whispered some more. Waited some more. Anne became more attuned to the sounds in the hall than to the words of Pastor Bendz, who sounded perfectly rational but terribly ordinary standing up there talking about the wedding at Cana, not very interesting. By this time, Anne was more interested in the murmurs around her, Mrs. Bogle's murmur behind her to the Havlics, that "it was really good last night, just wait."

People did wait, but with less and less of their beginning anticipation. The air in the hall gradually became dense, heavy, as they sat, waiting, patient now and politely quiet.

It did change. After uninspiring talk about the wedding at Cana and reciting several of Jesus' parables without any fire at all, Pastor Bendz was suddenly back with Jonah under the withering bush. Anne hadn't caught the connection but she *was* caught, because Pastor Bendz was coming more and more alive, getting fiery again, although weakly if compared to his fire at supper last night. And she was caught by the story: the story of Jonah was one of Anne's favorites, the punishment but final saving of a self-righteous and hard-headed, mean-spirited man. Pastor Bendz was obviously enlivened by the story too, suddenly throwing out his arms and calling on God to save us all, and then launching into *Revelations* (Anne didn't catch that connection either), with something close to his fervor of the evening before.

People around the hall came alive again too; Anne heard some hallelujahs and amens growing in number through Pastor Bentz' recounting, with feeling, of the trials of Paul, Paul's perilous journeys and numerous imprisonments and his words of encouragement to followers through the litany of all his struggles. "We are all in our own prison!" shouted Pastor Bendz with sudden fire, throwing back his face, which had been growing red again; "we need our God!" The amens echoed through the hall.

That was pretty much the end. Fortunately (for Anne) the wild man/quiet man didn't call for people to come to the altar and "receive the Lord." Mrs. Jantzen instead rose to blow once again on her voice harp — the four notes repeated, again — and to lead them in singing *The Old Rugged Cross*. Then Anne stood, with the Harbisons, listening to the people as they milled and talked — and as the judge greeted some of the important ones and Mrs. Harbison spoke to all or any of them — while people kept making their way out of the hall. People were still half-disappointed, Anne could tell; they had come for more, the ones who had been more inspired the night before and the new ones who had been inspired by friends and neighbors to come for the first time. But they had livened up a lot since the down point in the middle of the evening and were making do with what glimpse they had got, of something bigger than themselves. A real taste, Anne thought, of what they had come for.

She suddenly felt, without thinking, that they had come because they wanted something like that; they wanted, needed, something beyond the routine of day-to-day work on the farm. Something grand. Something to make meaning of the endless struggle with Nature that must be carried out just to have a decent life for a family. Something beyond endlessly plowing and sowing the dirt and watching the skies for weather and hoping and praying for the dirt and the weather to produce something and for the children to keep producing. Something big enough to make sense of it all, make sense of surviving terrible winter only to start all over. It was the first time that Anne caught a hint, only a hint, of the meaning of these gatherings.

Back at the house — and on the ride there — Pastor Bendz retreated again into his own dark space. "I need hours of prayer," is what he said to the Harbisons when he declined to lead the nightly (thankfully short), prayer always said by the family in the living room before each retired to their rooms. "I have no words now," is what he said.

But he had words for twelve-year-old Caroline.

Anne was near dreaming, maybe already asleep in her bed when the repeated tappings on her door brought her awake enough to peep out and find Caroline there. She was glowing again, Caroline was, with something of the radiance of the evening before. "I've got to tell you something," she whispered as Anne was opening the door wider for her to come in.

Caroline curled up on the foot of Anne's bed as Anne crawled back in. "Put that extra blanket around you," Anne told her. The room was cold. "I'm not cold at all," Caroline said, but she picked up the blanket from the foot of the bed anyway and opened it on her lap, twiddling its softness with her fingers, alive with an excitement that she was holding in: half ready to burst with it and half holding back to nurse it and treasure it for herself. Almost ready to do something like curl up and purr at moments, reminding Anne of the cat Hannah. Anne had never seen Caroline like this. Anne sat up in bed herself, pulling the covers up around her.

"What do you think of him?" Caroline was asking, keeping her voice down, near a whisper. Anne knew who she was talking about. And she knew she was going to have to take part in the ritual, or sort of game, that so many girls started to play right around Caroline's age and into high school. A game, or whatever it was, that usually annoyed Anne, where another girl wouldn't commit to an opinion unless you spoke first. And then hedging if they did give anything close to their own opinion in response. Nothing like the straight-out honesty of childhood. Nothing that led to real understanding, to really talking like she and Ellen could do, right through disagreements. Anne had learned, from seventh grade when she was first baffled by it, that there was no good way of avoiding this game and no way out of it once you got sucked in. The only thing to do was to ignore her one natural impulse and follow the other: you curbed your curiosity about why the other person was asking, didn't ask her any questions, but simply gave your own opinion forthrightly and hoped the other girl didn't keep up the business of coyly hedging around. So many girls obviously wanted something from the process other than exchanging opinions, something that Anne hadn't been able to puzzle out.

So she didn't ask Caroline anything; instead she pondered what to say that would be honest without just upsetting her. Because Caroline seemed enraptured and Anne had seen, more than once, how quickly any bit of liveliness or excitement in her could be dashed — often by nothing more than a look from her high-minded father.

"He's different from anybody I've ever known," Anne began, "a lot more alive. I thought, last night, that he's so in love with being alive — and with everything alive — that it's a bit scary.

"But," she went on, feeling cautious, "he has another side too. Something about him tonight was a bit scary too; he was so ... so withdrawn and *un*-alive. . . ."

"But he's not scary at all," Caroline broke in, "he's nice. So nice." She leaned in close to Anne and her eyes sparkled as she near-whispered, "he likes me. He said he really likes me."

"You've been talking to him?"

"I went to his room and. . . ." Caroline drew back, looking defensive, "I just went to be sure he didn't need anything. Like Mama does with a guest always, at the last minute, but she didn't tonight. And there he was left alone, with no one treating him like a guest at all.

"I only put my head in the door," she defended herself. "After I knocked, of course."

"There's nothing wrong with being helpful to a guest," Anne reassured her, though she did wonder why prim Caroline approached a man's bedroom with him in it, late enough that all the family had gone to bed and the man would be going to bed too, or already in it.

"He was still dressed," Caroline said. "Otherwise I wouldn't have gone in when he asked me."

"You went in his room," Anne hoped she herself didn't sound judgmental — she couldn't stand a judgmental tone — but Caroline must have heard that she sounded surprised, and probably concerned.

"It was all right. He was praying."

"He interrupted his praying to ask you to come in?" This was getting worse; she shouldn't sound so surprised by each of Caroline's revelations. She had learned over many months how quickly Caroline might retreat into some false place and start quoting Scripture. It had happened even in the garden last summer when Anne had tried to explain weeding and before she understood that Caroline not only didn't want to deal with realities like dirt or weeds but would become immediately defensive over anything she took as a suggestion she might be doing something wrong. But Anne *was* surprised by what Caroline was confiding; it couldn't be honest to pretend that she wasn't wondering which of the two Pastor Bendz's had asked a twelve-year-old girl into his bedroom at night: the flaming evangelist or the hunched dark man who said he needed hours of prayer. But Caroline seemed to be talking about yet a third Pastor Bendz.

"He said he was just finishing his prayers. And he asked if I wanted to say one last prayer, the Lord's prayer, with him. He looked . . . he looked so . . . he was so *nice*, and he looked like Benjie Williams."

This *was* a third Pastor Bendz. Benjie Williams was an angelic-looking young man who was the accountant for the Co-op. Who had been called "retard" by bullies through school, Anne knew, but he had graduated and gone off to Seattle and come home two years later with a degree.

"He was kind like Benjie." Caroline was saying. Benjie Williams was celebrated for his kindness. He showed a rare gentleness and helpfulness toward anyone, to the pride of his sturdy, quiet mother who was known for her kindness and good works too. Though she shunned all the churches — raising her last child, Benjie, alone after her husband had died when his tractor ran over him — Mrs. Williams was respected throughout the Valley. People bought her jams, jellies, pickled beets, quilts, aprons, and smoked salmon and other things whether they needed them or not, in order to be sure she made a living.

"He *was*," Caroline whispered, "he was kind just like Benjie. He asked me everything, about school and about Bible study — he asked me what I like and what bothers me . . . he asked me *everything* I care about." Caroline's eyes were brilliant.

"And you know what?" Caroline leaned close again: "he touched me." And she leaned back again, wrapping the blanket around her like it was something delicious. Looking so happy, so pleased, hugging herself.

"I . . . aren't you. . . .? . . . well . . ." Anne wanted to ask *where* the wild/hidden/angelic man had touched her — Caroline seemed to be inviting the question — but Anne was afraid of the answer.

But Caroline was dying to tell: "He touched me on my breasts," she whispered. "Both of them."

Anne was as much startled by Caroline using the word "breasts" as she was by the revelation. It simply wasn't a word to be expected from prim, tall, puritanical Caroline. In fact it was a word that still bothered Anne herself when she came across it in her reading — she would skim over it — and certainly not a word in everyday use; people didn't talk about breasts, either having them or noticing them. And Caroline didn't even have them; she had the budding beginnings (and Anne remembered, briefly, the soreness of those budding beginnings, and the complicated feelings aroused by them).

"You had your clothes on. . . ." was all Anne managed to say, making it a statement, not a question.

"I was still dressed," Caroline got huffy, sounded insulted, drew back and made it clear she had expected better from Anne.

"I would never have gone there unless I was still dressed," she said, sounding like the old self-righteous Caroline.

"I'm sorry," Anne said, "I just worried for a minute. But I know you're smarter than that. "But," she said, again, cautiously, "we don't really know him. He's only been here, what? Less than two days?"

"He was *kind*," Caroline reiterated, leaning forward again. "He likes me. He said my long dark hair is like the hair of Rachel, and Leah, and Deborah. And Sarah. The most revered women from the scriptures. Their natural, flowing, uncurled hair as God intended it to be."

"Well, of course he would be right," Anne said (those women couldn't have gone to a hairdresser anyway, she thought, and most farm women of the Valley didn't either). "And he's right that you have beautiful long hair." Which Caroline did have, her thick and richly-colored dark hair right now spilling around her face and over the blanket on her shoulders — hair that Anne with her fine and short hair that just wouldn't grow long had envied.

"That's when I let it down," Caroline said. "I didn't go there with my hair down; I wouldn't do that. But after we said the Lord's prayer together. . . ." and she stopped, looking at Anne.

Anne waited, hearing an owl outside even over the sound of the wind that was so constant out there. She heard some creaks of the house inside as it was losing its warmth to the outside January cold.

She may have lost Caroline. Who wasn't really playing a game but who did seem to be retreating after all. And Anne suddenly felt she would rather just go to sleep anyway; it must have been after ten o'clock that they all came home and it must be near midnight now, or even after. She pictured the January moon and knew it had set long since. But as she was turning her sight from the window — must have been listening there to the owl, for the owl to speak again — Caroline suddenly spilled it all: "he said I'll be a woman. He touched each of my breasts and said I'll be a woman. He told me to read the *Song of Solomon*. He read a piece of it to me, himself, and told me to read it no matter what anyone said."

Anne was speechless. She had been puzzled when the family had skipped right over the *Song of Solomon* in the nightly scripture reading with no explanation, as though it was something that didn't exist. Something ignored that, according to the orderly arrangement of the books of the Bible, sat right in the middle of these scriptures that the family, and the church people, were always reading and quoting as though they were the most everlastingly important words ever written. Anne had started to remind them of the omission, but then didn't, sensing it was deliberate. But naturally she had been curious and had tried to read the *Song of Solomon* for herself. Then finding it confusing and somehow distasteful.

She didn't know what to say to Caroline. The late-night talk that never became a conversation ended with Anne feeling inadequate, and lame in any parting words. Certainly grateful, as she curled back into her covers, that Caroline hadn't wanted Anne to join into some lengthy prayer with her, as Caroline had always asked for in the past when she came to Anne's room at bedtime.

Years later, when Anne was no longer afraid of the word 'breast,' the thought occurred to her that Pastor Bendz may have been the best thing that happened to pubescent Caroline. Certainly it must be better to be glowing with the knowledge that you were alive and turning into a woman than to be prim and self-righteous? Anne wondered where Caroline was, what she was making of her life by now, but somehow she never took the time or made the effort to find out.

Chapter Eight

Sometimes sitting in church Anne was moved by one of the stories from the Bible, or by a sermon, but mostly she just thought that very few of these people acted much like the Jesus they were always praising. It was obvious to her that this Jesus would have liked her mother, and liked her better than he would have liked many of these church people who talked one way and acted another. Jesus spent his time with ordinary folk and outcasts, was kind to children, and he berated the church-goers who were hypocrites. Though he seemed to be saying you were supposed to forgive anyone — even the ones who killed him — and not only that, but you had to *love* everyone. Anne was pretty far from that.

The minister, Reverend Wolfson, was okay, a man as tall as her father but with a friendly manner; she kept hearing that he did a lot of visiting with the poor and with people sick at home or in the hospital. She had gone to a couple of the youth group meetings that he led last summer when she was fifteen, but decided that was one more of the weird things about church people. Most of these kids, once they were in church, sounded so much like their parents and then acted so different at school. At church they talked like they owned Jesus — and they did own the character they turned him into, pretty much ignored the man described by the writers of the four gospels that Anne carefully read. Even the world, the way the kids in the youth group saw it, wasn't a world, wasn't the wide, interesting world that Anne read about and wanted to live in but seemed to be narrowed down to a bunch of people who tried to keep the world small with a small-minded and jealous god in charge of it.

Reverend Wolfson was better than that. He nudged the kids, here and there, into thinking about things. He seemed to like them, all the kids, including Anne. But she was put off by the way he hedged around about "what boys and girls must remember" when he brought that up a few times. It was pretty clear he thought it was entirely up to a girl to keep herself safe, not "encourage the boys." He might have talked to the boys better — he met with the boys sometimes alone — but he never said a word about grown men, how a girl was supposed to cope with the way men were always after you. Anne got no inkling he would have believed what she had been learning in her life about men or why she was frightened by the judge; never sensed she could tell the reverend about either the judge or what she began to have to cope with next, from another one of the trusted men in the church itself, another deacon of the church, the choir director.

It was music that brought about the trouble with the choir director. The only way the church could really appeal to Anne, did appeal to her, was with music. She loved music; she was hungry for it; had never had enough of it. Grooved in her head was the swinging, delighting sound of this rhythm or that coming from the old wind-up Victrola on the homestead. How magical it was in her childhood, in rare moments, to have the whole world changed by music! Lightened, suddenly brightened, imbued with fantasies of people celebrating. How she had begged, when someone, so seldom, took down the victrola and any of the few records from the high shelf where they were kept out of reach beside the Books of Knowledge, begged to have the record played over and over, to have any or all of the few records (were there five of them?) played over and over. "The Drinking Song," the only one her big brothers liked or wanted to take down to play, was so scratchy you could hardly make out the words but the exciting movement of it, the wildly joyous shout of its repeated refrain, was exotic, the sound of another world. Anne's own favorite, especially grooved in her mind, was "Zip-a-dee Do-dah": *My oh my what a wonderful day!*

She sometimes wondered what had become of the old victrola, and those scratched records, when the homestead was abandoned. She had a vague thought that Father had taken them away before that to the sawmill along with his own desertion, another loss before the final desertion of his dying. (Much later she learned that Beverly, her sister-in-law married to William, had Mother's old treadle sewing machine and the few other things Mother had left behind — she had had so *little!* — when Mother herself left the homestead. But Beverly was a close-mouthed woman about anything except gossip and evasive with the family, so Anne didn't question her having Mother's things, though Anne would very much have liked to have the sewing machine herself.)

"I'm afraid I'm not very discriminating about music," Anne would say over the years: "Whether it's church music or country western or classical or rock, or whatever, so long as it's not whiny or dull — so long as it has real rhythm and cadence — it can get to me, at least for awhile." Her enduring favorite came to be Bach. But along the way she was captured, in turns, by Handel, by Elvis Presley, by the Eagles, by Richie Havens, by Mozart, by the Beatles and Bob Dylan and The Rolling Stones and Credence Clearwater. By Beethoven — that was a long, long period of delight, the continual discovering and rediscovering of nuances in Beethoven at the same time that she listened to Dylan and then Glen Campbell and Patsy Cline, found John Denver, folk music, Simon and Garfunkel, Willie Nelson. Before she was able to afford recordings she listened wherever she could: to the radio, at friends' houses, at record stores, sometimes jukeboxes, brought records home from the library once she had a record player. As the best rock faded into acid rock and (in her opinion) into pounding, unmeaning noise, she turned more and more to classical. She hardly realized what she was leaving out, that she'd never cared for jazz and that her ears shut out the crying or crooning of most popular love songs and the poignancy of blues.

In the Valley, when she wasn't yet sixteen and living with the Harbisons, the only music reliably to be heard was church music. The judge banned listening to any radio music except on the "Christian Hour" three nights a week. So that, whatever were Anne's own doubts (unspoken to the Harbisons or to anyone but Ellen) about the church and church people, drawn by music and by the encouragement of Mrs. Harbison — and also very much drawn by the fact that she had half a crush on the choir director, Mr. Hansen, who was also her high school math teacher — Anne joined the church choir in the fall.

All the girls had a crush on Mr. Hansen, at school and even at church. He was handsome, younger than most of the teachers, with dark hair and warm dark eyes. He was married and had two little sons. That made him safe, in Anne's eyes. It was safe to feel a warm glow of love from afar for someone so helpful and beautiful who had an attractive wife usually near him at church, someone respected at church and school, someone who looked at you and listened, someone so unlike her father.

In the eyes of the world he didn't do that much; why would the rest of the world know how Mr. Hanson devastated the safety of the little corner of the world that Anne had been protecting for herself? When he offered to collect her along with some others, give her a ride to Thursday evening choir practice, she was happy. Warmly delighted to have that extra time near her idol. Safe among the others transported to the church and then home afterwards in the dark winter nights. But then he began to find a reason, when one woman was ill and stayed away from choir for two weeks, to deliver Annie home last and to squeeze her hand too much when he wished her good-night. She didn't admit her suspicions about that.

She didn't admit suspicion to herself either, when she found herself somehow maneuvered into the front seat on the way home even though that hadn't been the arrangement before. In the deep cold of February into March she was glad of the heater on her feet. And she loved the closeness to her idol. When he began, surreptitiously, to touch her hand, in his driving gloves against her own mittens, she was secretly pleased but denying it. It was still safe. And it was a kindliness, a warmth, that she had never felt with a man. He was helpful in Algebra class, regarded her as a star pupil, encouraged her to help the others. *So what if there's something secret about it*, she told herself when some part of herself accused her. Was warning her. The little secret haven of being cared about by such a man was precious to her; she safeguarded it, in spite of growing guilt.

Still, she was always shy around him, ducked her head often rather than meet his eyes. But in class she loved to watch, especially from the back, the way he moved as he made his way around the room, explaining, helping one student and then another. He was so slim and upright, in his soft, tan sweater buttoned loosely over long-sleeved shirt and neat pants of some soft dark wool. He had a way of bending his head of waving dark hair, tilting it sideways as he listened to someone, that captivated Anne, that she found herself often watching to see.

Then it was blown apart. He kissed her, long and passionately, while she went numb. While she let it happen. When he had somehow delivered her home last again, out of order, on a blowing cold March night past her sixteenth birthday.

It was all so quiet. The night, the whole world seemed to have become utterly silent as she stumbled out of the car, as she went numbly toward the house — the judge's house, Mrs. Harbison's house. There may have been some murmur of good-night from him but what she heard was the crunching of her own boots alarmingly loud and destructive on the crackling, brittle snow between the car and the front walk. There was a bit of moon, far to the northwest; *waning moon*, her mind registered automatically.

There was the usual light showing from the kitchen, making shadows through the dining room and into the living room as Anne entered the front door holding herself stiff and more than usually afraid of making the least noise. Mrs. Harbison appeared at the doorway into the kitchen; she always sat at the kitchen table with a book or her Bible and one small light beside her until any family member who had been out was safely home on a winter night, out of the cold. (In spring and summer it was different, everybody still up — and busy, even — past ten o'clock. But in winter the judge retired by nine and expected everyone else to do the same, wanted no noise once he had gone to bed.)

Mrs. Harbison said her usual good-night but waited while Anne mechanically shed her outdoor boots and set them carefully against the wall on the old towel kept there for the purpose of absorbing any melting snow. There was no porch at the front entry, only at the back door. And in winter, when there was no mud as in spring, or any of the dust and dirt of summer, the back door was kept closed after supper, to discourage the cat Hannah from her continual attempts to escape from the basement into the house. Anne found herself thinking of all this, how only Mrs. Harbison regularly used the back door in winter and how she, and Anne and Caroline, regularly hung the damp towels from the front entry in the drying room and replaced them with those already dry.

Anne tiptoed up the stairs and went through the motions of getting into bed. Then lying there through the night, unthinking, even in half-sleep living in pages that kept turning through a Book of Knowledge. Pages about far away places.

She stayed numb then. Blaming herself as she made her way through Friday classes, not meeting his eyes in class, escaping the moment the bell rang and avoiding him in the halls, doing her chores through the weekend at home.

It was on Sunday, singing with the choir — an anthem she loved but not looking to him for every cue as she'd always done in the choir, not for any cue — on Sunday she found that something was going very wrong with her voice: that sometimes, when she knew she was feeling a note correctly, the sound wouldn't come from her, or only a beginning sound that dried up. Near the end of the anthem her voice, her throat, felt so dry she was afraid to try to reach the note at all, just moved her mouth to look like she was singing.

She made her way through classes again on Monday, stoic, refusing to raise her head as he passed by her desk saying something cheerful and kindly. Feeling, right through her skin, his eyes on her.

For a long time the old nightmares had been coming only every few months. And her father hadn't been in them since he'd died, not that she could remember. But now the nightmares were back almost every night. Only different: as she was falling, lost, into dark water; as she was lost again and searching, searching endlessly through ancient dusty buildings only to be in awful, heart-pounding panic at the end of the search; as she buried her face in the dirt of a plowed field in the dark in her terrified hope to escape from Rudy, she felt her father lurking somewhere in the dream. Out of her sight. And sometimes his face would change and she would wake ice-cold with fear.

She missed Ellen dreadfully, tried to write her a letter but after the first couple of dull sentences she couldn't find anything to say. Ellen wasn't good at writing back anyway; Anne would wait a month or more to get a few lines from her, after spending an hour to compose an interesting letter herself. But she couldn't write anything about this.

Two times in her life Anne thought of ways to kill herself. This first time was an adolescent craziness. She had no way to understand the emotions Mr. Hansen aroused in her, how his welcome warmth had opened a crack in the wall of her long-tended defenses. She didn't even know a new betrayal could revive past betrayals. She had vowed, after Mrs. Zibota, after Mrs. Binch, never to let herself be betrayed again and she had conquered those betrayals with justified anger, with hatred. But of deeper betrayals, where hate had never come to her defense, and of love and hate yet deeper, she had kept herself ignorant. Her mind was always filled with righteous justifications of her mother and her heart a deliberate blank against the ancient looming presence of her father (*he'd never been around much anyway; of course he was a blank in her mind, how could she miss him?*). All else lay behind the wall she had built in the winter of abandonment, the wall that had kept her out of the pit of dread and aloneness she had buried under her pride and reinforced with determination and with successful hatred of Mrs. Binch. She was baffled by warmth that came too close.

One moment on that Monday, as Mr. Hansen passed along her row in class, an intense terror took hold of Anne, so powerful that her pencil shook in her hand and her eyes went blind; she couldn't see the equations on the page. The light in the room contracted itself and then split itself into a thousand tiny pinpoints sparking from the edges of a great yawning blackness, a huge black hole that opened in front of her, with the sparkle of those tiny, dizzying lights spinning and spinning — spinning more and more wildly — around the black hole. Further and further off, spinning away from the edges of the hole, the lights were flying by some centrifugal force that was going to leave her being sucked into it. She had never felt such numbing terror in daytime. Only in nightmares.

She fought against the blackness of that black hole with everything in her, with a fury against being beaten. Sucked in her breath, stared at Mr. Hansen's retreating back. And she brought hate to her rescue, because hate had long saved her. She hated him. For what was happening to her. She hated so many. Then she made her pencil move, to follow the exact course of a proper equation, forcing the light to come back, to become normal.

But then she felt an awful churning sickness, such fear and dread that she needed to run. She clung to the edge of the desk, clung to the numbers on her page, focusing on them, felt herself physically forcing down her sick stomach, forcing the numbers, the Ys and Xs, into place, demanding they become clear again in the orderly arrangements she had created.

By the time the class bell rang, she had turned all feeling against herself. Despised herself. What a disgusting low creature she must be to attract only wrong from good people, from a man as upright as Mr. Hansen! A mean and measly creature. She knew, suddenly, that she had to destroy herself. She would cut off all her hair. All her petty fussing with her fine straight hair, curling it, wanting to look pretty, trying to look like Elizabeth Taylor! How disgusting! She loathed the idea. She loathed herself. She would pull her hair out by the roots! Somehow end herself and everything.

She ran all the way home after school — no waiting for the bus — through the slush of a thaw that she knew would be followed by more freezing, more bitter wind. Looking for cars to throw herself under, wondering how it would feel as they crunched over her, mad with the knowledge that she had to somehow destroy herself. But the few cars that passed were traveling either too fast or too slowly — too fast for her to make the resolve and judge the distance before they were sailing past, or so slowly that it was even harder to judge distance, because they could easily stop if she didn't decide quickly enough at just the right moment. She tried to imagine the car crunching over her, the crunching of the snow. But the snow was slush, was a mess.

And she had books with her — what would happen to her books; should she abandon them first? How? Where? She had a new book with her that Miss Gorman had ordered, with pictures of Greek statues. She loved the poetry book her teacher Miss Dickson had given her, carried it everywhere as a prized possession; why hadn't she thought of that and dumped her books at school so they wouldn't be ruined by being flung into dirty slush with her? Why did she have her World History book with so many pictures she liked? Did she have any right to ruin books just because she herself didn't deserve anything?

Finally at Harbison's she ran into the house. She was alone, Caroline probably gone on some after-school activity. Putting her books down carefully on her bed, she found Mrs. Harbison's scissors and shut herself in the bathroom. She looked at her hair in the mirror, deciding where to whack first; she had wanted to, been planning to whack viciously. Savage all past attempts to make the fine, dark stuff look curly and Hollywood-pretty. And then do something as bad to the rest of herself, although she had no coherent thought as to what that might be.

Then, in the mirror, she saw her face: her dark eyes so like her mother's, the smooth skin her friends said she was so lucky to have. She leaned closer to the mirror, seeing her sisters, seeing her mother. Like them, her mother, her sisters, she *did* have smooth skin. Like them she had fine, dark hair and dark eyes.

But who is this girl in the mirror? Am I really like my sisters? Which sisters? And why do I have my mother's look in my own eyes? It was both frightening and yet perfect to think she would be like her mother. But she saw that her mouth and chin were hardly like her mother's; the firm set of the jaw was like little Jeannie's. And little Jeannie had a determination so like their father. Like Mary, who had so much fought with Mother and even with Almighty Father. A stubbornness. Refusal of anything easy.

As she kept studying her own face in the mirror, she got lost in all that thinking. The comparisons. Ellen: so often with a softness in her eyes, especially when she was with the animals (but so confident too "sure as a little bug," James had said once about Ellen). Anne was seeing something like that softness in her own eyes just thinking of Ellen. By the time she remembered the scissors, her self-destructive fury had lost so much life it couldn't rouse her again to anything near viciousness. Or to any action. She stood there, staring stupidly. Then she put the scissors carefully away and went to her room, tried to study for awhile before starting the usual after-school chores. But mostly staring out the window, off and on, into the clouding distance, not moving to do the things she should do until she heard Caroline and Mrs. Harbison come in and bustle around the house and the kitchen.

Next day he tried to waylay her, positioning himself by the classroom door before the bell rang. "Anne, I wanted to talk to you about the last assignment," he said. Sounding so innocent in front of the other kids. She knew it was a lie: "Will you come back to my home room at. . . ?" but, ducking her head, Anne took advantage of the boys pressing from behind her and got past him. She wasn't able to say a thing. Everything seemed to be taking place at some distance from her, the other kids chattering away, the teachers in front of the class, the Harbisons going on about all the usual things at home — it all seemed to have meanings far remote from her, meanings she was left out of. And when she tried, sometimes, to join into what people were saying, she was embarrassed that her voice sounded so dry and weak, panicked to know she couldn't start a whole sentence because her voice would crack and quake before the end. She knew they would see her, hear her, for what she really was.

She was sick of herself and yet saving herself, hiding from a fear that she couldn't name, the awful memory of that yawning black hovering just beyond anything she thought or tried to think. That might still open to swallow her at any moment.

She went with Brenda and some other girls over to Deb's at lunch hour. Feeling exposed as they crossed the space between the school and the café in brilliant sun dazzling off last night's new snow. Wanting to run back but clinging to Brenda, following her because there was no place else to go. She would rather be reading alone, hiding in the library, but was sure she would be caught there by Mr. Hansen because she knew, with all her senses on alert like an animal's, that he had been trying to catch her alone somewhere since at least yesterday.

At Deb's, the girls chattering away and the boys coming over to flirt with them kept all attention away from Anne. Except for Brenda poking her a couple of times and trying to tease, "wake up, Annie, this isn't the time for a "brown study." Laughing because she liked to bandy around words like "brown study" and get Anne laughing too. Calling her 'Annie' deliberately, to tease, to get a response. But today Brenda was mostly busy with her popularity and Anne was grateful to be invisible behind it.

Miss Dickson, in English class toward the end of the day, wasn't content to let her be invisible. Full of life herself, Miss Dickson brought to life the books and stories they read, and the kids themselves. In her class they loosened up like they never did in other classes, sometimes put on skits or acted out scenes to dramatize what they were reading, writing their own scripts under her direction.

Today it was mainly the boys, talking and then arguing about what was the most important scene in *Julius Caesar* and how many roles they could get into a 15-minute drama. The most popular boys were insisting — of course — on the stabbing scene. And most of them, even the ones who didn't outright admit it, wanted to be Brutus, the combination of getting to stab somebody and thinking they wouldn't have to learn many lines being for them the perfect appeal. But Miles and another boy were more and more stubbornly holding out to find a "lead-up" scene and making the stabbing almost anticlimactic. And nobody wanted to memorize Antony's speech, or recognize that Brutus had a speech too.

Anne felt so removed from them, and from the story, that the boys might just as well *be* in ancient Rome. Or on another planet. Anne heard them, she heard them as clearly as she had sometimes heard voices coming over the radio. But if she was thinking of the play itself, it was to think that it was a strange thing full of people making sounds like words about things that didn't matter. She had tried to go through the day unthinking about anything but her assignments, the life in her books. But the sentences in her World History book, about the Renaissance, had kept refusing to turn into sentences while she had tried to read in study hall, had become just words until, repeatedly, she had had to start the same sentence over. And she hadn't been able to bring herself to open *The Mill On the Floss*, which she had chosen for her book report; the painfulness of what was happening to those people in the book was impossible to think about *because what was it for?*

"Anne. . .?" Miss Dickson startled her. Expected her to say something? But another girl spoke up and then a boy, and Anne began to understand: Miss Dickson wanted some of the Roman women in the play: "At least in the background," she was saying. "Observing, commenting. And who are these women?" she asked.

Anne did immediately remember. A reason she hated the play was, what use were the women? Caesar's wife, Brutus' wife, what did they do? They did nothing. Caesar and Brutus and the rest of them cared nothing about their wives, or daughters, or any children. They were just bent on something that was only about themselves. And the women stood by and let it happen. She didn't want to be one of those women, silently resisted Miss Dickson trying to get her to be part of the girls writing some lines for themselves.

Then she erupted. The urge to destruction got hold of her again. Not until the day was over, not until all these days had passed without the rest of the world knowing her turmoil. Although in her adolescent confusion she didn't know it, she had come to the end of something. She couldn't go home. There was no home. No place to go. She had been unable to put an end to herself but she had to break out; she had to end something.

It didn't happen until the buses were gone and the halls were empty. She had gotten through the day and, thankfully, it was ending. She felt a tremendous relief, and release, when the last bell rang. She breathed again, for the first time she remembered that day.

Tuesday. She always knew what day it was. It was Tuesday; she had survived five days. But Thursday was looming. Choir practice. She could have just been waiting for the bus again, among her classmates, as she had done on Friday while she had been trying to keep everything looking normal. Or walked home with Dodie Foster as they so often did when the weather was good enough, barely a mile to Harbison's and Dodie going only a little further. But that day, feeling nothing but avoidance, she didn't think of Dodie, though she did know the skies were bright again outside. But she was going away from the brightness; she slid along the halls toward the library, away from the general rush to the stairs and buses, to keep from seeing Dodie or any of her other friends, and hid in an empty classroom.

Then she did break out. Not that she expected to do what she did. She went to his home room door not knowing why. Probably to weep. And she did weep. But then she was seized with such sudden fury that she ripped his metal nameplate from the door and beat with it on the little glass window of his door until the window cracked straight across. She kicked and kicked at the door, shaking, sobbing, only much later feeling the pain of bruising her feet.

The principal, Mr. Rich, found her there. Collapsed in a heap against the wall in a flood of tears. Utterly ashamed to have him see her like this; she hadn't guessed he was still in the building. If she had hoped anyone was still around to know her, it could not have been this slight, soft-stepping man with his comb-over of sparse sandy hair who, besides being principal, taught her history class. He was new to the school that year and though she knew that Miles and other boys respected him after awhile, Anne had hardly thought of him as a real person. And she thought she could not bear pity, especially from this stranger.

"What is it?" Mr. Rich kept saying, sounding kindly; "Annie, what's the problem?" Using her childhood name. But his concern made her weep some more. She couldn't talk. Then he led her, finally, while she let him lead her, up the stairs. To Miss Dickson's home room. And there was Miss Dickson, with that look of interested intelligence in her dark eyes that Anne so much admired.

If there was one person in the school, in the town, that Anne wanted to emulate, it was Miss Dickson, her other newest teacher, only here in the Valley for the past year herself. But Anne had been too shy ever to approach her. She had tried to copy Miss Dickson's slightly curled and perfectly neat dark hair, had longed for the loose but nicely-fitting soft clothes Miss Dickson wore, and had been the shining good student in her class. Proud of herself, memorizing poetry for extra credit, pages of it, putting the class through her recitations until Miss Dickson, who had offered extra credit for such recitation, decided to have Anne recite the longest poems to her alone: *O Captain My Captain. . . .; When Lilacs Last in the Dooryard Bloom'd. . . .*" And now, here, Anne stood before her, a shivering mess not wanting to be seen by her idol, sniveling through her runny nose and unable to speak at all.

Miss Dickson surprised her. Immediately put her arms around her, runny nose and all, and shooed Mr. Rich out the door. Then Anne found herself in Miss Dickson's lap, in her big chair by the desk, with a box of tissues and being coaxed into telling all of it. Weeping with shame, sometimes choking on it, "I . . . I know it's my fault . . . why didn't I see I couldn't . . . I shouldn't. . .?

"And I don't know where to go any more" she sobbed, "I can't go back to his class. I can't . . . do . . . I can't do anything." And she cried out: "There's no place to go. . . . I have no place. . . ."

"Oh my girl, my girl," Miss Dickson said, "it isn't your fault." And she kept saying it, cajoling out of Anne the next bit and then the next — even about the judge. But with the worst tears, and Anne's most awful shame, all the shameful details about her love of Mr. Hansen. "There, there," Miss Dickson kept saying, and "yes, I know," patting Anne on the head or shoulder, or offering more tissue, then holding her closer along the way, letting her just keep crying at the end.

Until Anne finally wept: "How is it I can go so wrong? What is the *matter* with me?" Then Miss Dickson lifted Anne's face by the chin, made her look into her eyes.

"There is nothing the matter with *you*," she said, her dark eyes sparking. "Do you hear me? Listen to me." And she held Anne's chin even forcibly when Anne tried to cast her eyes down again. "Listen to me, Anne. You've always listened to me as a teacher. And I know what I'm talking about as much as I know the poetry you and I both love. And I insist on *this*, that there is *nothing* the matter with *you* that makes these men misbehave. *They* are the responsible ones."

Anne wasn't hearing this. There was a whole lecture she didn't hear. Yet she took in something, something from the sparking eyes and the passionate insistence of Miss Dickson. Something that revived her. Then Miss Dickson softened: "Annie," she said with affection, "you've got to learn to look them in the eye. Stop acting like a doe in the forest" — Anne remembered those words — "You aren't a little doe in a forest. Stop ducking your head. . . .

"Or," Miss Dickson suddenly said with a quirky smile, "then *do* act like a doe in the forest and don't duck your head at all when a man sneaks up on your blind side. Instead, run. Recognize the sneaking and run. Run for your life."

Anne felt Miss Dickson's frustration, how this woman wanted to reach her, how, with all her helpfulness, she couldn't help but be impatient with words or with Anne. All the way home to Harbisons as Miss Dickson finally insisted on driving her, she felt how clear and sure Miss Dickson was while Anne herself was so foolish and incapable. But somehow, in spite of it all, not so bad as she'd felt herself to be. Quiet again.

Miss Dickson followed it up; she didn't just let things pass by or ignore them, as so many people seemed to like to do. She must have worked at it, because Anne was summoned to a meeting after classes before the week was over. Miss Dickson told her in advance two things: "Mr. Hansen will be there," she said, "to apologize to you." And she said that Anne should bring her two closest friends: "Bring with you the two girls you trust the most."

Surprising herself, Anne didn't ask Brenda, the basketball star, her newest friend. Instead, in fear and trepidation, she asked the two quietest girls who had known her from first grade: Janet, quick enough but so sort of stunted by alcoholics at home; Gloria, stolid and a moralist but so faithful to a friend, whom Anne had almost left behind in her rise to become star pupil and captain of the track team.

They sat there, the three girls — Anne in a fever — until the principal, Mr. Rich, came in acting solemn while Mr. Hansen had been fidgeting by the window shades and then Miss Dickson finally stood to explain: "We are here for an apology. A teacher has to apologize if he crosses the line with a student. And Mr. Hansen wants to do that."

Miss Dickson then looked to Mr. Hansen and he came, slowly, toward her at the front of the room. The same soft sweater, tan this time, the same dark eyes, the same beautiful man. Anne hadn't really looked at him for a week. But he was still the same. Squirming inside, she suddenly remembered Miss Dickson's insistence and tried to look him in the eye. But she immediately blushed, hot, and tried to look anywhere else instead. Tried to hold up her head but she couldn't look at Janet or Gloria either. Miss Dickson came and sat at the desk right behind her.

Anne didn't hear the words of apology. She heard the sound of Mr. Hansen saying some words and then, gratefully, heard Miss Dickson ending the awkward encounter. And then, dreadful as it had been to go through it, Anne felt something new inside her as she crept away. Under the turmoil of shame and awful embarrassment there was something like relief, a feeling of satisfaction even, that something, somehow, had been settled.

Her feelings about Mr. Hansen weren't settled. She was afraid to be near him, climbed immediately, determinedly, into the back seat of his car coming and going from choir practice when she did go back. Resisting his offers of help, feeling mortified but determined. What else was there to do? She had missed two choir practices, claiming to be sick, and didn't know the Easter anthem very well when they sang on Sunday even though the choir had begun practicing it more than a month ago.

Easter as seen by the church people had long seemed strange to Anne anyway — there was something disturbing in tales about a dead man coming out of a cave, out of his tomb. It had been just before Easter when she had come to live at the Harbisons last year and been promptly carried off to church, and she had liked the music. And on that day, her first Easter in church, the music was more than music; it had seemed like a live thing that day, playing upon and playing with something else: two white flowers placed before the altar. All through that service a year ago Anne's eyes had feasted upon those two white flowers, especially the one. An Easter lily. She had never seen an Easter lily, didn't know what it was until the service had ended but couldn't stop looking at the stately green stems holding up four glistening white, expansive blooms that at moments glowed like gold in the light of the altar candles. Then her eye would shift, with the music, to their delicate companions: tiny white blossoms like tissue clinging to a lacy network of fine green leaves and stems on the other plant.

How had such beautiful things been found, she had wondered all through that service. It was magical, was not believable, that there could be things so gloriously in bloom, reaching marvelous full life out of the frozen cold. Into the dirty snow of March. Something very deep in her had been stirred, that year ago, reviving her sense from childhood of her own birthday: how she had been born just before terrible March would start turning itself into warm April. Her birthday meant the soon return of the earth, warm again after it had been so locked up in freezing cold (like the cold of her father's grave soon buried under deep snow in October).

Sitting in church that year ago Anne had almost laughed out loud at herself to remember how as a child she had thought that people had simply made up the calendar and that they had made a terrible mistake by including February. "I can tell why they put in December," she had told Ellen, proud that she had figured it out when she was six or so, "because it's for Christmas. And January makes you want to be good, so the warm will come back again. Like making you work harder so you'll be more glad when it's done. Or punishing you so you will learn. And March is for some people having a birthday just when the cold is letting up, like James and me, when you know the warm *is* coming back."

Anne remembered how she had thought that adding in February, after you had already struggled through so much cold and dark of winter, was just too much punishment. That it was a big mistake, because it could make you start turning sour, feeling mean instead of wanting to do better.

The smell of warmth again was what Anne most deeply loved about the time that came right after her birthday. The sun. The sound of trickling water, the bursting pussy willows. But most of all the smell of the many, many — countless — things brought back by the sun and the water: the smell of earth, of the animals' lives; the fresher smell of people and even of their clothes; feeling her own smell more warm, alive. Drinking in the deep fragrance of grass suddenly fresh green out of dead brown. The fragrance of bluebells, of the growing grain. Even the smell of Bu-hac in the outhouse.

On that year-ago Easter day, so miserably cold outside, Anne had marveled at the sight of the living white flowers before the altar, but it may have been the fragrance drifting and floating about the church that moved her more than sight. Certainly moved her more than any strange words from scripture that she was obviously expected to be serious about, moved her as much or more than the music. But the scent and the music and the mysterious glory of those living white blooms were all one. That was when she had begun to take seriously, not yet as idea but as something deeply felt, a sense that there was something far more important about going to church than she had realized.

But her thoughts about cold, and warmth, and Easter, and of her father lying under frozen earth, were all entangled together. She certainly hadn't wanted to think, didn't want to think, of Almighty Father rising in his anger from that frozen grave. To do . . . what? To live again? How? William had told Anne what his friend Barney told him when they were teenagers, how Barney took the summer job of gravedigging when other boys wouldn't. Until Barney got a real job and younger boys came along. They always dug several graves in late July and August and then covered them with plywood, William had said, "because most people died in winter when the ground was too frozen to dig."

"Do you know who dug the grave Father was buried in?," Anne would ask her older siblings over the years, but nobody was sure. All the boys who had helped the old cemetery-tender by doing the gravedigging had gone off in the War.

That first year that Anne was in church at Easter, women had stood about the Easter lily after the service, congratulating Mrs. Bogle who, it turned out, had been planning this Easter surprise for some time, hoping to produce it earlier. "It was a failure last year," she said, and Anne almost winced at the sound of her voice — it had such a twang to it that Anne never knew whether the sound was more fascinating or more irritating. "It bloomed too early, en puny. So this year I carted in en ol' pig trough into the greenhouse — only thing that looked like deep enough — to mulct it down for the winter. En I made myself wait till the day after Christamas before I brought it out, into the house to warm it up en start it growin.'" She was very proud of herself, Anne could tell, but Mrs. Bogle was always matter-of-fact, no matter how pleased she might be over praise of her beautiful flowers and no matter what odd thing she might say, "I prayed with this plant, ladies," she said next; "I prayed over it and I prayed for it; I done everything but pray *to* it — that I could never do, pray to enything or eny living body 'cept Jesus."

This year — one year and some weeks later — Anne couldn't even see the Easter lily (another one? — the same one?) from where she sat up front with the choir, to the left of Reverend Wolfson. She *did* know the scent, the same lovely fragrance drifting toward the choir benches, and it heartened her, so that she got carefully through the anthem, listening closely to the other sopranos on each side of her and picking up peripherally on Mr. Hansen's directions without looking at him.

Then this went on, in class and at church, her avoidance. She did become a little closer to Miss Dickson — memorized the longest poem yet to recite to her: *It is an Ancient Mariner. . . .* — but still overawed by the woman's liveliness and quick expressions of interest.

Then a new rush of feeling took hold of Anne. After church one day that was sunny in April — the days now growing long and so often sunny — she saw Mr. Hansen tending to his two little boys, maybe five and seven years old, while his wife talked to some people at the church doors. Anne remembered that she had seen it before, how the beloved man talked and laughed with his sons as the boys ran around the church yard or around a parking lot downtown by some store, while he let Mrs. Hansen chat to friends or neighbors undisturbed. Happy, and patient and thoughtful, with his wife and with the boys. Playful. With a smile for all of them now in this sunny April as they loaded into their car. The car that Anne had been trying to bury among her other dreads, the car of secret sin that mortified her to think of but that kept resurrecting itself as a warm, dark haven of something she still wanted to have but also, terribly, in her latest dreams, something vaguely threatening.

She watched Mrs. Hansen, his wife, smiling in the passenger seat as they drove away, looking so comfortable and sure of her place. And from an awful mix of conflicted feeling Anne seized on the familiar one of despising herself all over again. She was appalled at what she had done to Mr. Hansen. At what Miss Dickson had done to him on her behalf. What shame and horror he must have felt getting through that forced apology! The father delighted with his sons, the man who was so good to his wife. In front of his principal, in front of Anne and her friends, paltry girls! Did his wife know? Had Anne ruined him? She knew, from books and from life, that women were easily ruined, but she saw for the first time how the almighty man could be brought down. And what a more mighty ruin it was for a good man to be brought low. Men climbed higher; they claimed, and were given, higher ground. But Anne knew how the "good" women talked; she had absorbed how boldly they condemned someone already low but how secretive they were in whisperings about anyone as high as the judge or the teachers. She had absorbed, from overtones, what they were saying after shooing out any children, about their own men; she knew they often banded together in a view that men were really "just little boys," at the same time that the women supported "those little boys," as having some higher place than their own. "You must feed them good," Anne had heard one woman proclaim while the others nodded in agreement, "and don't tell them what you're really thinking." Anne knew that through the women's talk, the women's whisperings, that people were either made high, kept high, or brought low. Anne's friends had been sworn to secrecy by Miss Dickson, and Anne had never let that day of the apology be talked about with them, had shut off any mention or hint of it. It was a closed book to her, one she never wanted to think about — except for that treacherous inner feeling of relief, that she had been taken off the hook, rescued from awful guilt. But had Gloria or Janet talked? Had Miss Dickson or Mr. Rich said anything?

Anne was overwhelmed with a new guilt, over the apology itself, over putting such a good man through a dreadful ordeal. She doubted Miss Dickson. She avoided her. She was filled with a world of doubt again about herself. That word "paltry," from some story, impressed itself on her, described everything about her, everything she did or tried to do, everything in her life; it was all so measly: petty, small and worthless. Paltry. She got sick, hurting all over, so miserable for days with something like flu that, for the first time in her memory, she actually wanted to stay in bed, shut out the whole world, stay hidden forever. She missed the last track meet, the big one.

Then track season was over; school would soon be ending. Even the lovely May weather seemed like it was reproaching her, blaming her; like it was made for people who deserved it and she would be a little wretch to try to claim any enjoyment from it. There was no future, an empty summer looming.

She did cut off her hair. Not in a frenzy this time, but in cold, deliberate strikes with those sharp scissors Mrs. Harbison kept in a kitchen drawer just for haircutting. Anne loved the clean, sharp *swak* the blades made as they sheared off a lock and then another. She had always loved scissors, both the perfect differences they could create in their cutting and the neat finality they made of things you didn't want, putting an end to them, leaving them to be tossed away and forgotten.

"Good heavens, Annie!" Mrs. Harbison said when she arrived home, "what's happened to your hair? Did you do that?"

Mrs. Harbison had known there was something wrong; she had tried, in her quiet way, to probe Anne over the last several weeks, trying to get Anne to talk to her while Anne hadn't been able to tell her any of it. Over the evening Mrs. Harbison shook her head with a little frown whenever she looked at Anne's hair. Then, when supper was over and they were finishing the kitchen cleanup together, she insisted that Anne sit in a kitchen chair: "So I can straighten this up. You can't go out looking like that." This was so like her. She had been cutting and trimming hair in her family for years, of course, like so many women did. With some pride in doing it. She was firm about insisting that Anne sit in the chair that she pulled into the center of the kitchen floor — firm in the way Mrs. Harbison could be about keeping things in order around her household — while she collected a towel, her scissors. Anne didn't know how to resist.

Anne didn't think her hair looked *that* bad. She hadn't wanted, herself, to go out looking like she had butchered it; she had cut it off straight, as straight as she could, all over.

The result at Mrs. Harbison's hands was astonishment, to Anne when she looked in the mirror, and to most of her friends. "I look like a boy," Anne said.

"You look like one of those flappers from the magazines," Gloria said, not approving.

"Like a pixie," Brenda said, flipping her own bob.

"I had to cut it so short in order to fix it," said Mrs. Harbison next day, "but it suits you. It looks good on you, sets off your dark eyes."

Miss Dickson exclaimed with something like delight and said almost the same thing as Mrs. Harbison: "it looks good; it suits you," and she teased: "What beautiful brown eyes you have." But then she studied Anne with her own dark eyes and patted her on the shoulder. "Come and talk to me, Anne, like I've said before. And aren't you going to treat me to any more of your recitations?" Anne knew she had been concerned about Anne avoiding her.

"You'll get through this," Miss Dickson said, letting Anne go as Anne kept edging away from her, "but you don't need that habit of getting through everything by yourself. You need to talk."

"And don't forget the poetry you love at a time like this," she was saying as Anne was getting away.

How could she go and talk to Miss Dickson when she blamed Miss Dickson for the ruination of Mr. Hansen? But couldn't blame her. Couldn't blame such a good person or such a good man, had to blame only herself?

Her haircutting brought her nothing but unwanted attention. Brenda and half the girls were talking about "pixie cuts," were buzzing about who could learn to do them. "My aunt cuts my hair," Dodie said, "and she knows Mrs. Harbison. I'll get her to talk to Mrs. Harbison about how to style it that way." Only the older women went to Mrs. Jarvey at the beauty parlor, "and old Mrs. Jarvey couldn't learn anything about style," the girls had long scornfully agreed. They studied magazines, cut each others' hair or wailed about how mothers or aunts or older sisters could "never get it right."

Hair styles, and her own "pixie cut," seemed to be all that Anne was hearing from morning till night, even after she made her way home to the relative peacefulness of the Harbison household. Where she still had to be ever watchful for the sneaking presence of the judge, who always seemed to know it if she needed to go to the drying room to collect clothes from the racks, or to the basement for a jar of canned vegetables, or outdoors for any reason. Who would turn up to "help" if his wife was safely in another part of the big house, getting his body close up against Anne's, leaning into her face while she turned it away, repelled by those rubbery lips trying to reach her own. Who came home early to surprise her in the basement one day, getting hold of her arm and managing to put a wet kiss somewhere near her mouth as she pushed and pulled to get free of him. She got up the basement stairs and fled the house completely, ran down to Dodie's.

Even the judge had his lowering, disapproving looks about her hair, quoted from Scripture about Deborah or somebody and made clear that it was immoral for a woman to cut her hair. Even Caroline, thirteen now, eyed Anne's hair and pursed her lips like a church woman. (Poor Caroline's habit was to try to behave like both parents at once, to speak like her father, or give his disapproving looks, but subdued and confused by trying to imitate the gentle tolerance of her mother, at least in her mother's presence.)

At school Anne tried not to squirm under so much new attention. She felt even Mr. Hansen was part of it, of people noticing her. And Miles, the boy she watched from afar. She had to struggle with a new sensation that the attention brought her. Because part of her liked it. She was pulled one way and then the other: she *wanted* to like the attention, to indulge in it happily the way Brenda did. She despised that part of her but she wasn't managing to hide it, even from herself. She felt herself glowing warm with liking it. "You're so . . . uh, you're so pretty," Harold Burney said to her, bumbling around trying to take her books from her after school, wanting to carry them for her without even making clear what he was doing, hadn't asked her. "Would you . . . um . . . would you, maybe, think of going to the movie on Saturday?"

She'd known Harold since seventh grade when he'd entered school as a new kid. Skinny then but growing bigger every year until now he was one of the sophomore big guys. Not terribly smart but a big guy who seemed like a nice guy. It struck her that he was asking her for a "date," this big bumbling kid she'd hardly paid attention to except to feel that he was "okay," a sort of classmate buddy who was okay.

She couldn't think in terms of "dates." Dates happened in movies; they didn't even happen in the books she liked to read. She became more confused than Harold was, and just as bumbling. Between them, in their confusion, they dropped most of her books on the floor.

Somehow they picked them up again; somehow she let him know she wouldn't be going to movies with him. She was so bad at it! She must have hurt his feelings, though she hated to hurt anybody's feelings. He stayed away from her for the last week of school.

On her way walking home afterwards the thought slipped into her mind: What if it had been Miles who was asking her out? Miles, her archrival for grades since grades had mattered; Miles who'd always been aloof with girls; Miles who was the best-looking boy in the class in Anne's eyes; Miles who'd been growing tall even in junior high and groomed by the high school basketball coach before he, with Anne, even entered high school. Who had been, this year, their sophomore year, the brightest new star on the high school team. And still the one, now more than ever the one, who easily solved math problems, explaining his equations and the steps in his solutions as though they were matter of fact. While Anne had to work hard, apparently so much harder, to arrive at the same result. But she outshone him in English class, and in World History. She knew, without their ever talking about it, that he struggled for his high grades there as she struggled for hers in math.

In fact he never really talked to her, about grades or anything. Never had talked to her except in the most casual way.

"Some boys don't get interested in girls as early as others," Brenda confided. "I read that in *Look* magazine. But Miles is getting interested this year. And he's interested in you."

Anne couldn't see it. Of course it had taken her forever, herself, to get interested in boys and she still wasn't that interested; that part she understood. But she was intrigued by something in Miles that she couldn't name until much later and didn't recognize as being like her father. It was his devotion to whatever he was doing that fascinated her. Devotion to the point, it seemed, almost of mindlessness. He could sit and read or do his work in study hall completely oblivious, it seemed, to the whispers, giggles, rustlings and restlessness around him, never raise his eyes from his book except to stare far off out the window. He drove down the basketball court with utter determination, racking up points as a high scorer in game after game. "The cheerleaders are a distraction," was a remark he did make to Anne. She understood that too, as she felt the same. Basketball season was the real high of high school life — there was no football, the deep snows starting in October — and the basketball games were raucous with teenage excitement and with the town's excitement. Sometimes, with her ears almost hurting from the shrill whistles and the gym echoing and virtually rocking with relentless shouting and screaming — the band and the constant thumping of the drum even when the band wasn't playing, the cheerleaders shrieking and leaping around — sometimes Anne had been so glad when a game was over that she wanted just to walk home alone in the night, to get her own senses back.

It seemed that Miles liked solitude. But she wasn't sure whether she liked it herself any more. Feeling she was too much inside herself. Missing her sisters, though they'd so often been too crowded together. Missing . . . what? After years of the close crowding of family into a little cabin and years of Mrs. Binch snooping and prying and leaving no room for Annie to breathe unless she fought for it — fought to keep herself to herself — now everyone was remote. There was no one close; she was stranded somewhere alone. And her springtime, the wonderful time of year when she had so often felt the world opening, had been ruined. She felt bottled up. She was resentful that she had been stranded, shameful and miserable, in the midst of her favorite months passing her by; that the warming and burgeoning of the world, that precious time that came only once a year, that came only after long struggle through cold and dark — that this wonderful time held nothing for her. And disgusted with herself for feeling resentful. She despised the feeling of resentment in herself, vaguely knowing it as an awful flaw that the family deplored in her sister Margaret.

She could still, thankfully, lose herself in a book but sometimes even reading, her favorite pastime, raised spectres of people's pain, people's meanness to each other. She re-read *The Secret Garden* at bedtime, several times over.

Miss Dickson waylaid her. After school, soon after the pixie cut. Anne felt, at once, that of course it had to happen, that Miss Dickson wouldn't just forget about it after she had said "you need to talk."

But how to talk? Anne was ashamed that, the first time she had talked, she had blubbered and sobbed, letting the most hidden shameful things just come out of her, out of her control.

Now she was tongue-tied. There was too much to say, and nothing to say, about the suffering she had caused, and Miss Dickson had caused, to poor Mr. Hansen. About how her haircutting had brought her into worse depths of confusion instead of putting an end to it. About Miles, or her hidden resentments of the spring in place of feeling hopes from it. But about how insidious were hopes anyway. About hating herself at the same time that she felt the swelling in herself of something like pride that she tried to put down. About what a complete wretch she was. How bumbling and how stupid about anything but books and yet proud because she simply couldn't get rid of the proud feeling. About how she half knew she had her mother's pride and her father's pride without being able to talk about either one.

"Are you still reading poetry?" Miss Dickson asked, "I have a couple of new ones for you." She was firmly guiding Anne back toward her big desk after class. "And did you like any of the last poems I gave you?"

Anne admitted she had been memorizing Edgar Allen Poe, *Ullalume* and of course *The Raven*: "*As I pondered weak and weary. . . .*" Those poems weren't the ones Miss Dickson meant and they weren't in the book Miss Dickson had given her last fall. That book had Emily Dickinson and Robert Frost and Edward Lear and such. Hopeful poems.

"Well . . . sit down, sit down, while I look for these two others. Poe's poems are . . . hmm. . ., . . . fun to memorize, aren't they? The rhyming is wonderful. Hardly anyone better at rhyming than Poe." When Anne didn't respond, Miss Dickson herself sat down, beside her desk instead of behind it. "So what did you think of the other poems I found for you, by Native Americans?"

"I liked them. . . ." Anne was hesitant. Because it wasn't true and because she didn't want to talk.   She felt she was mumbling. And disappointing Miss Dickson because she'd only read the extra poems without much understanding, and couldn't remember much about them. She knew there were four of them. She saw the four dittoed sheets in her mind and kept thinking of the number four: Four sheets, neatly folded, stuck in her poetry book. Four more days of classes — real classes before the playday picnic at the end — four days as something to hold onto before the emptiness of summer. Four problems to solve for tomorrow in Algebra — if you didn't count the makeup some kids were doing that Anne usually helped them with in the first free fifteen minutes of class. Four steps, times four, plus four, from this floor, from this room, down to the back doors where kids waited for the buses. . . .

"Tell me which ones you liked," Miss Dickson said, her voice very gentle.

"Really, I guess I have to say. . . .," Anne squirmed, but she had to tell her: "I . . . I guess I didn't really read them, not the way I read a book. They're more . . . they're more like Emily Dickinson. I think . . . I think. . . ." She didn't know what to say. "Maybe I just need more words to make me understand something. Like a story, I need a story."

She felt she was dumb not to have understood or liked the four poems. And worse: a disappointment to Miss Dickson because she had hardly paid attention in reading them.

"I just don't seem to know enough to understand something unless it tells a story," she bumbled on, feeling lame. "And those other poems are so full of . . . of . . . well, of things that are really hard, life being hard, just too much to think about when they pack it all into such . . . such a short, hard poem. . . ."

"But two of them, at least two, are so filled with a hopefulness, and a power of life," Miss Dickson said. "At least I felt that. But you didn't, so can you say why? Why they seemed hard?"

When Anne didn't answer, didn't know what to say she didn't press. Instead she tipped her head and suddenly smiled: "And Edgar Allen Poe is easy?

"Or maybe," Miss Dickson was teasing, "maybe isn't the gloom and doom of Edgar Allen Poe just a little bit *too* easy?" It was a look familiar to Anne from English class; the affectionate tilted head, the teasing followed by a slight frown that wasn't really a frown but a look of curious, expectant interest. Like Miss Dickson really wanted to know what you were thinking while you could see her own thinking was so alive and ready to add on to yours.

Miss Dickson touched her arm. "Edgar Allen Poe no doubt had his reasons, Anne, for dwelling on a dark side. But he wasn't living in Alaskan spring. It doesn't seem he was finding hidden bluebells in spring or gathering wild raspberries in summer, as you wrote about in your essay.

"Poe wasn't a track star either, so far as we know," Miss Dickson went on as Anne was silent, "and he wasn't sixteen with a whole life before him when he wrote that wonderfully rhyming poem about the raven. And you wrote in your other essay about how the raven was often a good sign to your mother's people.

"But let's leave Poe for a moment," she said as Anne still said nothing, "leave him to his own time and place. To whatever age he was when he wrote his raven poem. Let's. . . ."

But suddenly Anne, for no reason she knew, began to smile: "The fox in the night?" she said, "looking at humans?" She caught a spark from Miss Dickson's eyes. "That part of the one poem is really funny in a way."

"What if the mother fox had been looking at Edgar Allen Poe?" Miss Dickson said, and Anne laughed with her, to think of that cagey mother fox listening to the gloom and doom of the raven's pronouncements. Not of course while she was so seriously hunting for food for her newborn little kits. But snickering at the super-gloomy raven if she thought of him at all. Like Ellen would have giggled.

"'The fox dreams of mice in bountiful fields where her little ones play,'" quoted Miss Dickson from the last half of *The Fox* poem; "'she dreams that the dainty Wildflower Spirit has fooled the Winter gods so that they sleep. . . .'

"Can you remember the next lines?" Miss Dickson asked. Anne couldn't, but she had unfolded the dittoed page from her poetry book and she read aloud:

"'So that Wildflower Spirit takes from the Winter gods
    all the World to grow in,
To grow in the light of the great Spirit that feeds
    the fox and the bear and the people
Until we let her go back to her own rest.

We are not jealous that the gods are equal.
Thus we celebrate that the gods know each their own time.'"

How was it she had thought this poem was difficult or painful?
"It's a translation from a tribe in the Pennsylvania area, you notice," Miss Dickson said, "from a song or chant in their rituals, I think. Maybe a pretty loose translation from what wasn't written as a "poem" in our language. But it has that same feel as poetry, don't you think?"

Anne had been writing a poem of her own and she felt ashamed, that her poem was about feeling paltry instead of celebrating the bigness of the world. The wide wonderfulness that she had always felt in the world, especially in the spring. Dreaming about and longing to see and be more a part of.

"I have a story I want you to read," Miss Dickson said. "It's *The Merseys Tapestry*." She looked for it on her desk and then gave Annie a slim little book. "It's my only copy, and hard to find, but it's short and you can easily read it and either bring it back to me on play day or come and see me later, because you know I live in the Dorsey apartments, don't you? Of course you do." All the class, including Anne, had gone to

Miss Dickson's apartment for a Saturday tea two weeks ago, and a Christmas party last winter.

Anne left Miss Dickson's room feeling that she wasn't going to betray again the Wildflower Spirit, the bluebells she had deserted this spring.

TERESA

Chapter Nine

Alcohol was my boon and savior. At first I didn't care if it could also be my downfall. I needed a downfall. I never really liked the taste but with the first drink, followed so quickly by that slightly giddy sensation when cares start to melt, I had the feeling of life opening into a marvelous world hinting at a freedom I had never remotely felt. And the alcohol became delicious. It was balm to a work-worn, angry soul tired out from trouble, and I needed it. Wanted more, to feel that new world truly open, to keep living in it.

I knew what people said. But I knew how ignorant they were. I'd been watching and listening to the *kasaakaq* (white-eyes) for half a lifetime. There were some fine ones, a few, but I'd seen how most of them escaped every moment from knowing themselves or knowing the world they lived in, how they so often would run roughshod, like an animal scared stupid, over anything or anyone different in their path. How frightened they were of anyone different from themselves and how they covered over their fear by acting superior as soon as they got together in numbers. The old settlers weren't there in numbers and they had to learn some things; neighbors had to be neighbors in the early days. Though we never mingled even then, there was something like respect. But the new people, who built a town, respected nobody different from themselves.

I didn't feel difference from them about the hardships in the everlasting struggle to make and keep a farm. Though I never understood it myself — this fight to try to bring out of great acres of soil more than you could possibly need, using more and more machines to try to do it — I could see the work and respect them for it. I didn't mind the back-breaking work of clearing acres — I never minded work — but where I had grown, where we lived from the given bounty of a world we tried not to disturb too much, from the fish of the ocean and the berries and plants on land, along with a few vegetables we learned (yes, partly from the white eyes) to cultivate — looking at the white eyes from our way of life, the way of the white eyes was mostly a mystery.

It was my early delight and my later misery to fall in love with a man from that other world — Old B.A., as I came to call him. Bernard Allen Birnes. People have their special names for those they appreciate and those they put down, both extremes. They called him "B.A." because he never went by Bernard and they didn't see him as Allen either, like I did when we were young. Then they called him, more and more, "hard-working Birney." They called me a lot of names I won't bother to repeat — behind my back of course. At least old B.A. gave out with any of his disgusted feelings right up front, especially if I pushed him into it; he didn't have the white-eyes' usual way of covering over what they were feeling and thinking. He was never little and mean like most of the *mirikaanaaq*, the American white eyes. He was a big man.

When we met he was Allen. He had never liked his first name and signed himself always B.A. Birnes. When I was giving up on him, so much later, trying to argue against his hopeless love for a farm, I wasn't calling him Allen any more.

I had left home — which wasn't my home, because I never found my home after I was taken away from it — but I left the half-way, nowhere home I had been put into, to try to make a life for myself in the new world dawning when the American white-eyes were taking over Alaska. I couldn't have said what attracted me but I wanted a wider world beyond the little town I lived in. And I was ignorant. An older girl told me, when I was sixteen and it was nearing summer, that we could be hired at the fish canneries and have a whole new life.

I was very good, very quick, at the fish cutting and I never went back to try to find my village. By the end of summer I met this tall fascinating man who had his own sheet metal shop and we got married when spring came, when I was seventeen. It was only after that, after three years and a second baby on the way, that I learned he had an impossible dream to live again his childhood on a farm, to become a farmer with huge acres he thought he could call his own. I didn't see how anyone could claim part of Nature and think they owned it. Like putting your name on a piece of paper was supposed to mean something big. To me it was a little puny act in the face of the wide world that belonged to everybody.

156

It was certainly an impossible dream for Allen, because he wasn't a farmer. I knew it before I became a drunk but after I'd been a drunk for a few years I saw how deeply old B.A. was a conflicted man. He should never have tried to create his childhood all over again because he was a man who loved machines. The lure of any machine — how it worked, how to fix it for someone, how to make it work or make it work better — was too strong to keep him at home. We couldn't afford much machinery ourselves beyond the old tractor and truck he kept running and the generator and pumps and other things he fashioned, but other people could. The coal mines and the railroad and the Anchorage shipyard and people further and further away who had machines of any kind, they heard about him and they wanted him to come to them. Then the hundreds of colonists arrived with all their newfangled farm machines and Anchorage was a growing town and it was a lost cause to keep old B.A. on the farm.

But through all the twenty-four years that we struggled there, through days and weeks as I kept being left there alone with the children and the work, was left more and more alone, and through the last few years of outright combat between us with everything going to seed, he wouldn't give up the dream: We had to have the farm. He'd grown blind as a bat, old B.A., and I told him so. "We don't have a farm," I told him; we had him coming and going, going more than coming, while the kids were getting out of control without a father or a real family life. "There's no way to keep up a farm unless you're here," I told him. We had bitter words, especially over Martin, who was a wild child and needed his father's hand. "You and that child are just alike," I said, "you both think like machines, not like people. You might as well just finish turning yourselves into machines; you aren't human." He did work hard, too hard, whenever he was home, trying to make up for lost time. But it wasn't enough; it was less and less enough.

Finally I'd had enough myself. He agreed not to go away so much but then he immediately built a sawmill out of town where he spent most of his time. Making money, of course, which we needed. We needed it then because, creeping up on us without our realizing it, life had become a town life. We weren't raising what we needed for ourselves any more, or canning, smoking meat and fish. B.A.'s big excuse for running off everywhere had been that we needed to have money. But we didn't need much money in the early days; people didn't pay him much anyway and most of the time he fixed somebody's machinery for little or nothing or for something in trade.

It took me five tries to get away from him. The first time it looked like everything was going to go just fine. I had heard I could get hired at the Pearl White laundry in Anchorage and a friend knew of a little house right next door to her own. I took the girls with me but I left fourteen-year-old Martin because he needed his father — and he had his father's prejudices against me by that time — and I had us set up nicely in the little house that I cleaned from end to end. Had the girls in school that fall while I worked. But old B.A. came along in his high-handed way and made the girls go back to the farm. I tried to stick it out alone, schemed how I might get my daughters back again. But the truth was, I didn't have a lot of spirit. I'd been so long with old B.A. that I believed in his spirit more than in my own. So I gave up the job before another week was out and went back, back to our now even more neglected place in the Valley.

I tried again three times over the winter. I had some friends by then; I'd been refusing to be stuck on that homestead twenty-four hours of every day of the year. I'd met more people. And the Harleys — this couple with grown children; he drove deliveries back and forth from Anchorage to the Valley — he would take me to Anchorage and they let me stay with them while I tried to find a new place and a new life, a job in Anchorage. I knew I had to get that far away but I couldn't have thought how to get further — and *then* I would take the girls when everything was lined up. But the first time I got away I got such a blinding headache that I could hardly move for two days, spent two days lying in my friend Eunice Harley's darkened bedroom with a cold cloth on my head and wishing I could die. I had no spirit at all, even when the headache finally left me.

Then it took months back on the homestead for me to get up the courage to try again. But that next time and the time after that were the same story: I trudged all over Anchorage, first in the awful cold of February and then in the bitter wind of March, and there were no jobs. There were hardly any places that would hire a Native anyway, only places where you were kept out of sight of the public. I would have to wait for summer, I finally thought, when they hired us fast enough in the canneries because they knew we would work hard for little money.

Then I met Master Sergeant Kiley, when I went to Anchorage with my friends in May, on a warm and beautiful day that literally lifted you right up with new hope. We wound up at a party at Kiley's house in Mountain View. The birches were leafed out around the back of his little house, mixed in with the spruce so familiar from my childhood, and bluebells coming into bloom just off the shady side of his broad wooden deck. It was a day you wouldn't think a body needed alcohol, and I didn't, but as the day turned to warm and long-lasting evening I finally tasted what everyone else was drinking — a little crowd by then laughing and drinking and smoking while standing around on the deck or sitting with legs stretched out on its clean planks. So I tasted alcohol — bourbon, it was, a bitter taste — for the first time. So bitter I wondered why anybody bothered to make it, let alone pay money for it, let alone drink it. But that was only the first taste. With laughing Kiley I tasted it again, cautiously, and then a little more. And the warm May evening became the promise of an ever-beautiful life to come.

I fell asleep somewhere that night with such a dream still in my head. But not, I remember, not before I discovered something else that was new: a man who made love. Kiley, for all his other faults — and he had faults in plenty — was a man who made love. That was a new world to me; I'd never even read about it then, though I did several years later; — years later I devoured books of all kinds, discovering a world of things I'd never guessed at in more than forty years of living, discovering what a true innocent I'd been for those forty years. There had been passion with old B.A. when I first knew him as Allen, but our passions were different and his love passion always left off when mine was only beginning. In fact his passion for anything but machines and that farm mostly left off before I felt much more than a beginning. Or, maybe I should say that I felt a passion for that man Allen, who I loved from our beginning and couldn't stop loving, even more fiercely, even long after our end, but that our two passions hardly met even in the begetting of another child.

It turned out that what felt like a new passion was mainly a distraction, like alcohol. Everybody called him Kiley but I always called him "Master Sergeant," mocking him. He laughed at that, laughed at everything. That was new too. I knew from the beginning how careless it was; I knew Kiley didn't care that much about anybody or anything — that's why I jibed him by calling him "Master Sergeant," Master of nothing. But careless was what I wanted right then. And Kiley was clean:

he smelled fresh, never had the body odors or the griminess of the farm people. His clothes and underwear and uniforms were sent to the laundry. The shower that he had rigged, against the sunny side of his house with a plywood screen, had warm running water and he dashed into it twice a day. And so could I: what a luxury, what a wonderful thing, to feel always clean and sweet-smelling without having to heat water and carry bucket after bucket to the tub. Without doing it endlessly, for years, to bathe a succession of children or provide a bath for grown boys and husband. To be so tired that you hardly ever heated a clean bath for yourself. It was delicious to feel so clean. Delicious to be careless. And — make of it what you will, call it selfish — but what was most new, and most delicious, was laughing. Even with Kiley I never laughed until I had some of his alcohol — usually bourbon — but I loved the sound of my own self laughing.

"I lifted the heater from Base supplies," Kiley told me when I asked how the water could have been heated. And he laughed: "They'll never miss it. I do the supply sheets."

When I was drunk it came to me, sometimes, to see that I still loved only Allen. And still loved him as old B.A. I did know, drunk or sober, that I never loved Kiley; I loved only the man I'd first loved. But I hated him too, and called him old B.A. to tell him how much he had disappointed me. He was twelve years older than me anyway and started trying to be boss soon after we married.

"No Aleut needed a boss," I told my daughter Annie when she kept asking me questions about things when she was a mother herself. I was only a girl when I married Allen but I already knew the Aleut way of living life, not pretending to anything or making up a lot of words to try to justify yourself. I had been taken from my village but most of the town of Kodiak, where I lived and went to school, was still Aleut. Like my classmates at the Baptist school. I lived with the family of the store owner, who was also postmaster, and he was mirikaanaaq — you would say American — but even his wife was half Aleut (though she was haughty and didn't like to admit it). The mirikaanaaq were more powerful than we were. They claimed to own everything, but the rest of us were all around them. And some of us children had a second mother from our own people, because we would stop at her little house after school or try to sneak there on Saturday or on Sunday afternoon. She was old and full of stories, made us Russian tea with milk and added spices, told us tales of Raven and Salmon and Bear, how they had worked out the reasons for the world and were still working in it. How they made it beautiful but hard enough that you couldn't understand it unless you worked hard and kept up respect for them.

Nobody was supposed to be boss. Only the mother and the wise old men, the elders, knew what was best, and they encouraged you in the right ways. They let you learn, they helped you learn, and you learned what was most true to the ways that would help to keep everybody true.

I put up with Allen talking about being "right," but there was no such word or idea among my people. I let that word, that idea, baffle me as a young wife and mother; I let it puzzle me far too long. I knew in my heart that things in Allen's world didn't make sense but I didn't trust myself. What I *did* feel, couldn't get over feeling, is that you have to work to keep life going and respect the mystery of life and the mystery of the natural world that gives you what you need. If old B.A. had been able to keep up respect for one hundred sixty acres, the huge piece of land that we cleared and planted in our early years — and in spite of my fears that it was too much; — if he had kept staying and trying to understand the land that we took away from Nature, I would have stayed longer too, maybe to my death. Maybe by the end of my time I would have understood it. But even without understanding I may have worked alongside him, I think, forever.

But he wouldn't stay. He kept assuming I would keep the farm together, wouldn't see that I knew nothing (and I still know nothing after my years with him), of what is a "farm." It was for me an alien world, and when he refused to stay in his alien world with me I came to resent his refusal more and more, until I became bitter. I could have worked beside him but without him the work became meaningless. (Of course it's a two-way street, feeling alien. He seemed to think that I was the alien and I finally saw he had his own reasons to get bitter at me for feeling more and more like *he* was the alien.) When he leased out one field and then another to neighbors, half angry at me because I hadn't been able to keep them up and angry at himself for the failure of his dream, we didn't have a farm any more anyway. We didn't have a family life.

We came from far too different worlds; I knew that long before I left him and his dream but I didn't find anything to do about it except to leave. And then spend years trying to stay drunk, with him dead and no hope of repentance on either side. I couldn't mourn him; I was furious at him for his death, his final abandonment. I did mourn the last bitter years together; I thought over every last angry word and then I got drunk again to try to forget. I'd loved that man too much, still loved that man too much even when he was dead. I couldn't go back to my children because I couldn't bear being sober, remembering them. Or him.

Kiley was no longer even half a man in my eyes, if he ever had been, and I left him, I drifted. For almost ten years I drifted, trying to stay sober enough to work and trying to stay drunk enough not to agonize over the four little girls I had left behind me or be furiously angry over twenty-four lost years.

I didn't succeed and I should surely have known that; my Aleut ancestors would have known it well, that you don't escape what you have done. I was utterly untrue, for ten years and more, to what I knew was the truth.

ANNE

Growing Down

164

Chapter Ten

As she hoed and weeded in the vegetable garden, with school over and summer beginning, something unexpected but familiar happened for Anne: she began to dream again in daytime. Good dreams in daytime. Mrs. Harbison — and the family — realized that Anne liked the gardening, tending the growing plants and growing more, growing flowers, and they gave her free rein. Caroline hated it, would rather do the indoor work even if she shirked at some of it, while Anne mused over nature, able to forget unpleasant things for long stretches as she labored or puttered outdoors, liking again to be alone. The days were long and full of light, the weather perfect through the month of June. Often she worked late, after supper, or simply sat amidst the flowers at any time and surveyed the burgeoning garden, satisfied at the end of a day to see not a weed in sight. Lovingly she thinned and transplanted in the vegetable garden, enlarging it; started new flower beds, delving into the earth that came to feel more and more soft and rich and loose as she worked in compost and manure, finding the soil falling lightly from her fingers and her spade. She remembered hearing Mrs. Bogle, at the fair last summer — Mrs. Bogle of the Easter lily and with the most colorful flower gardens in town, winning blue ribbons for them at the fair; — she remembered hearing her say in her twangy voice: "My husband says I must be part gopher, the way I'm always digging in the dirt."

Anne didn't think she herself could be part gopher, or only slightly so, but she had read and heard that a person might have some animal spirit, or share a spirit with some animal. She wondered if she herself might be like a bird, hopping or flying around, happy when away from trouble. She loved to watch the birds, to hear them first thing in the morning and through the day in the garden. Her thoughts moved like a bird, lighting where they wished or lightly floating, drifting easily here and there.

Or maybe she was like one of the little bats. But something in her did love the earth, and the light and warmth of being in the sun. And she did have a deep, though sometimes very unsettling feeling for cats: Excited when she saw a picture of a big one — a lion or a sleek tiger or cheetah but staring at the picture while something moved inside her, too deep to get hold of. Something both frightening and exciting as she tried to imagine the life of such a perfectly beautiful and powerful animal. She shared an unspoken companionship with Hannah, the Harbison's cat, who spent hours with Anne in the garden, moving silently about as a brown-and-gray shadow or curled self-contained in the chair nearby while Anne sat reading or dreaming. Hannah never wanted a lap, was contented in her own chair, eyeing the world with her cat's eyes that never missed the slightest movement, sometimes slipping down to investigate or sometimes stretching out luxuriantly asleep and seeming unconcerned with anything. Sometimes Hannah rubbed herself, purring, against Anne's legs; that was as close as Hannah wanted to be.

Time seemed to go on forever as Anne lost herself in her work in the garden or as she sat out, late, until she saw the little bats fly. She saw Miss Dickson several times in the first weeks of June, and Miss Dickson told her to keep the lovely book, *The Merseys Tapestry*. She wrote in the front of it,

"For Anne,
    A poem can be like running a race;
    both have power and movement with grace."

They talked about books and poetry. But then Miss Dickson was gone for the summer, on a long visit back to Kansas and Missouri where she was from.

Anne liked to read in the garden in the afternoon but then she would just dream awhile, the book in her lap, as she thought over what she read and what she read mingled itself into the June sunlight and the growing life all around her. The woman in *The Merseys Tapestry* had had no growing things, no things to hope for from the outside world. But something very alive and peaceful had grown up, kept growing, inside of her.

An idea began to grow up in Anne's mind that let her begin to really wonder about the life of Mr. Hansen. The church choir was not meeting in the months of June or July, so she had some distance. First she thought about her brothers, how so many of the young soldiers flooding the valley during the war had reminded her of her brothers but of how she and her sisters had been so often warned about those unknown soldiers. How frightened they had sometimes been as children, not knowing which of those men could be trusted. How girls were so often warned not to trust any of them. Confused and frightened by the adults' air of looming, unexplained suspicion inspiring a sense of dread about some mysterious "thing" that might "happen to you" if you let some man get too close.

Not *all* men, she thought — not her oldest cheerful brother James who used to give you a piggyback ride or sometimes tell a story; liked to pop the popcorn for popcorn balls — *how had she forgotten about James making popcorn balls some far ago Christmas*?

But there had been the terrible stories from the playground and newspapers, and the very real drunken soldiers around Mountain View. There was murder; there was the killing by the thousands and thousands in the war. The awful word "rape." Anne thought of the judge, a deacon of the church who still often scared her but who Reverend Wolfson didn't think to warn her about at all. Didn't tell girls to watch out for grown men. She thought about Miss Dickson saying, "if a man sneaks up on your blind side, run. Run for your life."

Anne thought she saw why women had been so protected — even owned — by fathers and husbands in the books she read. Because males only respected something in other males, some power they thought they saw in each other. They lived by something like fear of each other, or by creating that fear, engaged in some constant struggle to prove themselves to each other. Or against each other. Liking to fight, which Anne hated, or to come frighteningly close to fighting. Most of them. Women and girls were like pawns in the middle of this picture, as Anne saw it, of males always struggling with each other. Except for your own brothers or father. But if you didn't have father or brothers or other men like them protecting you, then you were something like prey, like a doe in the forest who'd better run. Because men didn't see you as having any power of your own; they just didn't see it.

In that way were the "good" men so different from the soldiers that Anne and her sisters had defended themselves from in Mountain View?

Anne wondered. And those soldiers were "good" men too, at least some of them, in some way. Especially the two MPs, Bud and Wilson. But it was the MPs, Bud and Wilson, with their clubs and their threat of male force that had kept those other soldiers in line, not Anne and her sisters with their puny weapons. Without Bud and Wilson patrolling, and the awful consequences they could have brought down from the army onto men who got out of line, Anne and her sisters would have fallen prey as easily as any doe or any rabbit, or any creature that didn't scare a man.

There was something more in the "good" men, Anne thought, something she couldn't get hold of, something truly good in Mr. Hansen. But fear must be part of what had put a stop to his sneaking up on Anne? Would he have cared so much about being confronted by Miss Dickson, or the girls? But Mr. Rich was there for the apology, his principal. Another man.

She couldn't put it together. Not with her brothers. And she couldn't stop seeing Mr. Hansen with his little sons, how he loved them. How she still wanted to love him, and especially loved the way he tended to those boys, how he bent his head toward one or the other of his sons, or his students, in that listening way he had. She did love him.

It was confusing, how good and bad were so mixed up together. Some days Anne felt almost tender toward the bugs and cutworms eating her plants and hated to kill them. *They didn't really know the harm they were causing, did they?* Sometimes she talked to them, told them to go live somewhere else and felt foolish when Caroline caught her in earnest conversation with a bunch of worms she had dug out around the cabbage plants.

She had a new friend, Hazel, a little older, who had recently come from Outside. Who began to come by often to visit Anne in the garden. They talked comfortably, especially about books they were reading, and sometimes Hazel helped with digging or weeding.

Most days there was no sadness in Anne's garden. But sometimes it did set in: Sometimes she felt an ache over the pansies, her mother's favorite flower. Mother had grown pansies, and sweet alyssum, around the cabin dooryard until the end, threatening the children and the hens every year to keep them away from her precious patch of flowers. The pansies always reminded Anne of home and of how she missed her sisters, especially Ellen with her grins and giggles about everything. Sometimes Anne wanted to weep over the pansies; she gave them extra manure and tended them lovingly, bringing out huge, brilliant blooms, but some days a deep, aching heaviness wouldn't leave her until she lost herself in a book.

Her life in Alaska ended abruptly, with the peas getting fat and the flower gardens in a riot of bloom but before the vegetables — except for the perfect radishes, and the tender young spinach and lettuce and baby beets that she thinned and carried proudly in to be served for dinner — before most full-grown vegetables came into fruition.

It happened because she got her chance to go to the States.

Chapter Eleven

Mr. Riley, the plug-chewing neighbor who lived over the hill from the old homestead, had lost his wife in the winter. His niece named Hazel Birney had turned up soon afterward to stay with him. She brought him to church with her. It was kind of funny to Anne to see Mr. Riley "darkening the door of a church," as he himself said with a bit of his old chuckle. He looked like an old man now, bent, and without all the talking and chuckling he had been famous for. Not like the "champion cusser," of her childhood.

Hazel was barely twenty. She'd been through secretarial school in Wisconsin, where she was from, and where she'd had a job. "But I've always wanted to see Alaska and when the family said we couldn't leave Uncle Bird up here alone, I just said 'I'll go; I want to go.'

"I'm the adventurous one in the family," she laughed, talking to the Harbisons and Anne on the church steps after the service. She had a quick, bright cheerfulness and Anne noticed how her warm laugh, floating like her breath in the clear cold of the January air, seemed to have a pure note of its own and yet seemed to harmonize with the mellow sound of the organ drifting out of the church, still playing the final anthem. Anne saw that the cherry-colored wool of the skirt below Hazel's blue parka looked thick and rich, flecked with woven gray, and the tops of her brown leather boots had a gray fur that almost matched the fluffy gray beret perched on her head of wavy, shining brown hair.

Anne had long noticed people's clothes and she thought Hazel's were perfect, wondered why so many other people looked dowdy in the same simple clothes, even the same colors, while Hazel looked like she enjoyed walking around in them, looked free.

Hazel had come to Alaska with an older friend, a nurse coming up to work for Public Health in Anchorage, the two of them trading off driving the friend's Buick up the Alcan Highway. "It was such a great trip," Hazel was saying, "such gorgeous scenery, such nice people along the way. I'll never forget it, all our adventures, even the worrying a couple of times about whether our gas would hold out to the next station. We had to stay over an extra day and a half at this one lodge until they got their own gas delivered; their pumps had run out too, and people stacked up there, already stacking up there before we arrived, all waiting for the gas. So we made a vacation out of it, played in the snow and had a big party around a roaring fireplace." She laughed again: "I taught this truck driver how to waltz and he gave us an extra five-gallon can of gas after we all filled up and were all leaving next day."

"Well, you sound like true Alaskans yourselves," said an older man who had been on the edge of the conversation, "drivin' that highway for six days in the dead of winter, two women alone."

"Oh, we never really felt alone. And that Buick purred right along. A good winter car, already used to Wisconsin winter."

"There *is* the fact," the man said something Anne had heard too: "that highway when it's frozen in winter is actually the best time to be travelin' it, no mud or ruts or chuckholes, or dust, or flying gravel to break out headlights or windshield. And no mosquitoes."

Hazel joined the church choir and Anne was flattered but tongue-tied when Hazel kept trying to make friends with her through the last of that winter and into what became Anne's bad spring. Hazel was a reader; she devoured books even faster than Anne did. Not yet as frustrated by the pitiful size of the town library as Anne was. Anne later brought Hazel books from the school library, which was open two days a week in summer for a few hours.

"I'm mostly re-reading things," Anne told her when Hazel first asked what she was reading. They had been in the church kitchen that evening, drinking hot cider around the big black-and-white stove, two other women talking to a man nearby, all waiting for the other choir members to assemble for practice. "It's hard to get that many books around here," Anne said.

"One thing that may not be so great about Alaska," she added.

"But I do love it here," Hazel said. "Even the awful weather — this wind! — it isn't that discouraging." This was probably in February, when the Valley wind could be at its most bitter, or maybe March but before Anne's shameful kiss from Mr. Hansen. "You know," Hazel was going on, "I thought it would be worse; people talking about you living in igloos up here and not seeing the sun for half the year.

"Of course," and her lovely laugh pealed out, "I knew it couldn't be that bad. We'd had letters from Uncle Bird and Aunt Beulah and I knew they weren't living in an ice house! But I did wonder if we might be buried in snow. But it isn't really that different from living through winter in Wisconsin. Except the whole place is so gorgeous! I can't believe these mountains!

"So what are you finding good enough to be re-reading?" she asked Anne.

"Mostly Dickens now. The library has pretty much all of his." Anne didn't mention *The Secret Garden*, which she must have re-read two dozen times, wished she could get a new copy of, since hers was so worn and losing pages, but she couldn't find it in the Sears catalog, the only place she knew of where you could order books to buy. (Mrs. Harbison gave Anne two dollars each week, and Anne knew Mrs. Harbison wasn't accepting any money for Anne living there. "You do more than enough work," she had said.) Anne didn't talk to Hazel about her love of poetry either, because almost nobody shared it and she was pretty sure Hazel didn't.

"Well, I've read some Dickens," Hazel said. "I liked *David Copperfield* and some others. But Dickens does get wordy! Don't you think? I like the historical romances and *Gone With the Wind*. That's the one I've read more than once. I used to read all my brothers' books, *Treasure Island, Robinson Crusoe,* and the Hardy boys and everything else they had." She laughed again, "I used to think I wanted to be a boy."

"I used to read those too," Anne said. "I guess I never wanted to be a boy; I was just reading everything I could find in the library."

Hazel began to drop by Harbisons more and more often even before school was out, and it seemed to be Anne she came to see. Anne opened up around Hazel when she could hardly talk to anyone else. Hazel just got things out of you, got you talking when you didn't expect to. But she chatted just as easily with Mrs. Harbison or Caroline when Anne wasn't talkative, even with the judge if he was around. She wasn't put off by anybody. She was like Ellen that way. When school was out by the end of May, Hazel came by almost daily after Anne started the garden, for an hour or so right after lunch when she said her uncle was resting.

"I've seen pictures," Hazel said "of the huge cabbages and things grown here. Is that what yours are going to be?" She sat in the big wooden chair, on a cushion, her bronze-brown hair shining in the sun, lightly nuzzling the purring cat with one foot or the other clad in saddle shoes, watching Anne doing the first June thinning of carrots and then cabbage plants.

"I'd help," Hazel said, "except thinning is a job I really dislike. Hate to destroy the wonderful new little plants. And so I never leave enough space between."

"I don't like pulling them either," Anne said, "but I wait to take in baby carrots and beets and . . . and, well, take in anything later, to thin some more. Learned that from my dad, actually. And my mother wanted us to bring in the cabbage and kohlrabi and some others — the little plants when they were still young and tender — to flavor her soups. So a lot of the thinning keeps getting done along the way, leaving more room all the time for the others to grow big while you don't waste a lot of what you thin out."

She sat back on her heels and rested a few moments, swiping her damp fine hair off her forehead, thinking about that process of things thinning out as you go along. About how her own life had thinned down. From a big family to this one summer and a few friends. But with this new friend Hazel. Vague and unfinished thinking. But in the garden she didn't that much care about pursuing thoughts to an end; it was enough to let them wander, let them take as much time as they wanted to drift about. Light wherever they wished or not at all. Especially when she had Hazel for a companion.

Hazel was now wandering around herself, pulling a few weeds, as she often did. Weeding was something Hazel liked to do. "There's something so . . . so satisfying, isn't there," she had said, "in seeing a garden without weeds? And Uncle Bird's place is so *weedy*! You can't even find where the garden used to be."

"I'm not aiming for sizes," Anne said, finally answering Hazel's first question about huge vegetables as she was rising to sit on the wooden bench beside Hazel, who was back in the chair. "But the soil here is rich and the hours of light in growing season are really long — those are reasons for what you hear about these huge vegetables. Some people grow them as a sort of sideline. For fun, I think."

"I love these long days of light!" Hazel said. "I was actually still reading outside last night until after eleven o'clock! Didn't even notice what time it was and couldn't believe it when Uncle Bird called me to come in.

"I guess we are going to leave here soon though," she told Anne a couple of weeks later, late in June, as they wandered around the garden and Anne picked for her a bouquet of peonies and of snapdragons coming into bloom. "My dad is coming up. They thought — my dad and the whole family — they thought they were sending me here to persuade Uncle Bird to go back to Wisconsin. And he does seem so lost, sort of wandering around that big house and the yard. . . ."

"But you would *leave*?" Anne was suddenly feeling something plummet inside her. The sharp strike of a pain she was afraid of. "You just got a job." And she couldn't say more about it, shut out the idea of Hazel leaving, didn't hear Hazel telling her more. She had somehow let herself begin to think that Hazel would simply be here, counted on her being here, a friend who read books, someone who laughed, who got Anne talking and even herself laughing when everything else in the world, everything beyond the garden, looked so entangled that it was impossible to think about. After all, Hazel had gotten a half-time job in the office at the "new store" (everyone in the Valley still called it the "new store" though it had opened almost two years ago. Everyone went there and it was a bustling place, full of things like sheets and such that people had always had to order from the Sears catalog).

"My dad insists he's going to send me off on Alaska Steamship with Uncle Bird," Hazel said next day, "while Dad stays here to "wind up" things about selling the farm. And he has this time line.

"But I told him," and there was Hazel's laugh, "we've actually talked on the phone — twice — and I told him, 'good luck with winding things up on this farm by the end of summer! Which is his time line. The place is so full of *stuff*, Anne. And the yard! My dad wants Uncle Bird out of the way while he sells things off. And I'm supposed to pick out all the things for Uncle Bird to save — I've been trying to do it anyway — to take with us on the steamship. I told my dad it would take him two years to do what he's going to try to do, instead of the two months he's planning on. But he'll be here next week and he wants to ship us off right after."

Why is it that some people just keep having losses? Anne kept wondering as she sat out alone after supper — without even the cat Hannah — in the slanting, golden light of the sun hanging so long above the horizon, just out of her sight behind a neighbor's far-off barn. *Aren't there people who don't seem to keep losing everybody they care about?* She was thinking about *Mill on the Floss* and *Silas Marner*, neither of which she was willing to read again. *You can thin things out too much. What do you have left if you thin so much?* The thought of Hazel going away brought such a tight, dry, hard ache into her throat that it scared her; she felt her throat was closing.

If only Ellen hadn't gone.

And all her sisters.

She got up suddenly, and paced the vegetable rows. She had to make herself not think about it, about Hazel. About Ellen. She remembered Miss Dickson would be coming back. She walked the garden and then sat again and reopened *Can You Forgive Her?* — Miss Gorman at the library had recently gotten the Palliser novels. But the story moved slowly at the beginning, slow for her to get into; she didn't know any of the people in it yet and had read only one of Trollope's books before. After finding her place in the new book now, on only page twenty, Anne's mind wouldn't stay with it; after reading only one paragraph, she was blaming herself:

I didn't even offer anything to Hazel. She was shamefaced in the lowering sun. Mrs. Harbison called from the kitchen window but she didn't really mind Anne staying late in the garden — she was used to it — and Anne called back without having to think about it, that she would come in soon.

What did I ever do for Hazel while she kept trying to be a friend? So why should Hazel stay? But it felt like Hazel's leaving was something utterly final. Like Anne was always to be left alone, bound to lose everybody. The rays of the golden sun, the sun itself, seemed to be deliberately drawing away from her, glad to leave such a petty whiner as she was. Some dark pain began to close around her, the world growing heavily dark and the future looming before her like the dreaded empty places of nightmares where she was always desperately seeking. And always left unbearably alone.

Suddenly an alien sound, like the strangled last cry of a heifer dying, came from her own throat. Escaped from her mouth. And then another. And another. The same dreadful sounds. And more. She couldn't stop them. And then came hard, dry sobs, wrenching their way up through her, burning her chest and tearing the dry stricture of her throat.

She couldn't stop any of it. Her shoulders heaved and her whole body shook as she bent over the book in her lap, as the book fell to the gravel.

Her teeth began to chatter. Her chin, that she had so long held firm and determined, went into strange, frightening spasms.

She became awfully, terribly, icily cold.

She wrapped herself in her own arms against the cold and rocked in the chair, her will leaving her as all else had left her; her will folding in on itself and leaving her rocking and rocking, sobbing, hanging helplessly in the chair while her body did these terrible things, these terrible things that betrayed her — let her fall, hopeless and helpless, into the pit of pain and cold and dread and desolation that she had managed for all these years to stay out of.

But then, finally, the pain was pouring out of her in a steadier stream and she was only weeping. For a long time.

When she raised her head at last, she didn't know where she was. Then she saw her book on the gravel path at her feet and saw the cat Hannah. She heard Mrs. Harbison's voice again and realized the woman had come out the back door, toward the garden. Anne picked up the Palliser book.

"Are you all right?" Mrs. Harbison was coming closer. *She must have heard me, this awful crying.* Anne wanted to hide, was glad now that the west was darkening early — *she must have known for awhile that clouds were gathering there, over Anchorage?* That real dusk was coming early; *wasn't that the only reason for the sun darkening?*

"I'm fine," she said. With feelings so mixed, because she didn't want to be alone even though she wanted to hide, to have no one see her. "It's just . . . just that sometimes," she said, realizing she was mumbling but then trying to say it clear, getting too loud, "sometimes what happens to people in a book is so sad. You know?"

Mother would know how I'm lying. She always knew.

"I'm fine," Anne said again. But then Mrs. Harbison did something that started the tears again. With one hand Mrs. Harbison handed her a wad of tissues, unrolled from toilet paper (the only tissue Anne knew of except in Miss Dickson's room), and with her other hand was giving her two soft, white, lavender-scented linen handkerchiefs. Anne knew she wasn't being given a choice; she was given both: Tissue unrolled just for her and the lovely things women saved for themselves, Mrs. Harbison's own delicately-edged and carefully laundered handkerchiefs. Handkerchiefs so different from the big, square, blatantly red or blue cloths that they sewed and laundered for sons and husbands, Anne felt at once: like the ones Anne's mother had faithfully washed and dried and folded for her father, that Father had always had in some pocket. But Mother had never had the lovely opposite, never had anything like the soft and sweet-scented things Mrs. Harbison so easily handed to Anne.

Anne cried some more, for her mother and for the things Mother had never had. Glad of the tissues to try to clean up the long outpourings of her eyes and nose but unable to stop the new tears, holding the white handkerchiefs in her other hand as too precious to be used, while Mrs. Harbison stood by. But then Mrs. Harbison took back one of the scented handkerchiefs and with it she gently wiped Anne's face. "Keep the other," she said; "I'll put this one in the wash but you keep the other."

* * * *

Anne was utterly startled when, only two days later, Hazel and Mrs. Harbison came together into the garden to talk to her.

"You've always wanted to get to the States," Mrs. Harbison said; "isn't that right?" She was seating herself on the garden bench after Hazel had said hello and admired the flowers again. "You said you could live with your sister Mary in Oregon," Mrs. Harbison went on, "and want to go to college."

"Mary has told me so, in her letters. . . ." Anne began.

"And if you would come with us," Hazel broke in, "keep me company to take Uncle Bird on the steamship to Seattle. . . . It can be such a fun trip, Anne! The Inside Passage! Soon after Dad gets here; he'll be here in a few days."

"I need to write to your sister Mary right away," said Mrs. Harbison, always practical. "To see if she could meet you in Seattle. But Salem, Oregon isn't that far from Seattle. If Mary can't meet you there, the bus from Seattle to Salem can't cost much.

"There's money for the trip from the funds meant to support you," she went on, "or we'll pay." She said those last words like it was nothing to pay for Anne's freedom, Anne's release into the wider world that she had been longing for, it seemed, forever.

177

About the Author

Sarah Kavasharov was born and raised in the Matanuska Valley of Alaska. Besides raising three daughters, she taught English and later became an attorney and practiced law in Alaska. She has lived in Northern California since retirement.